THE DEAD SPEND NO GOLD

Bigfoot and the California Gold Rush

(A Virginia Reed Adventure)

by

Duncan McGeary

Dedication and Acknowledgements

Dedicated to my wife, Linda, who I met in writer's group and who has always understood my need to write. She has been my amused, bemused muse from the beginning.

Table of Contents

THE DEAD SPEND NO GOLD

Bigfoot and the California Gold Rush

(A Virginia Reed Adventure)

Duncan McGeary

Foreword

Virginia Reed Gerard, New York City, 1920

They don't want you to know the truth of what lured the Donner Party to their deaths in the Sierra Nevada, nor do they want me to speak of the systematic slaughter of the Indian tribes in California, far greater than in any other part of the United States. It is said that nine out of ten of the native inhabitants there were killed, all in pursuit of gold. But I cannot rest easy until the truth is told of that first eventful year of the Gold Rush, when I once again found myself confronted with the strange and mysterious. After long years of pondering my own journals and those of others, I have reconstructed the truth, as best I understand it.

Chapter One

Tucker's Journal, Autumn, 1848

In the mornings, a sliver of light winds its way into the cave through a curtain of trees. It is just a small ray, but it ignites the walls of gold and washes the darkness in a soft, silky iridescence. For a moment, I'm allowed to gaze upon the riches I will never spend.

After all, dead men spend no gold.

My partner and I labored for long, hard months searching for even a nugget of the precious metal, and yet here I lie, surrounded by more gold than any pharaoh, more than any medieval king ever had, more riches than Beowulf himself found in the dragon's hoard; here, in Grendel's cave.

But the monster will not let me leave. I know this now. He will never let me leave.

It should have been so easy. We should have found the precious metal glinting at us from the rocky streambeds. Having set out from our homes in San Francisco, Kovac and I reached the gold fields before most others. From the start, we heard stories of newly arriving miners simply plucking gold nuggets from the ground, but bad luck plagued us.

After some horrific experiences (that I may confess in this journal, but not yet!), we struck out overland in an attempt to distance ourselves from the others. The soft, sandy soil should have been easy to walk on, but the uneven footing exhausted us. Dust coated our trousers to the knee. The loudest noise in the quiet woods was the sound of our own grumbling bellies.

Though others seemed to be finding gold with every strike of the pickaxe, Kovac insisted on searching farther north. So it was that we climbed the cinder cone foothills, where landslides had laid bare the red and black lava cinders beneath the surface. The air was cool, but the sun was hot. At night, we camped among the ponderosas. I would idly break apart the orange jigsaw bark and then try to reassemble it as Kovac described the riches we would find. We were above the sandy desert soil by then, and the pine needles were so thick that they filled the spaces between the clumps of grass, making a soft carpet for us to rest on.

Eventually, we reached Bidwell's Bar, a town that had sprung up overnight at the base of Thompson Peak. After reprovisioning there, we continued on. We followed the North Fork of the Feather River farther up than any of the other miners, certain we would find the very source of the yellow metal, the mother lode. All around us, miners cried out "Eureka!" while we dug and scrabbled in bare, rocky ground.

"That's all downwash, I tell you," Kovac said, sneering at the riches of the others. "The mother lode is all ours. We just have to find it. "

All ours—all of nothing. I should have left Kovac to his delusions, but the wealthier others became, the more I wanted to believe that sooner or later we'd strike a vein richer than all the rest. Higher and higher we climbed. The wind whispered through the swaying pines, the dark green needles shimmering against the pure blue sky.

It was tempting, after everything that had happened to us, to believe that this place was paradise. Perhaps Eden itself. Perhaps we had returned as poor sinners to the very place from which God banished mankind. If so, Kovac was the serpent, leading me to the knowledge of riches I could never spend. It was a strange sort of paradise, for scattered about the ground were weathered bones, the natural charnel house of the wilderness.

But we were blind to the bones and the silent warning they held. Instead, we wandered farther up the creek until, at last, we found the wellspring. We could go no further, for an endless expanse of rock blocked our path.

It was pure accident that we stumbled across our destiny.

As darkness fell, we camped by the stream, utterly discouraged, unwilling even to speak. Kovac wandered behind a wall of trees to relieve himself, and there he found our cursed fortune. Perhaps on any other night, we would have missed it. But on this night, the moonlight curved inside just brightly enough to illuminate the darkness of the cave.

Inside was a miraculous grotto of gold. Oh, not a grotto with gold in it: no, this cave was made of nothing but gold, the walls lined from end to end with the gleaming brilliance of pure, silky metal. It was impossible. It was a dream.

I somehow knew from the start that we were cursed.

My partner was an older man, more patient than I. At first, he didn't load himself down with the gold, but watched and laughed as I snatched handfuls of nuggets.

"Don't be stupid, Kovac," I said. "Fill your pockets with as much as you can carry. I don't trust our damned luck." I didn't trust our friends, either; least of all my fellow miners. But most of all, I didn't trust the Fates.

"Hell, Tucker," Kovac said, trailing his fingers over the smooth golden wall as he wandered deeper into the cave. "We're gonna to be the richest men alive! A few nuggets ain't nothin'."

"If you say so," I muttered, shoveling nuggets into my rucksack.

"What's that smell?" Kovac asked.

Straightening, I breathed deeper, finally acknowledging what we'd feverishly ignored. The cave stank, and the floor was littered with gore and bones.

"Bear, probably," I answered him. "Maybe cougar."

We drew and cocked our pistols.

"Huh," Kovac grunted. I heard the clacking of bones as he moved toward me, toward the entrance. "Best we leave off for the night. Come back in the morning."

My pockets were full to bursting as I followed him out.

Daylight came after a sleepless night.

When we pulled back the branches that obscured the entrance, the cavern exploded with color, the sun illuminating the brilliance of the walls inside, reflecting an infinite mirror of riches.

We filled our packs and our pockets with loose nuggets—Kovac now as eager as I—hardly speaking, hardly breathing, unable to believe our luck. If we'd stopped then, it might have been all right. We might have gotten away. But I wasn't satisfied. I want to blame Kovac for everything, but it was my idea to strike the wall.

I took my axe and, with all my might, swung it against the gleaming metal. The head sank several inches into the soft gold, and with a cry of triumph, I pried a chunk of gold the size of my head from the wall. It fell out of my hands as its weight caught me by surprise.

I should have quit then. It was a sign. What use was a piece of gold so heavy I couldn't carry away?

But gold fever had taken me completely. As I struck the wall a second time, the metal walls boomed like a warning bell, growing louder with every echo. I dropped the ax, covering my ears until the reverberation stilled. In the silence that followed, we heard the sound of a single footstep, and our hearts stilled before beating in a wild staccato rhythm. The world seemed to pause, as if all creation waited with us for the doom that approached.

I don't know how we knew it was a footstep and not a falling rock, but we knew. It was only one footfall, but it shook the cave. Then came another step, and then…then we understood. The Beast approached, its footfalls rapid and thundering. The bones paving the floor bounced under the onslaught.

It burst out of the darkness. It had the shape of a man, but was impossibly big, taller and wider than any human, covered in fur, and all we could see were its glaring eyes and snarling mouth. *A grizzly,* I thought, until I stared into those eyes and saw the malevolent intelligence there.

We scrambled for the entrance of the cave, Kovac fumbling with his pistol. That must have been what slowed him, allowing me to push him aside as I got to the entrance before him.

I pushed Kovac, my friend, my partner, aside as if he was nothing, no one. Later, I would shudder at my craven actions, and wince knowing I would do it again. I wanted to live. I'd never known how much; so much that I'd push a friend into danger to save myself.

Kovac fell in the darkness, crying out for help, but I kept running. A single gunshot echoed behind me.

And suddenly, the wild mountain air was filled with throaty, guttural screams, which no doubt stilled every living creature for miles. The smell of blood rose and blossomed in the air. Such an act of killing might normally have drawn scavengers, but instead, it surely caused them to flee. They knew to stay away from that cursed place.

The screams stopped abruptly. I was alone. The only sounds were the scrabble of the scree shifting beneath my feet, pebbles sliding down the hillside, and my pack thumping against my body with every leap and step.

I didn't look back.

The gold wasn't heavy at first. My gibbering fear made the burden light. Then, as my breath rasped and my legs shook from fatigue, the gold became an anchor. But I couldn't let it go, in spite of the danger. The gold dragged me down, every step more difficult than the last.

Let it go, I thought. *There is enough gold in that cave to last a lifetime.*

But I couldn't. For six long, hard months we'd dug into the rocky soil of the High Sierra without finding so much as a nugget. I wasn't about to give up my treasure—more gold than anyone else had yet found, more riches in my pockets than I'd ever seen. These weren't rocks with tiny flecks of gold embedded in them: these were chunks of pure gold, unadulterated and glimmering.

I ran downhill blindly, stumbling and falling again and again, the heavy rocks slamming me harder into the ground than I expected, gouging into my legs.

It's mine! I'm not letting it go! The desperate thought repeated over and over again in my mind, even as the pounding steps of my pursuer grew ever louder behind me. *It's mine!*

My breath felt hot and dry in my throat, and there was a stitch in my side, but I kept going downward. My cave of gold was above the tree line, and the footing had been loose shale at first. The going was getting easier now that I was among the trees, but the trees themselves became an obstacle course. I slammed into the branches of a mountain fir, which pushed back just enough to throw me sideways.

A strangled sob escaped my throat as I almost lost my footing. I knew it was too good to be true. I knew my luck would desert me. I would never be rich. God was playing a big joke on me.

I sensed the monster's arms, those unnaturally long arms with human-looking hands and long, sharp claws on the ends of the fingers, reaching for me, mere inches from my back, ready to slice into me. I lunged forward, and it was as if the wind of the creature's strike gave me strength. Again and again, I felt the jolt of fear, but each time, my body reacted a little more slowly, and each time, I was certain that the claws had come closer, nearly catching me.

The gold became ever heavier. I could barely lift my feet off the ground.

Let it go! I shouted in my mind, but my arms wouldn't obey.

Falling was inevitable. Something—a tree root, a rock—caught my foot and sent me rolling. I was spinning, gaining momentum. I had the wild thought that this might be good, that I could simply tumble down the mountain and out of danger.

Then a rock caught the side of my head, and my thoughts became scrambled.

What am I doing?

The gold!

Even as most other thoughts abandoned me, I remembered the gold.

I'm a rich man!

The pounding of the monster's pursuit seemed to be inside my head. Strange. Rocks were rolling through my field of vision. I was lying on a steep hillside. The shale had collapsed, sliding downward, carrying me with it. I stared up at the clear blue brilliance of the mountain skies, panting. Then the sunlight dimmed and a huge presence loomed over me. Its features were shadowed and indistinct, but I felt its anger.

Gold nuggets tumbled out of my pockets and clattered down the hillside as the Beast lifted me by my feet, swinging me through the air, faster and faster, almost like my father had when I was little boy.

I sensed rather than saw the tree coming toward my head, feeling its shadow engulf me as the monster slowed my approach, saving me from a deathblow.

Behind the brilliant sparks of light was darkness.

Chapter Two

Virginia's skirt was hemmed above her boots. The other women of Sutter's Fort considered this odd—considered *her* odd—but she didn't care. It saved her from having to wash her clothes so often. A trio of old ladies was clustered on the wooden sidewalk ahead, staring at her from the corners of their eyes. They showed no sign of moving aside politely for her, so she veered out into the muddy road and trudged past, ignoring their whispers. Always the whispers.

She readjusted the wicker basket containing the day's bread from Johansson's Bakery. It was the biggest basket she could carry, and by the time she arrived at the hotel, her arms were like to fall off. As she passed Howard's General Store, a couple of men outside the store glanced up casually. They looked like a rancher and his son, in town for monthly supplies. An Indian dressed in white man's clothing stood behind them, and Virginia saw his eyes widen at the sight of her. She recognized that look.

He whispered into the older man's ear, and she had a sinking feeling that she knew what was coming.

The younger of the two ranchers was about her age, maybe eighteen or nineteen. He tipped his hat to her and smiled, and without thinking, she smiled back. His unruly dark hair and long lashes brought a pang to her heart. He looked much like Bayliss would have, had he lived. He started forward, perhaps intending to offer help with her burden. Virginia could have used a little kindness right then. She raised a knee to balance the basket on while she adjusted her grip yet again.

The older man grabbed the youth's arm and turned him around.

"What, Father?" the young man exclaimed.

"Leave her be, Frank," the older man snapped, his white handlebar mustache hiding a scowl on his weathered face.

"But she's so beautiful," the son whispered.

Virginia kept walking, trying to ignore what was happening. To pretend it wasn't happening.

"No, Frank...that's *her*," the old man hissed.

"*Her?*" The younger man looked puzzled. "What do you mean, 'her'?"

"*Her*, dammit. Remember? I told you she was living in these parts. You don't want to be alone with her. Some winter's night, hell, she might get hungry..."

Frank's eyes widened, and he turned and stared, then realized what he was doing and looked away. "Pity," he muttered, glancing over his shoulder at Virginia. "Such a beauty."

Virginia averted her face, blushing. Strange that after all this time, people could still make her doubt herself, men and women whispering, pointing, making her feel as though she had done something wicked.

She shook it off. *They can embarrass me only if I let them.*

She raised her chin. She had nothing to be ashamed of. She'd done nothing wrong.

Nonetheless, despite her brave front, Virginia was grateful to duck into the alley behind the hotel. It was her refuge. She spent most of her time staring out over this alley. Her tiny room at was the back of the hotel and had a small window from which she could see the far hills and forest.

Sometimes, on clear days, she could see the Sierra Nevada, snowcapped and rugged. On those days, she averted her eyes and closed the curtains. It was at those times that the trauma of that horrible winter gnawed again at her belly and the visions of the creatures she had fought nearly overwhelmed her.

Virginia shook herself, trying to banish the bad memories, blaming the crisp cold of the early September morning. She suspected that the cold would always remind her of that winter.

The kitchen was empty; breakfast wasn't yet being prepared. Virginia plopped the breadbasket on the counter and collapsed into a chair at the worktable, sighing with satisfaction at having a few moments to herself. It was rare that she was alone, and even rarer that she didn't have some chore or other to do.

A scurrying noise drew her attention. There was something under the table.

Virginia felt her old instincts take over. She sprang up, groping for one of the knives on the counter. Blade clutched in her hand and heart pounding in her ears, she stared at the shadow just visible beneath the hem of the tablecloth, wondering if she'd be able to strike before It—the creature she dreamed of every night—took her down.

She steeled herself to lift the cloth away, but then a small hand emerged and pulled it aside, and two wide blue eyes stared up at her. Virginia gasped, sagging against a cabinet as relief washed through her.

"Come out of there, you scamp," she said, not even angry, as she dropped the knife onto the counter.

Juliet Simpson crawled out, giggling. Virginia snatched her up and held the squealing little girl over her head. "You scared me nearly to death," she said, chuckling.

She sat back down at the table, the little girl settling into her lap.

"What are you doing he…" she began, but before should could finish her question, they heard raised voices coming from the front of the hotel. Virginia recognized the voice of the innkeeper, Mrs. Harrelson, and that of Clara Simpson, Juliet's mother. Clara was contracted to do the laundry for the hotel.

"You ain't got no one else, Mrs. Harrelson. I want more for a basket of laundry, or you can do it yourself," the washerwoman was saying.

Juliet tensed in Virginia's arms.

"That is not what we agreed to," Mrs. Harrelson answered, barely holding her anger in check. Clara Simpson was always trying to get a raise in pay, and Mrs. Harrelson had acquiesced twice already. "I don't doubt you deserve it, Clara," the innkeeper continued. "But I simply can't afford it. If I must, I will do the laundry myself. I've done it before and I can do it again, if that's the way it must be."

There was silence at that, and Virginia could feel Juliet trembling, as if the anger in her mother's voice scared her. Virginia hugged her tightly, trying to think of some way to distract her. She was a pretty little girl, but unkempt, her hair a tangle, her face smudged. Her mother was very diligent when cleaning the guests' clothing, despite her complaints about payment. She was less diligent about her daughter's appearance.

Virginia had to remind herself every day that it was none of her business. Her instinct to save people could get her into trouble.

The door burst open and a portly woman waddled into the room. She blanched at the sight of her daughter in Virginia's lap, and a look of horror flashed over her face. Then her anger returned, turning her face a deep crimson. "Juliet! Come here this instant!"

Juliet hesitated before sliding reluctantly off Virginia's lap. Mrs. Simpson met her halfway and grabbed her by the ear. "You come when I say so," she hissed, heading for the back door as she continued, "You stay away from that girl, hear!"

"But I like her," Juliet protested.

"She ain't right in the head. She done evil things…"

The back door slammed as tears sprang to Virginia's eyes. Footsteps echoed in the hallway and Virginia closed her eyes, struggling to compose herself.

Mrs. Harrelson came through the swinging door from the dining room and peered into the basket on the counter. "It's time for breakfast. Don't dillydally, Gina. You too, Feather."

Feather had silently followed the innkeeper into the kitchen. The Indian girl shared a room with Virginia, though sometimes it was easy to forget she was there, she was so quiet.

Mrs. Harrelson was a large old woman, gruff with the hotel's patrons but with a kind heart toward those in her employ. Virginia had gotten the impression that there was a Mr. Harrelson somewhere back East, inebriated and inept.

The innkeeper was the only person Virginia allowed to call her Gina, aside from her father. What's more, Mrs. Harrelson knew who Virginia was and professed not to care. She too had traveled by wagon train through Truckee Lake in 1846, but fortunately for her, her party had beaten the snows by a week. "There but for the grace of God," she had muttered when Virginia told the story, and never mentioned it again. Virginia was fiercely loyal to the woman.

"What's wrong?" Mrs. Harrelson asked, and Virginia realized she'd been staring at the table, remembering the glimpse of terror in Mrs. Simpson's eyes, and more, the look on the face of the handsome young man she'd passed in the street. She had given up flirting with boys, because they always found out what had happened to her, and their subsequent rejection always hurt.

"Nothing...I thought...I forgot something." She rose, straightening her dress.

Mrs. Harrelson missed nothing. "Was someone bothering you?"

"No," Virginia said, brushing her tears away. "I was just daydreaming, really." She couldn't meet her employer's eyes.

"Well, if they do trouble you, tell me. I won't have those men pestering you."

Virginia nodded, grateful as always that her boss understood and gently passed the blame onto something else, something other than what they both knew the problem really was.

Feather was at the stove, and though her back was turned, Virginia knew the Indian girl was listening intently to every word. It seemed that Mrs. Harrelson had a habit of taking in strays. Feather was even more out of place than Virginia. But while Virginia's problem was unique, Feather suffered the indignities that were all too common for her race.

Feather was small and precise in her movements, with delicate features, a sharp nose, and eyes that were always somber. Her hair was pulled back in a ponytail, revealing her high forehead.

Virginia hadn't known what to make of the Indian girl until the night Feather had found her stealing food. Now, that had been embarrassing. Virginia had been sneaking into the kitchen after everyone had gone to bed and salvaging scraps from the garbage. She couldn't help herself. She never ate the leftovers, and she threw them away when they went bad, but she wanted them just in case. She might need them.

One night, she'd looked up to find those solemn dark brown eyes watching her. Virginia had stood still for the space of a heartbeat, then put the scraps back. When she'd turned around, the Indian girl had been gone. Feather never spoke of it, for which Virginia was grateful. Somehow, the experience had turned them into friends.

When the Indian girl finally did talk, after days of silence, it was a complete surprise. Virginia had expected her to speak with a heavy accent, but instead Feather spoke with more refinement than anyone Virginia had ever met. The occasional "thees" and "thous" that peppered her conversation only made her seem more cultured. Far from being primitive, she was better read and educated than Virginia, having been raised by missionaries from childhood.

From their brief conversations, Virginia gathered that something had happened to Feather when she'd turned thirteen, and she had run away from the missionaries. She never spoke of it, but Virginia could guess, looking at that beautiful face and those dark brown eyes. The only thing Feather ever said, late one night while they were both in bed, was that she was alone.

"Thou callest me Feather," she said softly. "But my real name is Litonya, Little Hummingbird. Both names mean little. White people do not want me...nor do my own kind."

Virginia hadn't said anything. Tears had stung her eyes at the resignation in Feather's voice. She understood all too well. She almost unburdened herself, but was afraid to lose another friend.

Most of her own family was back in San Francisco. They'd managed to shake their past, to blend in with the bustling populace. In the bigger city, their name didn't stand out. But Virginia, for reasons she herself didn't understand, longed for the frontier, longed to forge her own path. It should have been the last place she wanted to go. Against her parents' wishes, she had taken the stagecoach back to Sutter's Fort. She hadn't known where she was going until she arrived.

To this day, she understood little of why she felt compelled to return to the frontier, to the shadow of the Sierra Nevada, where they had suffered through the bitter winter, to the place where her childhood ended and she became old in spirit. She was only fifteen years old, but she felt as if she understood life and death more than any of the adults around her.

Unfortunately, it wasn't long before someone in town recognized her.

She probably should have left when people's stares and whispers began to follow her along the streets. But something stubborn stirred within her, and she put up her chin and stayed. She would leave when she was good and ready.

Gold was found at Sutter's Mill in January of 1849, just north of the settlement. Thankfully, from that moment on, the girl from the Donner Party was no longer the first topic of conversation. Mrs. Harrelson was fit to be tied at first as the town cleared out. But then the flood of men from San Francisco arrived, and then successive waves of men from farther and farther away. All of these men, young and old, stopped in Sutter's Fort for one last taste of civilization before heading into the hills.

Virginia watched them leave with foreboding.

Many were fresh-faced boys who had lived in the lushness of the Eastern valleys all their lives and had no idea of the hardships they would encounter. Virginia had experienced the worst of them. Even if she had wanted to flirt with these boys, and even if they had, by some miracle, remained ignorant of her past, she simply couldn't. They were innocent boys, even the ones who were older and seemingly so much more mature. They just didn't know.

She saw it in their eyes when they discovered who she was. All of them had heard of the pass over the Sierra Nevada where, only two winters before, early snows caught a wagon train in a death grip, and whose members, it was said, preyed upon each other to survive.

They called it Donner Pass now instead of Fremont Pass. Virginia was grateful the wagon train had chosen George Donner as their leader instead of her father.

Virginia had found hidden strength in those snows, despite being led to the slaughter. She knew now that it had been planned from the beginning by creatures pretending to be human, creatures no one would admit walked this Earth. The wagon train was sent on foolish shortcuts and waylaid at every turn, yet she endured, protecting her family; but she was unable to save either of the young men who had been courting her. Bayliss died, and Jean Baptiste…changed.

Virginia was hearing whispers of huge, dangerous wolves in the Sierra Nevada, wolves unlike any others. Still, she hesitated, the memories of her last confrontation with the creatures fresh in her mind. She couldn't bear to approach the killing grounds. Here on the fringes of the wilderness, she waited for something to happen, though when she questioned herself, she couldn't say what.

She stared out the window at night and waited.

"Breakfast is only an hour away," Mrs. Harrelson said, breaking into Virginia's reminisces, her gruff tone back. "Hurry, hurry, you lazy girls."

Virginia was thankful to be lost in the tedium of cooking breakfast and preparing the dining room for their guests. There was something about preparing food, *plentiful* food, that gave her enormous comfort. Besides, with her head over the steaming stove, she forgot everything but the moment at hand, and if she was lucky, at the end of the evening she would fall into bed, her food scraps tucked away. Sleep inevitably found her too tired to allow for visions of wolves.

Feather and Virginia danced around the kitchen with practiced and fluid movements. Mrs. Harrelson left the preparing of meals to them now, after colliding with each of them more than once. As long as the customers didn't complain, she kept it that way.

The rest of the day passed by smoothly, despite its rocky beginnings. Before Virginia knew it, they were serving dinner.

She didn't notice him at first as she moved among the benches, serving stew.

It was a full dining room; all six long-planked tables with benches were occupied. All the diners wanted seconds, all except one man, who pushed aside the vegetables and left the bread untouched. He ate only what meat he dug out of the stew, though he seemed to find little enjoyment in the process. There was something odd about his chin, as if it was out of place, and his teeth didn't meet.

"Is the meal all right, sir?" Virginia asked before ladling another spoonful into his bowl.

He looked up at her blurrily, and she froze.

He'd been beaten, his face was wrinkled and bruised, and his jaw was out of line, but she recognized him. Strauss was his name. One of the Germans. One of *Them*. She'd never known whether he'd survived. Both humans and werewolves had starved that winter, each hunted by the other.

He didn't recognize her. She had grown a couple of inches and filled out since then. What's more, her hair was combed and her face was clean.

"Fine," he managed to say. "I just want meat." His voice was garbled, as if he couldn't get his mouth to work right, but the heavy German accent echoed in her memory. Virginia plopped the spoonful of stew into his bowl and turned away before he could see her expression.

No, no…

Her feet felt like lead as she moved away, heedless of other men gesturing and extending their bowls toward her. She pushed past them, ignoring their protests and almost running down the hall to the kitchen.

Feather gave a small cry of alarm as Virginia burst in. Stew slopped out of the stewpot, splattering onto the floor.

Feather stared at her. There must have been something in Virginia's face, for the Indian girl doffed her apron and handed it to Virginia without a word. She had to tug on the pot several times before Virginia would release it.

A moment later, Feather had gone into the dining room, carrying the pot of stew.

Alone, Virginia collapsed into a chair, staring at the wall, apron forgotten in her motionless hands until the sound of cursing brought her back to herself. Mrs. Harrelson was in the kitchen, which hardly ever happened.

What is she doing here? Virginia wondered, shaking her head slightly. The old woman was snatching pots from the stove and dropping them onto the counter hastily, as if even the hand mittens weren't enough to handle the heat. The smell of burnt carrots and beef filled the air.

The burnt meat had been part of her dream, Virginia realized. It was the smell she tried so hard to forget, the smell that had sometimes wafted over from the other cabins. She'd wondered, *How can they be eating meat, when there is no meat to be had?*

Mrs. Harrelson was standing over her, but instead of being angry, the woman laid the backs of her fingers on Virginia's forehead, taking her temperature. Her hand was rough but warm. Then she gently lifted Virginia's face between her two big hands and looked into her eyes. "Go to bed, Virginia," she said kindly. "I'll do the rest."

Virginia started to get up, to move toward the stove. "I'm sorry," she said. "I can do it." But it was clear from the tone of her voice that her heart wasn't in it.

"Go!" her employer commanded. "Don't make me goose you to get you moving. Nor do I want you to burn down my hotel. Get yourself together, girl. If I don't see you in the morning, I'll take care of the chores. You just get well."

It wasn't illness, and Mrs. Harrelson no doubt knew it, but Virginia didn't argue. She headed for the back stairwell, avoiding the dining room, and climbed the four flights of stairs, her shoulder rubbing against the wall for support. She made it to her bed and fell upon it fully clothed. She had just enough strength remaining to pull off her shoes and draw a blanket over herself before a dazed sleep took her.

Virginia woke in darkness, forgetting where she was. She remembered the cabin on the pass, the moans of hunger, the smell of human excrement, the constant cold. But this room was warm and smelled of freshly laundered sheets. Feather was breathing softly in the next bed. Sometime while she slept, in those dreams of hunger and cold, Virginia's resolve had returned. She'd hidden for too long, sheltered by family and friends and distance.

She threw off the blanket and rose quietly. She felt for the wardrobe, opening the lowest drawer. There at the bottom, underneath her undergarments, was the loaded pistol that she checked every day as soon as Feather went downstairs. The powder was dry.

It was about four o'clock in the morning, if her inner sense of time was right, and the rough wooden floors were freezing to her bare feet. She barely noticed. She made her way to the entrance of the hotel, where, on a small table opposite the front door, Mrs. Harrelson kept a ledger where she signed in the guests.

Virginia lit a candle and ran her finger quickly down the day's entries. There he was—Herman Strauss. He wasn't even bothering to hide his name. Probably thought none lived who'd witnessed his murderous deeds. But Virginia had seen him. She'd been there when the gunshot had nearly taken off his chin. She was the one who'd pulled the trigger. The wolf had run into the woods after that, and Virginia had believed him dead, but there was no mistaking him.

Room 14, the ledger said next to his name. She snagged the extra key from its hook.

She closed the book quietly and blew out the candle, then stood there for a few moments, letting her eyes adjust to the dark. He could see better than her, of course. He might even hear and smell her coming, if he was wary. But she was almost certain he hadn't recognized her. In the past year, she'd turned from a starving waif of a girl into a well-fed, well-groomed young woman. Maybe he'd spent the evening in the bars and now enjoyed a deep, sodden sleep. Maybe he wouldn't know it was over before she fired a bullet into his brain.

Virginia climbed the stairs, her bare feet making no sound. She knew all the creaky spots and avoided them. She took her time creeping down the hallway, aware of every loose board, but it was impossible to get to *Room 14* without making a little noise. This floor was almost empty. Mrs. Harrelson had stuck him in the end room, where she tended to put people she didn't like.

Would he hear her, lying in his bed? Virginia wondered as she cocked the gun. Would he be rising in silence to meet his attacker, Changing even as she drew near? Would he be waiting for her on the other side of the door?

She turned the key. The click sounded louder than thunder to her. She reached for the doorknob and felt the cool brass in her hand.

Chapter Three

"Thou art welcome here, Chief Honon."

Litonya hid behind her father's legs, for the white man was loud and fat.

"Who is this?" the man boomed. He dressed funny, smelled funny, and spoke funny. Litonya did not know the English language then, for she was only five years old, but this meeting was forever etched in her memory. It was impossible that she could have understood the conversation, much less conversed herself, and yet she remembered it.

Her father's gentle hands disentangled her from his legs, pushing her toward the thunderous giant. There was an equally large woman behind him. Litonya had never seen anyone so fat.

The stranger scooped her up, and she barely restrained a scream as he set her down on top of an outside table. Her father would want her to be brave. Both her father and the strangers examined her, as if she was a prize horse.

"She is as light as a feather," the man said. "And so shall she be called…Feather."

"My name is Litonya," she said, very clearly.

"No, Little Hummingbird," her father said. "You must speak as these people speak, and learn all you can." He did not give voice to what he must have thought, that a feather was an adornment that the Miwok gave their dead.

"Why?" she asked. She managed to keep the mournful wail out of her voice, which sounded flat to her ears and yet desperate, too.

"We must learn their ways, so that we can live among them," her father explained. "Stay and learn everything you can, and when you have grown, return to me. Teach us what you have learned."

Father left, taking a little bundle of her clothing, her buckskin moccasins and her manta dress.

From then on, Feather dressed like the other girls and tried to act like the other girls, and as the years passed, she forgot what her father looked like, forgot even her own language. She learned, as her father had commanded, attending the missionary school and reading every book the Cumminses owned. She learned the Bible and the white man's religion, but she never completely believed. She learned to love the books and to value them, but she knew she was missing the Tellings of her people.

The missionary couple was kind to her, protecting her as best they could from the taunts of the other children, but they were already old when she came into their lives, and sickly. She was only thirteen when Charles Cummins died, and Sarah Cummins soon thereafter. Feather was put into the care of another missionary, but he was not kind, nor did he protect her. Instead, he had…

She never let herself think about that.

She left the settlement that had once been Yerba Buena and was now called San Francisco.

At first, she could not bear to return to her own people, the Miwok. She wasn't ready. Instead, she remembered a story from when she was small and lived among them. It was one of the few stories she remembered, and she often thought about it long into the night, after the white man's lessons threatened to overwhelm her. She clung to the myth, for when she thought of it, she remembered how it felt to belong to the land.

It is said that after Coyote and Lizard created the world and everything in it, they argued. They agreed that humans should be created, but they fought over whether The People should be allowed hands. Lizard won the argument in the end, and thus humans have fingers and hands to grasp things and get into mischief.

But Coyote was angry. He went away and created a place of his own, hidden from humans and all other creatures, a paradise that the humans would be allowed to enter one day, but only once they had learned the lesson of bearing hands.

Until then, men would be clever and lord it over the other creatures, but they would die alone, and turn to stone.

It was a silly bedtime story, perhaps, and she didn't quite understand it, but it fascinated Feather. She spent months walking the trails of the High Sierra, looking for this paradise, knowing it for a myth and yet still wanting to believe it existed.

Eventually, she found her tribe, her people. They'd been driven high into the Sierra Nevada by the encroachment of white men. Her father had grown old, but remained chief of the Miwok.

"I am happy to see you, daughter," he said in Miwok.

Tears sprang into her eyes as she understood his words. But even if she had not, the look of kindness on his face would have made her weep.

And so had come a second learning period as she reimmersed herself in the culture of her people. Their language returned to her as though she had never left, but the comfort she had once felt among them was gone.

She didn't feel as though she belonged with the Miwok, but she stayed for her father's sake.

Litonya quickly discovered that her people, except for her father, did not want to learn what she had to teach them about the white man, his religion or language. Most importantly, they did not wish to learn about what the invaders wanted. She almost despaired, for she saw how many more white men sailed into the harbor of San Francisco every year and understood more would come.

The miners crept ever closer, following the stream, until they neared the sacred valley. Then her father sent for her. "The Skoocoom is upset," he told her. "You must go to the white men and warn them they are in danger."

When Litonya had first returned to her people, she had not believed the beast to be real. She vaguely remembered childhood tales of the Skoocoom, but as an adult, she thought them superstition. The white man's attitude had affected her more than she knew.

But one day, she saw the Skoocoom staring at her from the trees, as if Litonya was suspicious and possibly threatening.

She went alone to talk the white men, knowing they wouldn't believe her. "Thou art in danger," she told them.

"*Art* we now," the leader of the miners laughed.

"Thou must stop," she insisted.

"Who's going to stop us?" the miner asked.

"There is a Being who lives in these mountains who will take offense at thy intrusion. We cannot protect thee."

They were amused by how she spoke their language, but it was clear they didn't take her seriously—not until Chief Honon and the men of the tribe appeared on the hills above them, fully armed.

The white men fell silent at the sight and conferred anxiously.

"We will mine the lower reaches of the stream first," the leader said, finally. "It's what we planned to do all along."

For a time, the miners stayed away. But they could not stay away for long. It might have been only one or two of them at first, but inevitably, they climbed too far. The Miwok found out about the trespass one night, when there was a loud bellowing from the mountains. A wind swept through the village. Shelters were knocked down, cooking pots overturned, and fires broke out. Amid the confusion, children cried out in fear.

In the morning, a young boy and a young girl were missing.

They were never found.

Litonya was summoned to the Council.

The next morning, she reluctantly donned the dress of a white woman and descended, alone, into the valley.

***

Strauss, or rather the creature pretending to be Strauss, waited behind the door. Virginia didn't know how she knew, but every primeval instinct that her ancestors had bestowed upon her was screaming a warning about the danger. It was the thing in the dark, the monster in the basement, at the bottom of the stagnant pond, just beyond the turn on a dark path.

It waited.

She'd seen werewolves transform: the flow of saliva over the sharp fangs, the wild aspect to their eyes, the transformation into the rawness of nature, of tooth and claw, without thought, only hunger. The Change was most frightening not upon its completion, for she'd seen wolves and they fit into her perceptions of what was natural. No, the truly terrible part was when they were neither man nor wolf, but something worse—something unnatural and without the redeeming aspects of either species. Something dark and malformed.

Imagining him Turning in the darkness only made it worse.

She opened the door.

It cracked like a shot, and Virginia fought the impulse to run. There would be no stealthy attack; this was her only chance. She threw the door open and leapt into the room.

It was pitch black. The werewolf had completely covered the window. Virginia felt a sharp pain in her hand. The pistol flew out of her fingers and into the darkness, landing who knew where. She instinctively put up her arms, and again there came a slashing pain. She felt the blood start flowing from her wounds.

She ducked, not even thinking how or why, and felt the wind of a slashing blow pass above her head. Then she rolled to one side and heard the smack of a blow on the floor next to her. She scrambled to her feet, feeling a compulsion to jump. As she did, she sensed the passage of another attack, this time below her.

Virginia marveled at her ability to guess her opponent's moves. But unfortunately, there was no way for her to attack. Her weapon was gone. All she had were her fists. She swung wildly, and amazingly, she struck something. There was a howl of pain. By some kind of wild luck, she had connected with Strauss's misaligned jaw. She struck again, moving forward, and again connected.

Then he was attacking again, with a shriek that seemed to shake the walls of the room. Virginia dodged in the dark, each time sensing where the next blow would be before it fell. But each time, the strike came closer. It was only a matter of time before he'd have her.

A blinding light flared in the room. Virginia's eyes adjusted faster than the werewolf's. She glimpsed Feather holding a lantern in one hand and a butcher knife in the other. It was a knife Virginia used every day, and when the Indian girl threw it to her, she easily plucked it out of the air by the familiar worn handle, turned, and thrust it into the darkness.

The werewolf almost impaled himself on the blade, but at the last second, moving faster than any human, he twisted to one side and the blade struck him in the shoulder. He winced but held the young women at bay with a snarl and red, glowing eyes. Then he ripped the knife from his shoulder with his teeth. A toss of his head, and the knife clattered into a corner.

All of Virginia's courage and resolve fled. She knew all too well how fast the werewolf could strike. There was no way to escape.

She drew herself up to her full height, resolve steeling her spine, determined to hold the monster back for the sake of the Indian girl. She moved between Feather and the beast. "Run, Feather!" she cried. "Get help!"

Feather did not move.

The werewolf opened his crooked mouth and a sound came out that was like words, but also like the growl of an animal. Either way, the meaning was clear. He was promising them a painful death.

Virginia clenched her jaw. *I was spared that winter in the mountains*, she thought, *so I could destroy these creatures. But Feather doesn't deserve this fate.* She gathered herself to leap at the creature, into its jaws if need be, anything to give Feather a chance to get away.

"No, Virginia," Feather said, her measured, calm voice, pulling Virginia back. "Let me…"

Again, an intense light filled the room. Virginia closed her eyes involuntarily. When she opened them again, she saw the lantern fly past her, toward the werewolf, who drew back, seemingly blinded. The lantern burst over him, and he emitted a half-human, half-animal cry. He batted at the flames, which only spread the fire. He turned and glowered at Virginia before leaping for the window and smashing through it.

Virginia and Feather ran to the window in time to see the werewolf land in the middle of the muddy alley and roll in the puddles there. They watched the creature transform back into the shape of Herman Strauss. Disoriented, he stumbled to his feet, glaring up at the broken window before staggering out of the alley.

***

"We have to get out of here," Virginia said, turning away from the window.

She felt Feather's small but surprisingly firm hand on her arm. "Stay," Feather said calmly. "It is too late."

As if in response, they heard a question from the doorway. "What happened here?"

Mrs. Harrelson was wide-eyed and pale. She wore a nightgown and a sleeping bonnet and resembled an oversized child, but her sleep-bleary eyes quickly gained focus.

"We heard a strange sound from the room below us," Feather said. "It sounded like some kind of animal."

Virginia nodded. *Room 14* was on the third floor, at the end of the corridor. Their own room was directly above it. There was a rickety fire escape running down the side of the building. It was just possible they could have gotten here before anyone else.

"When we knocked on the door, a man opened it and grabbed us," Feather continued. "He looked terrible; vicious. We were afraid for our lives, and for our…" She gulped and fell silent.

Virginia finally spoke up. "Feather threw our lantern at him. He…he was on fire. He thrashed around and fell out of the window."

Mrs. Harrelson looked skeptical, but as the hotel guests crowded around her, she apparently decided this wasn't the time to question the girls' story.

"Pardon, Miss, but what happened to your hand?" one of the guests asked, pointing at the blood dripping down Virginia's fingers. He was dressed in some kind of velvet smoking jacket and had an arch tone to his voice.

"She cut it on the broken window shards," Feather answered.

Virginia saw what were clearly claw marks and hid her hand in the folds of her dress.

"What was it? What made that infernal racket?" asked Mrs. Peterson. She was an old woman on her way to San Francisco, the mother of a rich miner, though her accent was Midwestern dirt poor. "It sounded like a dog."

Mrs. Harrelson bent over and picked a clump of fur up off the floor. There was blood on the end of the tuft. "Did he bring a dog into the room?" she asked. Then the innkeeper went to the window, gently moving aside Virginia, who stood in a daze, her legs shaking. She wanted to sit down, but, glancing at the werewolf's rumpled bed, couldn't bear the thought of sitting on it. Mrs. Harrelson looked down at the muddy alley, saw that the puddles were red with blood, and frowned. Then she turned and shooed the guests away, her take-charge manner fully restored.

"There is nothing we can do until morning," she said. "Go back to bed." She practically pushed the last of the gawkers out and slammed the door. Then she went over to the corner of the room and picked up the pistol, which was still loaded and cocked.

"How did this get here?" she muttered aloud, as if mystified. But she gave the two girls an appraising look that belied her question. She gingerly lowered the hammer into a resting position and placed the gun in the pocket of her voluminous robe.

Mrs. Harrelson turned and, before Virginia could react, grabbed her wounded hand and inspected it. She glanced sharply at Virginia, who avoided her eyes. "Do you know who it was?"

Virginia didn't answer.

"One of the miners, perhaps." Feather answered for her. "He was rough looking. I do not doubt he might have done such a thing before. They forget about civilized ways up there in the mountains."

"But if he survived, why run away?" Mrs. Harrelson wondered, clearly expecting no answer. Her gaze fell on Feather. "Feather, you've spoken more in this past hour than in the entire year I've known you. And you, Virginia, are singularly silent." Her sharp gray eyes missed nothing as she looked from one girl to the other. Then she shrugged and put her arm around Virginia's shoulder. "Come, girl. Let's bandage your hand."

***

Mrs. Harrelson led the girls back to the kitchen, closing the doors to give them privacy. Now that the fight was over, Virginia couldn't stop shaking. Feather got up and grabbed a towel and draped it over her friend's shoulders like a blanket.

While Feather bandaged her hand, Mrs. Harrelson went off and came back a short time later to announce that the missing guest from *Room 14* was a man named Herman Strauss, and that she would inform the local constabulary first thing in the morning. She stared at her two charges in silence for a long moment, as if she wanted to question them further, but they both looked intent on their tasks, so she subsided.

"I think there is more to this than you say," she said, finally. There was a brief pause before she added dryly, "Men can be real beasts."

Mrs. Harrelson arched one brow at them before sweeping out of the room, leaving the girls in awkward silence until Virginia caught Feather's eye. Suddenly, they were giggling, and then erupting into full-throated laughter. They could have died; they could have been found out; but they had survived. Still, their laughter had a tinge of hysteria to it.

"Beasts indeed," Virginia said, which set them off again.

After a while, Virginia realized she was chuckling alone. Feather was staring her with a serious expression. "Thou art a Hunter," she whispered.

"What do you mean?" Virginia asked uneasily.

"That is why I came to work here," Feather said. "But I had to be sure. Now I am. No one but a Hunter could have survived a fight in a dark room with a Skinwalker, especially not an unarmed girl. It is no accident thou didst survive the Donner Party. Thou art a Hunter, Virginia."

"A Hunter?"

"My people have a word for it: *Canowiki*. Hunter is the closest English word," Feather explained. "In every generation, some few are born who can fight the creatures of the dark; not only the Skinwalkers, but all manner of beasts. We were told there was such a one among the party that was trapped in the mountains. My uncle, Salvador, went to see if it was true, but he never returned. I fear he fell to the beasts."

"Salvador was your uncle?"

"I knew him as Sewati."

"He was brave and kind," Virginia said. "He and his companion, Luis, helped our family. But…I don't know what happened to them. They went off with the last escape party, but never returned." She bit her lip, remembering the two silent Indian sentinels who had brought her family food and stayed near their cabin, protecting them from the werewolves.

"The survivors of that group came to my village," Feather said. She was blinking as if trying to hold back tears. Her voice sounded constricted, almost hoarse, as if she was having a hard time speaking. Virginia was surprised by the show of emotion. "We knew from the look in the white men's eyes that they had killed them, but we took no revenge. That winter took so many of my people, with or without the help of the white men."

Feather's eyes were turned away, and her voice, so strong and confident a short time ago, was soft and low.

Virginia was amazed that the Indian girl was opening up after all this time. "I thought you were estranged from your people."

"I was…I am. But I still belong to them, and they to me." She hesitated for a moment before she explained. "After I left the missionaries, I went to live among my people. Not long after, the miners came, invading our territory. But they drew too near the territory of…another. This creature took revenge upon my people, carrying away several children.

"I, having been raised by the white missionaries, was sent to look for thee, and I was *glad* for it. I feel more comfortable among thy kind than mine, but I am not fool enough to believe I am one of you. I need but walk out into the street and listen to the calls of the men and see the scorn of the women. That is why I stayed in this place, because thou didst not treat me thus. I had thought a Hunter would not treat me that way."

Virginia wanted to deny that she was a Canowiki, or whatever they called it. A Hunter. *I'm just a fifteen-year-old girl!* she wanted to protest. *I'm no slayer of monsters!*

But when she looked inside, she hesitated. Everything since Truckee Lake had seemed to happen in a dream, a daze, and so she had left her home and her family, seeking she knew not what. She knew only that the humdrum life she had been living was not the life for which she was destined. As terrible as it sounded, the thought of battle called to her, drawing out a restlessness she didn't know how to quell.

She had recognized it as she'd stalked and battled the werewolf, Herman Strauss. It was like shedding an overcoat that had grown too tight across her shoulders, and shedding it gave her freedom at last.

"I have been seeking thee," Feather said, her dark eyes calm again. "We—my tribe—need thy help. We are being stalked by a terrible creature."

"A werewolf?" Virginia asked, feeling her pulse quicken.

"No…something far worse."

Chapter Four

I live.

I expected to die when the monster swung me against the tree, but I awoke with a deep gash to my head, bleeding and dizzy, but still breathing.

I am beyond terror. I am numb.

It is a mystery to me why the monster let me live.

I have this journal, where I recounted our travels, and the stub of a pencil. When daylight leaks through the narrow opening of the cave, it is reflected and redoubled, giving me enough light to scribble a few thoughts.

Kovac was vainglorious and delusional. He'd been so certain that we'd be rich, and I...I was a fool. What possessed me to follow such a madman, I do not now understand.

Well, we found gold, that is for certain: more gold than King Midas had, but it doesn't matter. Kovac is dead, and I will follow him to the pits of hell, if I'm not there already. The cave reeks of death, but even more, it has the taint of the creatures that live here.

I awoke in the darkness, and the foul smell smothered me until I gagged and vomited. I struggled for breath, then gagged again, emptying what was left in my belly. I kicked out in agony, and the bones scattered and rattled, and something scurried away. There was a rustling sound. I sat frozen in fear, listening to the movement, until I realized that it was insects feeding on the decaying carcasses that litter the floor of the cave.

I tried to rise, but my legs gave out under me, from weakness or from a wound, it is hard to say. There is surprisingly little pain, but I am beset by an overwhelming weariness.

The miasma of the smell has coated my skin and my clothing until I have become part of it; a wraith, wallowing in filth.

I am an educated man. Kovac and I were different from the other miners. We left good jobs in San Francisco, he an accountant and I a teacher in a school for the children of those who own the town. Perhaps it was proximity to wealth that made me so greedy, for I grew weary of teaching *Beowulf* and *Hamlet* to ungrateful children. Because of my education, I know too well what holds me captive, and my fate.

When I saw the shadow of the creature, I heard Beowulf's lament:

"The monster rose, from demon-haunted halls,

Spawned in slime, evil banished,
By God, forever punished,
Hell is his home, Hell on Earth."

***

Unaware of the events in the hotel, Frank and Thomas Whitford left Sutter's Fort early in the morning, their Indian ranch hand, Hugh, driving the wagon. Thomas sat with Hugh while Frank was left to sit in the back, holding onto the crates of supplies. No one else was on the road to stir up the dust that usually hung over it, which gifted them with clear, cold skies stretching all the way to the mountains. The puddles they'd had to flog the horses through on the way into town were drying up.

Frank wished he were on horseback, but that wasn't the kind of trip they were on. Once a quarter, they came into town for the few things they couldn't make or grow themselves. They had most of what they needed at the ranch, for it was a huge spread, with many capable hands.

It was Frank's first trip back to town since coming home. He was still trying to regain his bearings around the homestead. It seemed as if only Hugh was unchanged. The half-breed Indian had always been there, a steady, reliable presence in the lives of the Whitford boys. Frank hadn't even known the tall man was an Indian until someone had shouted a slur at him once in town.

Frank wasn't sure which had changed more, the ranch or him. He hadn't wanted to come back, and had hoped to work with some of his friends in Boston during the summer. But his stepfather's last letter was so strange that he'd felt compelled to return home.

Surprisingly, the ranch seemed to have fallen on hard times in the two years Frank had been gone. Most bewilderingly, the property boundaries had shifted, and no one could tell him why.

"Father?" he ventured. The old man didn't seem to hear him, but Frank continued anyway. "I've been wondering why you sold the bottom pastures to the Newtons?"

From the driver's seat, Hugh glanced over his shoulder with a strange expression. He gave Frank a slight warning shake of his head.

"That is none of your concern," Frank's stepfather snapped.

Frank wanted to object that it was very much his concern, but something about Hugh's warning glance told him to stay silent. Frank examined Thomas's stubborn posture, looking for a chink in the iron facade.

Nothing he'd seen since he'd returned home surprised Frank more than his stepfather selling the Bottoms, especially to Henry Newton, whom he disdained. The Newtons had arrived several years ago, flush with money, and had begun buying out the smaller ranches in the valley. Worse, they had begun to push into territory that had been given, by unspoken agreement, to the Indians. Henry Newton had been agitating for the removal of the Indians ever since arriving in California. Until then, Thomas Whitford and the other early ranchers had always gotten along well with the natives.

"Father," Frank began again. "I need to understand what's happening…"

"I don't want to talk about it." The scowl on Thomas's face was impenetrable armor, so Frank fell silent. The buckboard rattled endlessly, and it was too noisy to do much talking anyway.

His stepfather had changed while Frank was back East. He'd always been a grim man, but the death of Frank's mother had made him shut down completely. Now he seldom talked, never laughed, and spent much of his time holed up in his gloomy office, leaving the operation of the ranch to Patrick.

Frank couldn't remember any father but Thomas Whitford, and yet…he still couldn't quite get himself to leave the "step" out of the "father."

Patrick, who was bigger and more outgoing as well as being Thomas's natural son, had always seemed like the older brother. He was tending toward fat, with the broad, weathered features of a Western rancher. Their youngest brother, James, was smaller and quieter. Red-haired and cheerful, he was almost always reading a book or daydreaming.

It didn't take long for Frank to realize his father needed his help saving the ranch, but every day, he regretted leaving Massachusetts. It wasn't the sophisticated community of Harvard that he missed. He'd stuck out like a steer with one horn there. It was more that the ranch sorely lacked female companionship, something Frank had enjoyed as a star member of the Harvard rowing team.

None of the neighboring ranchers had any suitable daughters—except maybe Patsy Newton, who was as shallow as Dry Creek. There were prostitutes in town, most of them intimidatingly forward, and some old widows running hotels and laundries. The Donner Party girl was the first female since his return to catch his interest.

Frank couldn't get her out of his thoughts. Virginia Reed was her name. The girl was a classic beauty; blonde hair and clear blue eyes, a petite figure and dignified bearing. It was her smile, disarmingly candid and fresh, that had caught his attention. He couldn't forget how quickly that smile had disappeared and her expression had closed down when his father had grabbed his arm and hissed, "That's *her!*"

Such a pity, he thought. *She is a beautiful girl. And in the face of such scorn, she has an indomitable spirit.*

Maybe he would put up with his brothers' ribbing and his father's disapproval and go see her. The alternative seemed to be Patsy, that old washcloth of a girl, who had managed to come by the ranch three times already, making a worse impression every time.

One thing Frank had learned at school among all those Easterners was that others' opinions didn't matter. He'd come to realize he didn't really fit in anywhere; not with the rough ranchers at home or with the more refined families of the East. He was, forever and always, an outsider.

So what did it matter if his father and everyone else disapproved of his courting Virginia Reed?

Besides, not everyone in the Donner Party had resorted to cannibalism. Of all the families trapped in the snows, the Reeds were one of the few to hold their dignity intact. But there was always that lingering doubt and the unspoken presumption of guilt by association, and the sense that it was the Donner Party's fault, through foolishness or laziness, that they had been trapped.

But Frank knew from personal experience how quickly the weather could change, how quickly the snows could trap the unprepared.

As a child, his friends had invited him on an expedition into the mountains, but his stepfather had kept him home to do chores.

One of the boys never returned. Billy Thomson came out of the mountains alone, wet and delirious, with no memory of what had happened to Jeremiah Fleming, only a strange story of how they had lost the trail when it began snowing. Jeremiah had torn off his clothing and run into the woods, but Billy had managed to stumble across the trail. Rather than pursue his friend, he made his way back to the valley.

By the unwritten code of the West, Billy should have gone after his friend. But if Billy had done that, both would have died. After enduring years of scorn, the Thomsons moved from their homestead. Like many of their neighbors, they sold out to the Newtons.

Before he left, Billy Thompson implied that something else had happened to the Donner Party; something that had been hushed up. Billy had whispered something about wolves. "But not natural wolves," he had said in his portentous way. "These were half-man, half-wolf, thems that did the eating."

Frank had laughed at that, but since then, he'd heard other rumors, even more outlandish and unbelievable.

An image of Virginia Reed's face came into his mind.

That girl fought her way through hell, Frank thought, *and yet has the smile of an angel.*

***

Patrick waited at the gate, looking grim. This gate had once been the entrance to the Whitford ranch, but now the land beyond it belonged to the Newtons, and Frank felt its wrongness each time he passed this stretch of road.

Worse, Henry Newton was riding alongside Patrick, accompanied by his foreman, Dave Martin. Newton was a huge man in girth, and Frank always felt sorry for the horses that had to carry him. He was bald on top of his head, but let his white-streaked hair grow long on the sides and back, and it merged with his heavy beard.

Frank had immediately disliked the man, even before he'd spoken and made his odious opinions known. Newton made it clear he wanted the Indians gone. Martin was even worse, speaking ill of the Miwok every chance he had. He was a dark, ruddy-faced man, always scowling.

"It happened again," Patrick said when the Whitfords' wagon rolled up. "Three head of cattle rustled this time. Oliver and James are tracking them."

Frank's heart dropped. Oliver Newton was about the same age as James, but much more outgoing. For some reason Frank couldn't understand, James had fallen under Oliver's sway. It was an unhealthy influence.

"Just the two of them?" Thomas cried. "I told you not to do anything until I got back."

"Don't worry, Father," Patrick said. "I told them to keep their distance. Besides, I have no doubt that it's the Miwok again."

"Three head of cattle?" Frank said. "Is that all?" He regretted it the instant the words passed his lips. His father looked almost puzzled by the remark, for to him, losing one cow was as bad as losing a herd, but Patrick caught his meaning right away.

"Because we have hundreds?" Patrick sneered. "How about we give a few head to the wolves, maybe some more to the Paiutes, maybe some more to the Maidu? Hell, McCarthy could use some cattle to replenish his stock."

Why not? Frank almost asked, stopping himself just in time. Old man McCarthy had been kind to them years ago, when they had fallen on hard times. The wolves? They took a few head each winter, and for that they were being hunted to extinction. As far as the Indians were concerned…

"They're starving," Frank said. "The miners have pushed them too far into the mountains."

So far, Newton had said nothing. He didn't need to with Patrick there. Now, the older man scoffed at Frank's concern over the Indians. "That's not our problem," he snapped. "They should stay where they belong."

"They *let* us settle here," Frank said. He turned to his father for support. "When you arrived in this valley, you were starving, that's what you told me. The Miwok saved you."

Thomas looked away and didn't say anything, which seemed to encourage Newton. "Well, the savages certainly steal like they own everything," he said.

"This land was once theirs," Frank insisted.

"No longer," Patrick joined in heatedly. "The land belongs to those who make use of it."

Frank sighed, trying one more time to be reasonable. "Starting a war over a few head of cattle hardly seems worth the cost."

Newton snorted and shook his head.

Patrick seemed to grow larger in his saddle. He was a burly man to begin with, and in that beefy body, Frank could sometimes see the vitality of his stepfather as a younger man. "Is that what they teach you in your fancy schools?" Patrick sneered. "To buy off your enemy?"

"Of course not, you…" Frank began, feeling his anger starting to rise.

"Enough!" their father roared.

Frank was glad the old man had stopped him. Frank had almost called his brother an ignorant ass, which would have been a bad thing to say given the volatile tempers, no matter whether it was true or not.

"We should send a search party after James and Oliver right away," Newton said in the ensuing silence. His air was commanding, and Patrick nodded agreement.

"Who's stopping you?" Frank asked.

Newton flushed, recognizing Frank's implication. Without the elder Whitford's blessing, most of the local ranchers would refuse to go along. Despite the ascendency of the Newtons' spread and the decline of the

Whitfords', there was no comparing the relative respect the two patriarchs enjoyed among their peers.

"Hitch your horse to the wagon, Patrick," Thomas commanded. "Get in back with Frank."

"But Mr. Newton wants me to go along..."

"Patrick!" the old man admonished, and Frank felt a swell of pride at the familiar tone of command in his father's voice. It was one the boys never disobeyed.

Again, Patrick turned red, his round, open face clearly showing his embarrassment.

"You go along, now, Patrick," Newton said easily, as if it was his own idea. As if he was giving permission. His cold eyes bored into Frank as if he'd never seen him before. "My daughter has been expecting you to come calling, Frank," he said. "I told her you just got back and were settling in, and you'd be along soon enough."

Frank nodded, but said nothing. He sensed Patrick glaring at him, and something that should have been obvious suddenly became clear. Patrick was jealous.

It would be so much easier if Patrick was the eldest son, Frank thought. Then Patrick could take over the ranch and marry Patsy Newton.

Well, why not?

What if Frank renounced his inheritance?

It might break the old man's heart at first, but he'd see the wisdom of it eventually.

Patrick got off his horse and opened the gate for the wagon.

"Don't wait too long to send a search party," Newton said to Thomas. "If my boy is in enemy territory, he needs our help."

Newton urged his horse around the wagon and galloped away. Hugh, with a silent Thomas Whitford beside him, drove the wagon through the gate, continuing toward the homestead. The strained silence remained until they reached the veranda of the ranch house an hour later. The moment the horses were put to pasture, Patrick started up again.

"Henry...Mr. Newton says we should follow the rustlers. Teach them a lesson, once and for all. Most of the neighboring ranchers will want to join in, and will send a couple cowhands each. Henry says we should finish this."

"What else does *Henry* suggest?" Frank asked. "That we slaughter the entire tribe?"

"If needs be," Patrick sneered.

"Enough," Thomas warned, following them slowly up the steps.

Frank kept his tone calm and reasonable. "If you take our ranch hands that close to the gold fields, half won't come back. We've a hard enough time keeping them as it is."

"Maybe they're more loyal than y…"

"I said *enough!*" Thomas's voice broke through their argument again, this time sounding tired and resigned instead of angry. But there was no mistaking the finality of the tone. He trudged through the entryway and into his study, his sons trailing behind him. Thomas sat down heavily behind the desk and looked up at them tiredly.

"When James returns, I want you all in the study. We need to treat with Chief Honon and resolve this rustling problem once and for all. See if we can't find some solution. Frank is right; we don't want a war. But Patrick is right too. This can't go unanswered."

Thomas Whitford stared at his two sons until he was sure he had their attention. "No more of this bickering, hear?"

"Yes, Father," Patrick said.

Frank nodded in agreement.

"Good. Now go see Cookie about supper."

***

Henry Newton rode home shaking his head. He'd heard tell that the younger Thomas Whitford had been a man to be reckoned with, but all Newton saw now was a withered old fellow, grieving for his wife, letting his weak-minded son run his ranch into the ground.

He was still taking the measure of Frank Whitford, to whom he'd paid little attention when he was younger. Frank had returned from school a grown man; worse, his *own* man. And he was getting in the way, distracting Patrick just as Newton began to play him.

All might still be well if Frank married Patsy. *If I could make that happen,* Newton mused, *then I'd get the Whitford spread without a fight.*

Newton had arrived in the valley several years before, but he was still an outsider to the other ranchers. His inheritance, which had been a modest legacy back East, turned out to be a substantial amount of money in the West. But his ranch could only grow by absorbing other ranches, and for that to happen, the other ranchers had to be willing to sell. So Newton had set out to systematically weaken them, by whatever means possible. His biggest obstacle was the Whitfords; no matter how many ranchers Newton bought out, his ranch was still never going to be as big as the Whitfords'.

The other possibility was…

"This is your chance, Boss," said his foreman, Martin, interrupting his thoughts. "You play this right and you can get rid of the Indians, expand your ranch even further."

Newton's thoughts exactly.

One night, Martin had told him about how he and his two friends had been part of "regulator" troops in the south of California, and how the civilized folk were taking care of the Indian problem down in those parts by killing the savages wherever they found them.

It hadn't all gone smoothly. Martin had a price on his head. But no one had come searching for him.

Bud Carpenter and George Banks had an aura of lawlessness about them, but Martin was forceful enough to handle the unruly ranch hands, freeing Newton for other things. It made Martin an ideal foreman.

So far, the other ranchers in the valley were unwilling to wipe out the Indians, and so Newton's hands were tied. His relations were rocky enough with his neighbors, some of whom, especially the Whitfords, inexplicably *liked* the savages.

"Let me think on it," Newton said, putting Martin off again.

***

The frigid silence between Patrick and Frank lasted through dinner. They went to their rooms without exchanging another word. Frank tried to read for a while, but gave up and turned out the light. He lay in the dark, his thoughts swirling about Virginia Reed and his brother James and his father's strange behavior.

Frank finally gave up trying to sleep and slipped quietly out the back door. Between the main house and the bunkhouse where most of their employees slept, there was a small shack. Frank knocked softly on the door, and it immediately opened.

Hugh seemed unsurprised to see him. He motioned Frank inside and pulled out a chair at the little table where a single candle flickered. The room was otherwise bare except for a small bed in the corner.

"I expected you hours ago," Hugh said, sitting down across from Frank. He folded his arms and waited for Frank to ask his questions.

His eyes were deep set, and all Frank could see were the shadows across his face. "What's happened here? Why is Father acting this way?"

Hugh didn't need to ask what Frank meant, although he sat in silence for a long moment before answering. "Mr. Whitford ran out of money..." he began.

"How is that possible?" Frank exclaimed before the Indian could finish.

Hugh didn't react, allowing Frank's impatience to grow in the silence that followed. Finally, he said, "We have been having troubles with rustlers."

This time Frank stayed silent, realizing that Hugh would reveal the details in his own way and at his own pace.

"They blame the Miwok," Hugh continued.

"They?"

"Mr. Newton and the other ranchers," Hugh said.

"But you don't think it's them, do you?" Frank said. Hugh was not a Miwok, but from a friendly tribe farther south.

"The rustling began soon after Henry Newton arrived," Hugh whispered. He let his words hang in the air.

Frank let that sink in. Was that possible? That Newton would steal? "Doesn't Father see that?"

Hugh shook his head. "He can't conceive that a neighbor could do such a thing. But he also resists blaming the Miwok. So when he ran out of money, he was forced to sell the Bottoms to Mr. Newton."

"Why does he need the money?" Frank asked.

"You don't know?"

Frank shook his head, frustrated.

"Your college education was far more expensive than expected."

Frank was stunned. He sat unmoving, watching the flickering candle, trying to absorb what he hadn't wanted to know. "I thought there was a fund for that. From my mother's family."

"It is true your mother requested that you go to school," Hugh acknowledged. "But there was no fund. Mr. Whitford promised to send you to Harvard."

"I didn't even *want* to go!" Frank objected. "If he was going to send anyone back East, it should have been James. He wanted to go so badly."

Hugh shook his head sadly. "Your mother wanted you to have an education, Frank, and your stepfather is a man of his word."

It explained a lot: why James was so aloof toward him, and why Patrick was out and out hostile. While Frank had been back East rowing sculls and only half applying himself to his studies, his adopted family had been struggling to keep him there.

Hugh seemed to know what he was thinking. "Patrick has fallen under the sway of Mr. Newton," he said. "He resents you, Frank."

"I heard what he said about Chief Honon," Frank said. "That's not the way I remember Patrick talking."

"Mr. Newton's hate is strong and simple. It explains everything...while it explains nothing."

Frank bowed his head, wondering how his old friend could make so much sense and at the same time make none at all.

***

It made James nervous, how Oliver kept talking, and how loudly, no matter how far they ventured into Indian Territory. There had been a time when the Miwok and the Whitford family had been peaceable neighbors. Their father had allowed the Indians to hunt on his land, and Chief Honon had allowed them to graze their cattle on Indian land. But that had been years ago. With miners searching for gold on both their lands, things were a mite tense between them. The interlopers killed off wildlife, and food was scarce in the mountains.

James suspected the rustlers were miners, who seemed to respect nothing but their feverish desire for gold. Whoever it was, they'd left the strangest trail he'd ever seen. It took time to notice the pattern; it meandered pointlessly, sometimes even backtracking, sometimes climbing into the mountains, and consistently went through thick undergrowth. If there was a choice between a straight dirt trail and a winding sideways route over stone and gravel, the rustlers, whoever they were, always took the roundabout way.

But there was no point to it. The rustled cattle couldn't help but leave a trail, blundering along, breaking branches, stomping on bushes, leaving their excrement everywhere. Still, even past the foothills and into the bracingly cold air of the ridgeline, it was unclear whom they were tracking.

"What we ought to do is join the miners," Oliver was saying. "Just for a day or two. Maybe we'll get lucky."

"What's the point?" James answered, almost under his breath. "All the good sites have been taken."

"Not all of them," Oliver said. He reined in his horse, turned around, and grinned.

"What do you mean?" James asked, uneasily recognizing the mischievous look.

"Well, the way I see it, the Miwok owe us for our cattle…" Oliver began.

James started shaking his head. "No, no, no."

"I bet there's gold there, just waiting to be picked up. And no one knows about it but us."

"We promised," James said. "Chief Honon and my father shook hands on it, on our sacred honor."

"What do Indians know about honor?" Oliver scoffed. "Stealing cattle ain't exactly part of the deal."

"We don't know it was them."

"Hell we don't. It's only fair they pay us back."

James pulled up his horse while his friend rode on. "They're expecting us back, Oliver. We don't want them to send out a search party. How would that look?"

Oliver only scowled and set his spurs to his mount, urging it up a ravine.

It was perhaps not the best thing to say to Oliver. Not long after the Newtons had arrived in California, Oliver had disappeared, and the whole valley had hunted for him for days. They'd found him playing with the Indian children, as brown and dirty as they were. They'd accepted him so completely into their tribe that they had tattooed a mark on the back of his hand. It looked like two lightning bolts crossing in the middle.

Henry Newton's face had been dark with fury when he'd found his son.

Oliver had never lived it down, and wore gloves whenever possible.

"We don't need to go back right away," Oliver insisted. "Frank can do your chores. He'll jump at the chance to cozy up to your old man."

James frowned. For some reason, both Oliver and Patrick disliked Frank. He had to admit, he resented Frank too: not because his oldest brother had it easy, as Oliver and Patrick seemed to think, but because James envied his education. Books and learning had held little interest for Frank, at least before he went East, but at night, James invariably curled up with a book while his brothers fooled around.

They kept riding, despite James's misgivings.

Despite the warmth of the sun, the boys bundled up against the insects and wore their hats low. The horses suffered even more, quivering and twitching, and giving an occasional whinny at the sheer relentlessness of the attack. The horses dropped their manure while walking, as if the piles of dung were offerings to the insects, as if they were trying to placate them. If so, it failed, for it only attracted more of the pests.

The path was covered with white pumice, shining brightly in the sun, causing the boys to squint as they peered into the bright day.

The mountain above was spotted with snow, beautiful from a distance, and as they drew closer, it loomed over them, a world of its own. The path wound along the base of high cliffs, their walls growing ever higher, the boulders at their base ever bigger; the tops of the cliffs bent over the riders, rock falls tumbling downward. Even in this landscape of broken stone, sumac and pine seedlings were growing.

The cattle tracks continued to meander back and forth across the hillside, but always climbed upward. At the top of the final tree-lined wave of hills was a massive tree fall, all the toppled trees pointing downward, the stripped logs looking like fortifications protecting the crest of the hill. *Stay back!* they seemed to be saying. *Go no farther!*

"These trees were stripped and placed here intentionally. Who would do this?" James wondered aloud.

"Indians," Oliver sneered, guiding his horse past the fortifications. "Obviously."

But James remained, gazing in wonder at the stockade. "I've never known them to do such a thing."

Oliver snorted. "Who knows what the savages might do?"

The two boys were close to the tree line, higher up than any miner or Indian would want go. The temperature dropped with every few hundred feet. As James noticed where the trail was heading, he stayed silent, remembering all the times they'd turned back at this point. Now he regretted ever showing his friend the secret canyon.

As the horses clambered up onto the shale shelf that was the highest they could be ridden, Oliver slid from his saddle, grinning at James. "Well, I guess we're heading for El Dorado after all!"

James had peeked into the narrow canyon once, and it indeed seemed like El Dorado; a magical place, with waterfalls and sylvan glades. The Indians called it the Sacred Place, and it was absolutely forbidden for any white man to enter. The trail led into the narrow opening, a still-steaming cow pie right at the entrance.

James chewed on his lower lip, knowing he wasn't going to be able to stop Oliver from pursuing the rustlers, but he had to try. "Oliver," he said. "Let's go back. We know where the trail leads. What if there is a whole band of them?"

Oliver didn't answer. He pulled his rifle from its saddle holster and cocked it. The metallic snap echoed eerily, bouncing off the hard shale of the hillside.

James tried again. "We should turn back, Oliver!"

Oliver hesitated, but didn't even look back to see if his friend was following as he disappeared into the canyon.

James sighed and dismounted. He was biting his lip so hard, he feared he might draw blood. He forced himself to relax. He tied his horse's reins to a withered juniper tree, pulled out his own rifle, and followed Oliver.

James could touch the boulders on either side of the entrance. They were worn so smooth that he suspected generations of Indians had done exactly that. Their most sacred ceremonies had been held in this place, out of sight of prying eyes, for as long as anyone could remember. They left offerings to one of their gods here.

It was lush and warm, and James had to remind himself that a moment before, he'd been shivering. The bright valley opened up just past the entrance and descended in a gentle slope to a small pond. From the tallest cliff poured a small waterfall, splashing into a pool that overflowed into a creek, which disappeared into a crevice on the downhill side of the valley.

With steep cliffs surrounding the pond on the valley floor, there should have been little light, especially this late in the day, but a warm glow came from somewhere James couldn't determine. Pines grew along the edges of the canyon, taller than any James had ever seen, seeming to reach up to the peaks of the mountains, wreathed in clouds.

James had an overwhelming sense of trespassing.

But it was more than that. It was as if the stones and trees of the canyon threatened them—which was strange, for it was so beautiful. A neighbor had once showed him drawings of Yosemite Valley, several days' ride south, and while it was glorious, there was a shimmering and fragile beauty to this canyon that made it even more awe-inspiring.

This place is not natural, James thought. The brittle splendor here was sharp, dangerous. *Blue waters can drown, and deep snows can smother, and the cliffs are filled with boulders.* All of it could simply pluck him from existence, leaving its beauty untouched.

He stared while Oliver hiked down the green meadow toward the pond. Then he gagged at the stench of something dead lying near him, hidden in the underbrush. It couldn't be the cattle, since they'd been missing for only a few days.

Oliver seemed oblivious as he strode toward two lumps near the edge of the pond. James hurried after him. The remains of the slaughtered cattle were strewn about in the mud near the water; tufts of fur and broken bone and scraps of red meat. A skull, horns intact, was split in half; another two were smashed to pieces, the brains extracted.

No human did this, not even Indians, James thought, *certainly not in the time they had.* They hadn't been more than an hour behind the rustlers. *And where did they go?* There was no way to get off the mountainside without being seen, unless there was a back entrance to this canyon. He looked around, but the cliffs were huge and solid. The trees didn't offer enough cover to hide anyone.

"Well, I still say they owe us," Oliver said. He kicked at a bone and it flipped over, the marrow glistening. He turned his back on the carnage and went to the side of the pond. He crouched in the shallows, sifting the gravel with his fingers.

The canyon suddenly became dark, and James looked to see if a storm was blowing in, but except for a few wispy clouds, it was clear. The sun was still bright, and yet it seemed dim.

There was a loud whoop. James looked down to see Oliver holding something that was glinting brightly even in the dim light.

"Biggest nugget I ever seen!' Oliver shouted. "We're rich, my friend. The pond is full of it, right here in the water, James! Last time we ever have to chase after stinking cows!"

James approached, trying to see what Oliver was holding. Something splashed into the pond, sending huge ripples across the otherwise still surface. Oliver must've thrown a big rock, skipping it across the water in his joy. Strangely, wherever the rock landed, a red splotch appeared on the surface of the pond.

He turned to Oliver just as his friend's body toppled over, his head gone. James stared in shock, turning back to see the detached head, not a rock at all, still bobbing in the pond. The light went out of Oliver's eyes as it sank, a large bubble breaking the surface with a pop.

James turned to run and found a tree behind him, a huge, moss-covered mass with two large branches, a thick trunk, and a knobby top. James couldn't take it in. It made no sense. It was unmoving, but it hadn't been there moments before. No, that wasn't moss; it was fur. Now the tree moved toward him. Eyes glared out of the round knot on top, intelligent and malevolent, bearing down on him.

James fired his rifle, certain of his aim at such close quarters, but the creature neither faltered nor flinched. It kept coming toward him. He dropped the rifle and ran from the clearing. The ground shook, the light dimmed further, and he felt the wind of the creature's approach. There was a roaring sound drowning out his shouts, and the growl of the monster filled his ears as an ever-increasing stench filled his nostrils. He felt himself snatched up, and then he was flying toward the tops of the trees.

James floated through the air in a moment that seemed to last an eternity. He closed his eyes. He could almost believe he was back home, in bed and dreaming.

And then something struck him in the back of his head, and he fell into a dreamless sleep.

Chapter Five

I heard the monster pass in the darkness of night before ever seeing it. Its tread was heavy but certain, as if it could see in the dark. The smell was overpowering. It hesitated beside me, and I dared not move until it continued on.

The pain in my head made me dizzy. When I tried to rise, I felt boneless and blind. I wondered, because of the pain, if I was permanently crippled. But somehow, I slept.

Awakening a second time, I glimpsed the small one. The first light of day flashed into the cave, revealing the creature watching me from the middle of the cavern. I say small, for it had a miniature shape, as if undeveloped—but in truth, it was nearly as tall as a juvenile human. Only in comparison to the other monster, the one who had captured me, did it seem diminutive.

Yet I sensed from the beginning that it was young. It didn't move at first, so I had time to examine it. It had two arms and two legs, and stood upright. It had a huge head, and what neck it had was obscured by a covering of long hair. The creature that had captured me was dark and could have been mistaken for a bear standing upright, but this one was pure white, with red eyes, which could have made it look demonic; instead, the eyes had a softness to them, the innocence of a small child. It is an albino, I am certain. It has large canines protruding over its lower lip. Its tongue sometimes hangs out when it concentrates. My fear of it had almost vanished when it finally approached me. I let it touch my face without wincing. It has large, square hands, with four fingers and a thumb.

I suspected I have been spared for one thing: to be this monstrous child's playmate.

***

"Something worse than werewolves?" Virginia repeated.

Feather looked solemn. She simply nodded. Virginia waited for her to say more, but Mrs. Harrelson returned just then, followed by a tall, gangly man with long black hair that was gray at the temples, giving him a shaggy dignity. He was dressed elegantly, with a silver star on his chest, but his clothes were stained with many days' wear.

"This is Sheriff Pike," Mrs. Harrelson said. "He has some questions for you."

He approached Virginia, but ignored Feather. "Virginia Reed?" he asked with a slight bow.

Virginia inclined her head. He seemed to know her, though she was certain she'd never met him before.

"I know your father," he said. "Fought with him in the Mexican War. A brave man. Apparently, his daughter is too."

Virginia felt her cheeks burn hot at the mention of her father fighting during the Mexican-American War. It only reminded her of that horrible winter trapped in the mountains. She'd never forgive Colonel Fremont and the other soldiers for conscripting her father for that silly battle instead of organizing a rescue mission to set off over the mountains.

Pike glanced at Feather, then dismissed her, and took a seat near Virginia. "Describe the man who attacked you."

Feather answered instead. "He was small and scrawny." The sheriff looked over at her as if surprised she had spoken. "He was quite dirty, and he stank," she continued.

"And?" Pike asked, turning back to Virginia. "Did he have any unusual features?"

"A broken jaw," Virginia said. "It seemed like it was at the wrong angle."

The sheriff slapped his hand on the table. "I knew it! You were lucky. He is a very dangerous man. We've been looking for him."

"Why?" Feather asked. Virginia almost smiled. Shy little Feather was so put out at being ignored that she was being uncharacteristically forward.

Pike frowned. "He claim-jumped some miners on Barrel Hill. Killed them, took their gold. But one of them managed to get away and describe him. I wasn't sure it was accurate until just now, because the survivor was delusional. Talking about monsters and such. I can almost understand why, because the carnage in that camp was like nothing I've ever seen. The men weren't just killed, they were eviscerated, taken apart. Wolves had gotten to them."

"Sheriff Pike!" Mrs. Harrelson exclaimed.

The man looked puzzled for a moment, then turned to Virginia. "I beg your pardon for the description. It was shocking, and I shouldn't have upset you."

Feather and Virginia managed not to look at each other.

"So, I've been keeping an eye out, but not really expecting him to show up here," Pike continued. "I'm sorry for that, Ma'am. Perhaps if I had been more alert, this attack wouldn't have happened." He stood up and once again gave Virginia his strange courtly bow.

"I'll find him, you can be sure of that," the sheriff said. "From the amount of blood in the alley, he can't have gone far. Thank you for your help, Miss Reed." At the last second, he gave Feather a glance and a slight nod.

"What happens if he comes back, Sheriff?" Feather asked.

"He wouldn't dare," the man said dismissively.

Mrs. Harrelson saw him out, and the girls were left alone again.

***

"He didn't seem to want to acknowledge you were here," Virginia said.

"Being ignored is preferable to being scorned," Feather shrugged. "It is of no matter."

"I'm sorry," Virginia said.

Feather shrugged again.

"You were about to say," Virginia finally said, breaking the ensuing silence. "What could be worse than a werewolf?"

"A creature that has always lived alongside my people," Feather said, settling back into her seat. "As long as we stay away from the Sacred Place, except to leave it ceremonial sacrifices, it leaves us alone."

"It?"

"My people call it the Ts'emekwes or the Skoocoom," Feather said. "Both names are borrowed from other tribes, as we will not use its real name—for if we say the true name aloud, the monster will hear and carry us away to be eaten. Some of my people think the Ts'emekwes are gods."

"Do you?" Virginia asked.

"I was raised a good Christian. I should believe in only one God. So when I feel safe, I do not think the Ts'emekwes are gods. But when I am scared and alone...then I believe as my people do."

Mrs. Harrelson bustled into the kitchen, scolding them for chatting when the guests were already clamoring for breakfast. Feather rose to slice the day-old bread. Virginia gathered the coffee beans and began to fill the mill for grinding. "Make extra," the innkeeper ordered. "As soon as word gets out about what happened, everyone will come flocking to gossip and gawk."

Just as dawn was breaking, the girls slipped upstairs to dress.

"You certainly have a lot to say all of a sudden," Virginia observed as she put on her work apron.

As if to be contrary, Feather didn't answer.

"It's a lot to take in," Virginia mused. "'Skoocoom doesn't sound so scary."

"That is why we call it that in the brightness of day, when surrounded by others," Feather said. "'Skoocoom, Skoocoom,' we chant. But at night, alone, we call it Ts'emekwes, for it can tear thy limbs from thy body and devour them before thou knowest they are missing."

Virginia shook her head. "Sounds like werewolves to me."

"No!" Feather said emphatically. "Werewolves can be killed, like any natural creature. But the Skoocoom is tricky. You never see him in time. You never hear him. All you can do is smell him."

"Smell him?"

"If you smell death approach, you must run. You must never let him get close enough for you to see him, for he will kill you for the sacrilege."

Virginia listened intently. It all seemed so unlikely, but then, who was she to doubt? She had just fought a beast that was supposed to be mythical. "But if you never see the...the Skoocoom, what's the problem?" she asked.

"He has...emerged," Feather said. "He has begun feeding again. We have failed him, and he is taking retribution." There was a distant look in her eye. She sounded like a proper schoolgirl, with her diction and her vocabulary, but she said things no typical schoolgirl would ever say. She was Virginia's age, but her solemnness made her seem older and wiser.

"At first, I did not believe in the Skoocoom," she said. "When I was a child, I did not credit any of my people's beliefs, thinking them superstitious nonsense. So I was told by my foster parents. I was raised a Christian, but in my secret heart, I found those beliefs to be equally strange. But my own eyes have shown me what the Skoocoom can do. Hence, I was not shocked to see the Skinwalker last night. I knew such creatures existed."

Virginia mulled this over. Werewolves probably existed in every region of the world, but this was the first time she'd heard of Skoocooms or Ts'emekwes.

There was a commotion at the front of the hotel, and the girls dropped their knives with a clatter, hurrying to see what it was about. Mrs.

Harrelson stood on the sidewalk, arms crossed, protecting her hotel, but the clamor was coming from across the street. A crowd of men had fanned out around the entrance to the small building that housed Mrs. Simpson's laundry on the first floor and her home above.

"What's happened?" Virginia asked over the shouting crowd.

"It's that terrible man, Strauss," Mrs. Harrelson shook her head. "He's grabbed Clara Simpson and little Juliet."

The shouts grew louder, and men waved rifles and pistols in the air. Sheriff Pike showed up just in time, hurrying down the street with long, lanky strides. He bent his head toward the men in front, arguing urgently and motioning the mob back. They took a couple of steps backward, but before the sheriff could even turn around, they edged forward again. They fell silent, however, so Pike's voice carried across the street as he knocked on the door of the laundry.

"Come on out, Strauss. I promise you a fair trial. These men out here won't wait for any such thing."

"Do what you want!" called a voice from inside. "I don't care!"

Virginia shivered. She recognized the slurring of the voice: the distorted muzzle of a werewolf was mangling the human words. Pike stiffened at the sound and looked around uneasily.

"Let them go, Strauss," he said. "They didn't hurt anyone. They won't save you."

"You can have them, Sheriff. But I want something in return."

"You can't make any demands, Strauss. You come out now or else."

"I'll let them go, but I want that bitch, Virginia Reed, to take their place!"

That silenced the mob. Virginia saw everyone's eyes turn to the hotel, and one by one, they focused on her, standing there by the door. Feather and Mrs. Harrelson turned to stare at her.

She found herself stepping off the sidewalk and into the street, almost as if someone else was inside her, forcing her forward…because her mind was screaming for her to run away.

The crowd parted for her. The sheriff met her on the sidewalk in front of the laundry. "No, Miss Reed," he said, shaking his head. "I can't allow you to go in there."

"Two innocent souls are in there," Virginia said, forcing the words out past the constriction in her throat. "There is only one of me."

"I'm sorry for them," Pike said gravely. "But the course of events has swallowed them up, and they must take their chances with fate. I can't allow you to sacrifice yourself."

"I have no intention of sacrificing myself," Virginia said. Her voice was steady, and her tone surprised the sheriff, who backed up a step. "I beat him once; I can beat him again."

Pike towered a good foot over Virginia, and, looking up, she could see that he wanted to scoff, but something stopped him. "Perhaps you could, Miss," he said. "Perhaps you could. But I can't take that chance. Seems to me that this fellow has nothing against Mrs. Simpson or her little girl. They're innocents, as you said. But it's clear he has it in for you. So I reckon they might survive, but you certainly won't."

"But..." Virginia began to argue.

"No, Miss Reed," the sheriff said bluntly. "I've decided. Now go back to the hotel before I have these men carry you back."

Virginia turned and walked across the street, her head down, blushing. She wasn't aware of the looks of respect from the men or the wide berth the bystanders were giving her.

"Bring the Reed bitch to me!" Strauss yelled. In response, the crowd began murmuring and shouting uncouth replies.

Pike held up one hand for silence, and the crowd quieted. "I'll give you one hour to come out!" he shouted. "After that, we come for you!"

Virginia went to her room, barely aware of navigating the stairs and the hallway. She was almost surprised to find herself sitting on her bed. The crowd outside grew louder.

She knew what she had to do.

The knapsack under the dresser she shared with Feather hadn't been opened once since Virginia's arrival at Sutter's Fort. Inside were the men's clothes Virginia wore on the trail; trousers, shirt, and coat. Beneath it all was the bowie knife her father had given her at their parting.

He had tried hard to keep her home, but after their experience at the pass, both of them considered her an adult. "I can't stop you," he'd said gravely. "And I know you can take care of yourself. This knife has kept me alive more than once. It will comfort me to know you have it."

Virginia dressed quickly, topping off her outfit with the workman's cap that was crushed in one corner of the drawer. She looked in the mirror and nodded. From a distance, she could pass. She only wished she had time to find the pistol Mrs. Harrelson had retrieved from the werewolf's room.

She turned to leave and found Feather standing in the doorway. "Thou art going after him," the Indian girl stated.

"There's a back door," Virginia said. "If it isn't being watched, I'll be able to get in."

"I am coming with thee."

"No, you're not," Virginia said. "I don't want to have to worry about you."

"I have helped thee before," Feather said stubbornly.

"Yes, and you surprised both of us, hunter and prey."

Feather, apparently unmoved, crossed her arms.

"You can't come." Virginia pushed past her and headed for the stairs. She hadn't gone more than a few steps before the Indian girl started following her.

"I told you, I don't want your help!" Virginia exclaimed.

"I understand," Feather said calmly. "However, you need someone to create a diversion. I doubt Sheriff Pike has left the back door unguarded."

Virginia didn't say anything, just kept walking through the dining room and the kitchen and out into the alley. Feather silently followed.

The alley was empty. The crowd was so intent on the laundry that no one noticed them…that is, almost no one. A small child at the back of the crowd spotted them, his eyes growing wide. He tugged at his father's coat, but the man angrily cuffed the child away. The two girls walked across the street and into the alley on the other side.

The alley ran behind the buildings and ended only yards from the back of the laundry at a nondescript door that was indistinguishable from all the other doors. Virginia only knew it was the correct door because sometimes the load of laundry for the hotel was so large that she had to bring a cart to pick it up. When they reached the back of the building, Virginia poked her head around the corner.

Feather was right. Two deputies with rifles stood near the back door. Their attention was directed toward the laundry's interior, so they didn't notice the girls. Virginia pulled the bowie knife from its sheath, glancing at Feather. The Indian girl nodded. She was so quiet, she was nearly on top of the deputies before one of them noticed her.

"Hold off, there, girl. Stand back." He stepped toward her, hands out.

"Come for laundry," Feather said, assuming a thick native accent.

"No, you can't. It's dangerous here. You must leave now."

"Laundry!" Feather repeated, as if she didn't understand the man. "Mistress send me. Beat me if I come back, no laundry…"

The deputy turned to his comrade. "Damn Injun's gonna get herself killed. Shamus, haul her outta here."

The other man reached for her, and she rushed between them, shouting, "Let me in!"

One of the deputies caught her, lifting her into the air as she screamed. Virginia darted behind them to the back door. She slipped inside and ducked behind the counter near the door. Just in time, for Strauss poked his head into the back room, probably wondering about the shouting.

Virginia caught a glimpse of his face.

He was still half-man at that point. His muzzle was beginning to protrude, and it was raw and glistening from his burns, his teeth and mangled jaw even more noticeable. His eyes were glowing red, and his face was covered with black fur. But he was fully clothed, and his hands were still human enough to hold a pistol.

The werewolf turned back to the front room, and Virginia heard Juliet sobbing. That hit her hard. Even if she'd wanted to back out, she couldn't. She knew only too well the horror that little girl was feeling.

It was dark inside the laundry, and it smelled of soap, but overlaying that was a wild, gamey odor that was only too familiar. Memories flooded back; memories of waiting at the entrance to the cabin, the creatures approaching, with only her gun to protect her family and friends. The same fear and resoluteness filled her now, and she raised the knife and walked swiftly into the dark room before she could change her mind.

Strauss wasn't expecting her, that was clear. His head—his snout—was pointed at the front window. Virginia was halfway across the room before he Turned. He transformed instantly, his clothes ripping as his larger muscles and thickening chest burst from the fabric. He could have just shot her, but the gun dropped out of his paws. She could almost feel his ravening need to tear her apart with tooth and claw. His jaws were already snapping as he leaped.

That moment seemed frozen in time. Wide-eyed, Juliet clutched at her mother's dress. Clara Simpson's eyes were closed, probably in prayer; she was oblivious to Virginia's presence and the werewolf's Turning.

Virginia stabbed upward at the wolf's chest, but he twisted away, so she only caught him with a glancing slice. They both fell backward into the outer room.

"Run, Juliet!" Virginia cried as she and the wolf landed against one of the counters. The structure collapsed under their weight and tangled them in shards of timber, but it gave Virginia a chance to get to her feet.

The foes faced off. The wolf was charred over half his body; raw, red flesh was already beginning to decay and fester. Without clothing to contain it, the odor was overpowering. Virginia gagged even as she leapt toward the werewolf again. He was there, welcoming the attack, and at the last second, she dove toward his legs and cut at his tendons.

She missed, but he was forced backward, into the front room. She rolled and shot a glance into the corner. The mother and child were gone, the front door hanging open. The wind slammed it shut just as the combatants landed in the middle of the room and again faced off.

Something trickled down Virginia's face, and she licked at it. It was salty and tasted of iron.

She was no longer frightened. Indeed, she felt exhilaration, joy in the chase, the hunt, and the kill. He was hers—*would* be hers. The creature that had once been Strauss saw her excitement, and she saw a moment of doubt pass across those glowing eyes. Then he snarled and lunged at her.

This time he didn't dodge, but forced his way through her next slash and started to close his mangled jaws on her neck. She shoved the knife into his chest with all her strength. The wolf grunted and started to rise, then fell backward with a strangled sound like a kicked dog.

He thrashed once or twice, and then the light went out of his orange eyes. Within seconds, the creature had Changed into a man, a naked man covered in shreds of clothing. Virginia was standing over him, her knife dripping blood, when the front door burst open and men rushed into the room.

***

Virginia found herself outside before an awed and silent crowd. On the wooden planks of the sidewalk, Mrs. Simpson and her daughter were still crouched in fear, Mrs. Harrelson beside them. Pike gently took the bloody bowie knife from Virginia's hand.

Everyone's eyes went to the knife, which dripped blood onto the worn gray planks, and then back to Virginia. She felt nothing; she was numb. It was as if she was waking from a dream.

She heard a cry of joy, and then Juliet was running toward her, grabbing at her legs and looking up at her with a shining face. "Thank you for saving us," she said.

Virginia started to feel again, and that was a mistake. Suddenly she was shaking so badly she could barely stand.

"Juliet!" Mrs. Simpson screamed, rising to her feet. "You get away from her this instant!" She pulled her daughter away. "You are a witch," she hissed. "Don't think I didn't see. You and that creature…both of you are *unnatural.*"

"This young woman just saved your life," Pike said. "Show a little gratitude."

Clara Simpson whirled on him. "He wanted *her!* He only took us because of *her!*" She took Juliet by the arm and clomped down the sidewalk and down the steps to the street, dragging Juliet behind her. Juliet turned her head and beamed at Virginia over her shoulder, her gratitude undiminished.

The sheriff was still holding the bowie knife. He suddenly remembered it and absently wiped the blood off on his trousers before handing it back to Virginia.

Mrs. Harrelson emerged from the crowd, followed by Feather. She put her arm around Virginia. "Come, girl, let's get you home."

They walked slowly across the street. Virginia's legs didn't want to work. She walked mechanically, stumbling, but Mrs. Harrelson's strong arms caught her each time. She didn't lead Virginia to her small cubicle of a room, but to the kitchen.

This is my true home, Virginia thought, looking around the room.

"I have some lemonade made," Mrs. Harrelson said. "You sit right here and I'll be back with a glass."

Feather sat next to Virginia and took her hands, her voice low but triumphant. "Thou *art* a Canowiki."

Virginia certainly didn't feel like some mythical Hunter. She felt like a very young, shaky, and entirely average girl.

"I need thy help, Virginia Reed," Feather said solemnly. "I humbly ask thee to come to the aid of my people."

"I was lucky," Virginia said, shaking her head. "I caught him by surprise."

"No," Feather answered. "Only the greatest of warriors can kill a Skinwalker with only a knife. Thou art a Canowiki."

"That's impossible."

Feather didn't look disappointed, but then, she rarely showed emotion at all. She sat unmoving, her dark eyes serious but not betraying anything. It seemed as if she was simply waiting for Virginia to change her mind.

Canowiki.

"I just want to stay here, work quietly, and live in peace," Virginia insisted. "Or if I must leave, I want to go to a place where no one knows my name."

But that was not to be.

Later that evening, Mrs. Harrelson came into the kitchen and helped the girls fix dinner. Virginia was only too happy to stay in the kitchen and let the others serve. They had an extraordinary number of guests, and Virginia preferred to avoid the stares. With dinner served, she began doing the dishes. When the last diner had left the dining room, Mrs. Harrelson came in and sat at the table.

"Leave off those dishes, girl," she said. "Come sit with me a moment." When Virginia obeyed, the innkeeper pulled an envelope from her apron and handed it to Virginia. In it was more money than she had ever seen in her whole life.

"This is three months' worth of wages," her boss said.

"I don't understand." Virginia protested. "Are you...you *want* me to leave?"

"What?" The older woman looked startled. "Of course not. You're one of the best workers I've ever had. That's just the problem. You're no kitchen drudge, Virginia. You have more important things to do."

Suspicion bloomed in Virginia's mind. "Has Feather been talking to you?"

"She didn't have to," Mrs. Harrelson said. Her voice suddenly took on a strong Scottish brogue. "In my home country, we call girls like you Daughters of Andraste, the goddess of war in the ancient religion, of whom there are a few worshippers even now. There was one such in my village. She was burned as a witch."

"A witch?"

"Instead of being grateful for your intervention, Clara Simpson is saying that she saw you and Strauss transform into those...creatures." She snorted in her indignation. "The simpleton is mistaking the one for the both of you."

"You know about the..."

"...the werewolf?" Mrs. Harrelson completed her question. "It's pretty obvious, isn't it? But what Mrs. Simpson is saying is dangerous. I've seen it back in Scotland. Rumors take hold and...well, combined with what happened to you before..." She shook her head, and the lines of her face seemed to deepen.

"We are beyond witch burnings, surely," Virginia protested.

"Perhaps," Mrs. Harrelson said. "But not beyond ostracizing those who are different and strange to us."

Virginia hung her head. "I understand. I...I would hurt your business."

"Hurt my business?" Her employer gave a belly laugh. "Dear girl! Folks would be filling my dining room for months just to get a look at you. But I won't do that to you, Virginia. You aren't a sideshow freak. No...it is time to move on."

Virginia tried to hand the money back. "This is too much."

"Nonsense," Mrs. Harrelson said, getting up from the table and wiping her hands on her apron. "The gold miners are overpaying for everything, and I've seen enough hard times in my life to take their money."

Still Virginia did not move.

"Virginia, I couldn't save my spirit-sister from the flames, but I *can* help you," the innkeeper said gently. "Now, off to bed with you. You too, Feather. I'll finish up. But I want you gone by morning, Virginia. I insist."

Chapter Six

By noon the next day, the ranch house was ominously quiet, leaving Frank to await the eruption. Patrick made himself scarce when their father looked like he was getting ready to explode.

But when Thomas Whitford emerged from his office, his voice quiet and controlled, it alarmed Frank more than if he'd shouted his fury. He was thin lipped and white faced. His handlebar mustache, which was usually proudly waxed upward, drooped. Only twice had Frank seen his father this grim: once was upon the death of his wife, Frank's mother. The second time was when gold was discovered in the hills above the ranch.

"Get the crew together," the old man said. "Find Patrick. Tell him to ask the Newtons to join us. We leave at noon."

"We should take care of this ourselves," Frank said. "I don't trust Henry Newton."

He expected his stepfather to be angry over the comment, but Thomas didn't seem upset. "Oliver is his son. He needs to come along. In fact, I think we need to include as many men as we can get. Tell Patrick to round up volunteers from the other ranchers, like he suggested."

"I'll tell him, Father," Frank said. He turned to go.

"Oh, and Frank?" Thomas's grim resolve softened for a moment. "Remind Patrick this isn't war…it's a search party. Nothing more."

That isn't going to happen, Frank thought. The moment the men got together, they'd be itching for a fight, no matter whether they found the missing boys or not. They were waiting for an excuse to drive away the Indians once and for all. But he didn't argue. *If the savages have done anything to Oliver or James,* he thought, *why, I'll be right there with the rest of the men in exacting revenge.*

If only Oliver had been missing, Frank wouldn't have worried. Oliver had a habit of shooting off his mouth about searching for gold, so it didn't surprise Frank that he'd disappeared. But James was conscientious; he wouldn't just run off without warning.

Frank found Patrick in the barn. Frank was halfway through his explanation when Patrick dropped his pitchfork, jumped on the back of his favorite horse without saddle or bridle, and rode off with a whoop of excitement.

Strange he should so hate the Indians, Frank thought. *Sometimes he seems almost a savage himself.*

Patrick was known and liked by all the neighbors, which is why Father had chosen him to gather them. Frank would have had to start with introductions. He'd lost touch with some of them, and others had moved in after he'd left for school.

He sighed and started ringing the dinner bell. The sound of the bell at such an odd time would signal something amiss, and the ranch hands would come running. When they started showing up, most were more than willing to join the search party.

"Pack up your gear," Frank said when they were assembled. "We're going after Oliver and James."

"Everyone?" Fred Carter asked. He was a short, stout man who lived for his sons. He sounded worried.

Frank hesitated. Jesse and Emanuel were probably old enough to go along with the search party, but then, someone had to stay behind. "We'll leave your boys to take care of things," he said. Carter looked relieved.

"Why the hurry?" Ben Torrance asked. He'd showed up late. He was a slow-moving man and deliberate in his actions. Quick, fast-talking Joe Foster was beside him. "What's happened?" Foster chimed in.

"Maybe nothing," Frank said. "But Father's worried that James and Oliver may have gotten in trouble with rustlers."

"Rustlers?" Torrance drawled. "Or Indians?

"Most likely both," Foster laughed, slapping his friend on his back.

"It's only been a couple of days," Torrance said. "More likely, they couldn't resist panning for a little gold up there in the mountains."

"Oliver, perhaps, but James would have returned, or at least sent word," Frank said.

"How long are we gonna be gone?" Foster asked.

Frank made a quick estimate. "We'll need…a week's worth of supplies."

"Why a week?" Foster asked. "Let's reprovision at Bidwell's Bar."

"We're going to bypass the town," Frank said. "It's getting a bad reputation. The riffraff have taken over."

Foster frowned. He had a taste for liquor and gambling.

"Father's orders," Frank cut off Foster before he could object.

"Should we take our guns?" This from young Johnny Hawkins, who had arrived from New York a couple of years before, completely enamored by the lore of the West. Frank reluctantly nodded.

The men split up, most of them running for the bunkhouse, others for the barn to saddle the horses.

Old Persimmons hadn't spoken. He was their oldest ranch hand, and always got along with the Miwok. He sidled up to Frank and said in a low voice, "Are you sure about this this? Some of these men are pretty jumpy. They think the Indians are going to scalp them in their sleep. It wouldn't take much to set them off."

Frank wanted to blurt out, *No, I'm not sure about this at all!* Hawkins's question about guns had him worried that the weapons would be used. But Father had made his decision, and Frank wouldn't undercut him by expressing doubt. "It's what Father wants," he replied.

Persimmons nodded knowingly, as if he knew what Frank had wanted to say. "I hope the Boss knows what he's doing."

By the time the party was assembled at midafternoon, they numbered twenty-seven. The Whitford ranch accounted for nine men; Henry Newton brought nine more, including himself. Of the neighbors, all four Jordan brothers came along, as well as old man Partridge and his man Carl Dutton. Peter McCarthy brought along his foreman, Harve Jeffers. Preacher MacLeod came alone.

Most of the ranchers brought along only their hunting rifles, but all the Newton men carried pistols as well as rifles. Dave Martin had two guns holstered at his hips, adding credence to rumors of his gunfighting history.

Thomas Whitford never spoke, simply surveyed the grim-faced and heavily armed men before mounting his horse and riding out at the head of the column.

I wish Father would remind them not to get trigger happy, Frank thought unhappily. *Before it is too late.*

He fell into place behind Thomas, feeling a sense of misgiving that bordered on foreboding.

***

Jameson was luckier than most miners, having found a small vein and worked it hard for a day or two before the others noticed. He was a small man and easy to overlook. Even luckier, he'd managed to set aside a nest egg by sneaking the tiny nuggets and dust into town before anyone could hit him over the head and take them away.

He surveyed the little valley that his fellow miners were working. It had been beautiful when they'd gotten there: basalt rock cliffs with pine trees and brush, and a small, pastoral meadow in the middle where they'd camped. Now everything was churned up, the soil, water, and trees stripped, cut, dug up, and thrown aside. All the beauty was gone.

Sometimes Jameson felt as if they were industriously trying to recreate hell.

Everyone's head was down; everyone was either panning or digging. A couple of the fellows were getting ambitious, cutting down the last of the junipers from among the rocks to build bigger works, mimicking their more successful brethren on the main river. Everyone below these men would be left with nothing, so everyone was hurrying to finish their claim before moving up the stream, leapfrogging those who had leapfrogged them.

There had been a small group of Indians camping in the meadow when they'd first arrived, and the miners had chased them off. They'd surrounded the Indian camp one night and fired their weapons in the air—though Jameson suspected that a few of them had also shot into the camp. In the morning, the Indians were gone. There had been a small pool of blood in the clearing, and that image often came back to Jameson as he tried to sleep, his tired muscles and aching bones keeping him awake at night.

Enough of this, Jameson thought. *I hate it. I feel dirty, inside and out.*

Most of the men who'd arrived with, after, or even before him were as destitute as when they'd begun. More destitute, really, for they still owed on their equipment and their grubstakes.

Old Johnson, who had been the first to stake a claim on this small tributary, had sold out the previous week for pennies, only to watch the new owners strike it rich a few days later, almost without breaking a sweat.

Peterson, who dug harder and faster and smarter than any other miner on the creek, was worn down and discouraged. "I'm going home to Utah, boys," he announced. "Tilling the soil is easier than this, and at least it feeds me in return."

Halsey and Planter had died from the same smallpox that killed many of the local Indians. Holliday had frozen to death inside his tent that first terrible month. Salazar and Estes were better off than most. They'd joined the big mining cartel down by the main digs, where they earned hard laborers' wages.

Jameson was the only one in his group still healthy and still willing, and he was teetering on the edge of giving up before his tiny gains were depleted. They may have gotten here sooner than most, but for most of them, it was still too late.

The stories of finding gold lying on the ground were still told around the campfires and in town, but Jameson doubted them. He'd seen nothing of the sort with his own eyes. Meanwhile, more and more men showed up every day, staking claims on sites that had most of the early, more experienced miners rolling their eyes. What was maddening, though, was that a few of them had gotten lucky.

Jameson rose from the muddy creek bank, hearing his bones crack with the effort.

He wandered away from the others, following a dry gulch up to a crumbly cliff. It was soft clay, not the most promising surface, but Jameson had taken to hacking at most anything with his pickaxe out of idle curiosity. Or maybe he was just mad at the earth and it made him feel good to gouge holes in its once pristine beauty.

He sank the blade deep into the clay and pulled it away. The whole bank seemed to come with it, and he jumped back, barely avoiding being buried. He closed his eyes, coughed, and waited for the cloud of dirt to filter to the ground.

When he opened his eyes, he couldn't understand what he was seeing at first. Light glared into his eyes, but the sun was behind him. It was a golden light. He stepped forward, filled with a wild hope, his heart pounding its way up into his throat. He glanced behind him nervously, but he could hear the others exchanging desultory chatter down by the creek.

Beneath the clay surface was solid granite, and down the middle of it was a seam of gold, gleaming in the afternoon light. A chunk of quartz hung by a shred of clay. He plucked it free and turned it over in his hand. There, shining like a lightning bolt down the middle of the translucent rock, was a thick vein of gold.

Jameson wanted to shout, to jump up and down, to show the world his discovery. He only barely managed to stay quiet. He looked down at the clumps of dry clay and had a wild impulse to glue it all back to the face of the cliff.

He filled his pockets with all the gleaming gold he could carry, but no matter how much he shoved into his pockets, there was more, each nugget bigger than the last. He replaced his first gleanings with bigger nuggets, burying the discards under loose clay. Just one of the discards would have sent him into a state of euphoria only hours before. Finally, most of the surface gold either filled his pockets or lay buried under the clay.

He knew—he just *knew*—that if he was to take his axe and strike at the vein of quartz, he'd find an even bigger lode.

Jameson could barely stand, he was shaking so badly. How long had he been away from camp? If he didn't get back soon, they'd send someone after him. Nevertheless, he sat down on the clay and put his head into his arms.

My God, he thought. *What am I going to do? My God...my God.*

He couldn't rush off to town—that would raise suspicions. But how long would it take until one of the miners wandered over to water one of the nearby trees and saw the quartz vein?

My God, how long before one of them comes looking for me?

Trying to compose himself, Jameson rose to his feet. His pockets were bulging, but that wasn't unusual. Most miners filled their pockets with likely looking rocks, examining them later in the evening by firelight. Once or twice, someone would cry "Eureka!" and produce a little pebble of gold.

Jameson tried not to laugh, because he suspected that if he started laughing, he wouldn't be able to stop. The others would recognize the sound of triumph and come running. Darkness was falling. He'd leave early in the morning, get to town, and stake a claim before the others were done with breakfast. With any luck, he'd be back with a loaded pistol and a fresh mining kit before the others even knew he was gone.

I can't do it alone, he thought. *I'll offer Peterson a small share if he'll go in with me—which will still make him richer than any other miner. Maybe old Johnson, too. Old sot deserves a break.*

***

"You all right?" Peterson asked when Jameson walked back into camp.

"Sure," Jameson said. He turned his face away, pretending to be examining the digs.

"You don't look it. You look like you saw a ghost."

"No...I was just thinking how lucky I've been compared to some of the others."

"Jesus, fellow," Peterson exclaimed. "Don't never say such a thing out loud! You want to jinx yourself?"

Jameson managed to keep his laugh from sounding hysterical.

It wasn't quite real. Nothing was quite real. Everything looked dirty and shameful somehow. All the backbreaking labor, the grubbing he'd been doing, and for what? A few dollars of gold dust. In his pockets was enough for him to go home. He'd never have to come back, never have to spend sleepless nights worrying about protecting his claim.

An even louder laugh escaped his lips.

Peterson also laughed. "Yeah, you're right. Can't be much more jinxed than we already are."

Strange how ambition suddenly changes, Jameson thought. *I don't want to be a little rich anymore. I want to be a lot rich.*

Peterson was eyeing him doubtfully. "You could come back with me, Jameson," he said. "I'm leaving in an hour. We can go part of the way together."

"Hey, why don't you hold off until tomorrow?" Jameson said. "Then I'll go with you, OK?"

Peterson stared at the ground, looking discouraged. "Wait a day for the company? I can do that. Company is all I'm coming away with from this pit of hell."

The others were giving up for the night, wandering back to the camp, too bone-tired to do much chatting. The miners skipped the usual small talk about nearly making the big strike, just missing it by a few feet; all the ones that got away. All nonsense. Most of the rich strikes were down on the main Plumas River, on claims surrounded by fences and guards.

We're small-timers, and we all know it, Jameson thought. *But that's about to change.*

By God, he'd hire all these fellows and give them a good wage. He wouldn't work them like damn slaves; he'd share the wealth.

Just as soon as he got enough for himself and his family.

Not much.

A few million, that's all.

***

Jameson wasn't sure what woke him. Whereas normally he fell instantly asleep after a hard day, this time he'd been too excited to sleep until long after the camp was filled with the snores of the others. Before he'd gone to bed, he'd dressed to leave early in the morning and surreptitiously transferred his gold to the bottom of his rucksack. Finally, he'd dropped off, and strangely, dreamed of being home in his modest farmhouse, happy with his wife and children, content with his meager life.

He opened his eyes as a strange cry faded away.

Old Johnson sat bolt upright, clutching his blanket to his neck like a maiden protecting her modesty. "What was that?" he hissed. His face was white and his mouth had dropped open. Night spittle ran down his chin into his scraggly beard. It was almost a full moon, but it was also cloudy, and the moonlight came and went.

The call came again, a booming voice from the top of the cliff. It wasn't a wolf or coyote, nor was it shrill enough to be a mountain lion. Bears sounded nothing like that. More than anything, it sounded like a man's voice, but deeper, garbled and echoing, as if the voice was somehow that of many men inside one throat.

He glanced over at Johnson, but Johnson wasn't there. Where he had been, a huge boulder had landed with a ground-shaking, wet thud. Jameson could see only the soles of Johnson's boots, pitted with holes that were leaking blood. All the men were on their feet now, snatching up their rifles; half were clad in long johns, half in their work clothes, having fallen asleep fully dressed.

Jameson sensed something moving toward him, and he jumped away at the last second. It was another boulder, this one even bigger than the one that had squashed Johnson, a boulder so big that it should have taken three men with long levers to budge it.

Indians? Jameson wondered. *We were warned not to come here. Sacred ground to some local god of theirs.*

Even as he thought it, the voice resounded again, echoing down the narrow valley. It sounded as if it was on the cliff on the other side of camp, which was impossible unless there were two of the creatures.

The first voice answered, and another thud shook the ground. A strangled cry abruptly ended. Something splattered across the ground, hitting Jameson's face, and he knew as he wiped it away that it was blood.

He suddenly understood that guns weren't going to do them any good and that they were all going to die.

Abandoning everything else, he grabbed his rucksack full of gold and ran downstream. He had gotten no more than a few steps when a boulder crashed into his primitive little lean-to, smashing everything within.

He ran.

He didn't look back, just kept running, tripping once on a dead body and slipping on the man's entrails. He cried out, looking frantically in every direction. It had grown quiet. No more rocks pounded the camp into the ground; there were no more screams. Dark clouds slipped across the moon, and it was as black and silent as a tomb.

Keep going, Jameson told himself. *Don't stop.*

He stood rooted to the spot, like a child hiding under a blanket, as though, if he didn't move, he was somehow hidden from the monsters. It wasn't Indians, he was sure of that now. He would have heard their war whoops, or seen their arrows riddling the bodies of the dead, or heard their gunshots.

No, this had been the crash of falling rocks, each bigger than any man could throw, big enough for a siege engine to use to demolish a castle. The human body was terribly soft and vulnerable to such an onslaught.

An awful stench reached him. He gagged, and the sound of his own coughing broke his paralysis. Because he'd made a noise, he sensed, he was no longer invisible. He ran, and the stench became overpowering. The earth shook with a shuddering drumbeat.

The clouds drifted away from the moon, and Jameson saw a huge, human-shaped figure only yards away. The monster had a large, shaggy head and fur covering its blocky body. It was twice the size of any man, with huge eyes and long canines that glistened in the moonlight.

The creek ran fast through this part of the narrow canyon. One of the men had been swept away by the current, never to be found.

Jameson didn't hesitate; he jumped into the swirling water. A massive hand snagged him by the hair, and he hung over the edge of the creek bank, his feet caught in the current, which twirled him around and around, and he realized the creature was on the verge of plucking him out of the air and throwing him back on the bank like a grizzly catching a salmon in mid-leap.

His hair grew tight at the roots. He pulled out his knife and slashed at his scalp. There was a flashing pain, and he fell into the rapids and was dragged under. He was swept down a narrow chute and slammed against protruding rocks. He sank all the way to the bottom, and he realized it was sandy there, that the savagery of the current couldn't reach him.

He'd been so frightened that he hadn't taken a breath as he was falling, and now he felt an overwhelming urge to breathe. He slammed against the sides and bottom of the gorge, tumbling so that he couldn't tell which way was up and which way was down. It was darker than the darkest night at the bottom of the creek.

Jameson slammed hard into a rock and took a huge breath of cold liquid that shocked him into immobility. Then…he gave up, and let himself flow. It was peaceful as he bumped along the bottom.

Am I still holding my breath? he wondered as the strain in his chest eased. He felt as though he was breathing. *I should let the backpack with its burden of gold go,* he thought idly.

His final thought was *I will die rich and no one will ever know.*

Chapter Seven

The child sleeps near me, and despite the stench, its warmth is welcome.

There is raw meat beside me when I awake, but so far I have resisted eating it. Kovac's canteen is also always by my side and always seems full, though I never see Grendel fill it.

Yes, I named the monster Grendel, but I am no Beowulf. I have not tried to confront the creature, nor tried to escape, for it would be useless. When I finally looked into the eyes of the beast, I saw its intelligence. It has an angry countenance, as if it longs to kill me. But when Grendel looks toward the child, its expression softens, and I can almost see humanity in the monster.

I am dying. My body fails more every day. Something in the air is killing me, or perhaps it is the infestation of insects, rats, and other vermin that scurry over my slumbering body, feeding on me while I sleep. My legs are too weak to stand, so I crawl to the corner to relieve myself.

What I didn't notice at first is the young one is injured. There is a wound on its shoulder, which was covered by a kind of mud. Today the mud fell off, revealing the wound, undoubtedly from the bullet Kovac fired trying to escape.

Now I understand the murderous look in Grendel's eyes. I suspect my continued survival rests on keeping the child happy.

I've started speaking to the albino. I point to myself and say, "Friend." And strangely, I've begun to think of it as a friend. Here in Grendel's cave, surrounded by gold, I've reverted to my old occupation. My teacher's instincts have arisen, and I speak to the child as though it is one of my students.

Today it looked at me and said, "Friend."

The sound was so strange that my heart seemed to stop for a moment. And then I did something even stranger; I smiled and gave the little monster a hug.

"You are Hrothgar," I said. It might seem odd to give the child the name of a king, but somehow it fits.

***

Thomas Whitford put the half-breed, Hugh, in charge of tracking.

"You sure we can trust this Injun?" Dave Martin, the Newton ranch foreman scowled. Henry Newton seemed to attract men who had grievances against the Indians. Martin had lost a brother on his trek West, and made it no secret that he thought the Indians should be banished from California, and if they wouldn't leave, should be killed off.

Patrick whirled on the man. "You leave Hugh alone," he cried. "He's one of the good 'uns."

Frank shook his head at his brother's angry shout. No one hated Indians more in general, but less in particular, than Patrick. It was as if his mind had decided against the Indians, while in his heart he was still in love with them. What's more, he seemed completely unaware of the contradiction. Frank couldn't help but wonder what his brother would think without Newton's influence.

They reached the Plumas River, and the sight astounded Frank. He remembered this stretch of the river as a meadow lined by aspen trees, with a soft layer of flowers that looked as if they'd been painted there.

Now it was all dirt and mud. Gone were the gold miners who had used picks and shovels, replaced by teams of men working like ants. The skin of the earth was peeled back, leaving a raw, deep wound. The hills above were stripped of trees, the lumber used to build crude fumes and dams, trestles on stilts, stealing the life's blood of water from its channels, imprisoning the flow as if it was their slave. The water struck against the earth, washing it away, leaving piles of gravel and boulders. The terrain was pockmarked and defaced, and alongside the devastation were the mounds of waste pilings.

The ranchers were silent as they passed the diggings, exchanging wordless greetings with the miners. Patrick went over and had a few brief words with some of them, but none had seen Oliver or James.

The searchers rode on, a vague disquiet in the air.

It troubles all of us, Frank thought, *this desecration of the land.*

But it was none of their business.

The search party continued up the waves of foothills and deeply cut canyons until they reached the base of Thompson Peak.

Hugh held up his hand. "They stopped here," he said. He got off his horse and walked the perimeter of the small clearing. He knelt down and pulled a cow skull out of the dirt. "They found the remains of one of the rustled cattle, but…" He shook his head.

"What's the matter?" Frank's father asked.

"These remains are fresh, but they've been completely picked clean, broken and scattered. I do not know what creature would do that…" He stopped and shook his head, as if suddenly realizing he might know after all. "There are no tracks," he said.

"Creature?" Henry Newton said. "You mean the Indians, don't you?"

Hugh shook his head again, but didn't answer. He looked frightened.

"But where are the boys?" Newton asked impatiently. "Did they backtrack?"

"They kept going upward," Hugh said, waving his hand further up the mountain. "Toward the tree line."

Everyone in the party looked toward the summit. There, the ground was gray and bare but for scattered boulders and a few scraggly trees that had managed to find footholds in the nooks and crannies of granite. The summit was wreathed in storm clouds. It was early in the fall, but a sudden snowfall was possible.

"I bet they went up the North Fork," Newton spoke up. "Oliver was just itching to pan for gold."

Thomas Whitford turned a level stare on Newton. "I promised Chief Honon," he said. "That creek is out of bounds."

"So's rustling cattle," Newton answered. "But that didn't stop them from doing it."

"We don't know that," Frank objected. "Besides, if I know Oliver, he was bored the minute he squatted to do his first panning. He and James are probably headed home by now."

Newton turned in his saddle. He had a way of turning his whole rotund body, his long hair and beard along with it, as if he couldn't turn his neck. He examined Frank coldly. "Maybe you don't know my son as well as you think you do."

"Frank's right," Gerald Persimmons said. It was clear that the burly old ranch hand was unhappy about having to come along and wanted to get back to the ranch. "The boys are probably already home, wondering where we all went."

"Unless they ran into the rustlers," Frank said, and instantly regretted it. He'd meant to take the suspicion off the Indians, but his words seemed to galvanize the search party.

"If the Indians can't survive without stealing, they should just leave," Johnny Hawkins said as they set off again.

Behind him, Preacher MacLeod snorted. "And go where, young man? We've already taken the fertile valleys, driven them away from the rivers with their bounty. We've killed their deer and elk. Just where on God's green Earth are they supposed to go?"

"They aren't God's creatures," Bud Carpenter said.

MacLeod turned in his saddle and stared back at the man. "Are you so sure?"

Carpenter scowled and looked away.

"Well, we can't both live off the same land," Hawkins said stubbornly.

"And who'd you think was here first?" MacLeod demanded.

Carpenter's friend, George Banks, wasn't so easily intimidated. "I hear they are taking care of the problem up north," he said. "Permanently."

Old Persimmons nudged his horse up beside them. "And how are they doing that?" There was a dark look on his face, but Banks didn't see it.

"If they get in the way, they are hunted down."

"So we murder them?" Persimmons asked, his voice rising. "Men, women, and children?"

Banks looked surprised at the anger in Persimmon's voice and didn't say anything.

They rode in silence for a time.

Newton cleared his throat. Frank realized that everyone had been waiting for him to say something. "The Indians have to go," he stated. "Either voluntarily or by force."

"I refuse to go along with that," Frank said. He looked to his father to back him up, but Thomas Whitford was riding ahead of them, as if avoiding the conversation.

"Oh, come now, Frank," Newton said. Frank was surprised to hear a tone of pleading in the rancher's voice, as if he was trying to win Frank over. "We are only the first settlers. Others will follow, in their multitudes. The savages will simply have to get out of the way."

Frank wanted to argue that the Indians and the white men could live together. But to his shame, he stayed quiet.

Gold had changed everything. No longer were words and treaties being used to move the Indians away from their ancestral lands. Now, more often than not, it was by the long, cold steel of a rifle barrel. Already weakened by the white man's diseases, the Indians became easy prey.

Frank felt the premonition of disaster stronger than ever. They'd set out to find two missing boys, but it was becoming clearer with every mile that something else was going on. Men like Henry Newton not only wanted a share of the gold, they also saw the gold rush as an opportunity to be rid of the Indians once and for all.

Frank's father had always done his best to keep the miners from crossing his land into Chief Honon's land, but lately, it seemed as if he had quit trying. And whether he knew it or not, by coming along, Whitford lent his prestige to the endeavor.

Now, as the party left the foothills behind and climbed higher into the mountains, they were approaching the sacred creek, which the ranchers in the area traditionally avoided. The Indians reacted violently to trespassing on this land, and even the miners avoided the area. As long as there was any part of the lower stretch of the river and its tributaries still available to the ranchers and miners, the mountain elevations were left alone. But everyone knew it was only a matter of time.

Frank spurred his horse to his father's side. "We shouldn't go higher, Father. We promised."

Thomas shook his head tiredly. "We won't go into the sacred valley. We'll turn away before that."

Frank started to relax, but then his father added, "Unless the tracks lead there."

The men grew more and more tense as they wound their way into the open space above the tree line, as if they thought being out in the open on the side of the mountain made them more vulnerable.

"I don't like it," Johnny Hawkins said. "We're too exposed."

Patrick spoke up. "We are better off out of the forest. From here, we'll see them coming from a long way off."

Some of the other men started to relax. They'd been just as concerned as Hawkins, but unwilling to admit it.

They are ranchers, not Indian fighters, Frank reminded himself.

In his eagerness, Patrick took the lead, with Hugh right behind him. As they reached the last of the scraggly trees, Frank saw the Indian look to the north, toward the valley held sacred by the Miwok. Patrick turned south, and Hugh's relief was evident in every line of his body, as was Frank's.

They reached a small, steep creek with a narrow path winding beside it.

"This is the North Fork. This steep little stream runs into the Plumas River," Patrick announced.

He turned down the path and the others followed in single file, all twenty-seven of them. Once again, it seemed to Frank that Hugh hesitated, his brow furrowed. But again, the Indian stayed quiet.

The creek broadened, and by the time they rounded the bend near the mining camp, they were riding three abreast. The men in the lead stopped abruptly, none of them moving. Then the wind changed direction, and even those in the back smelled the death before them.

Frank dismounted and tied his horse's reins to a nearby juniper tree limb. He grabbed his rifle from its saddle holster and hurried forward, reaching the carnage of the mining camp before most of the others.

His eyes couldn't make sense of the bloated flesh strewn about the demolished camp until he saw something resembling fingers on one of the lumps of meat. Gradually, he made out shapes, until he realized that they had once been people. He turned away, not wanting to admit to himself what had happened here. Massive boulders had left trails of smashed tents and equipment. Blood and entrails gave silent witness to where the men had lain. Other rocks, impossibly huge, seemed to have fallen into the middle of the camp from directly above, as if tossed by giants.

Several men bent over, throwing up. Others, white faced and with clenched jaws, walked to the edge of the camp, pretending to examine the cliffs above.

"I don't understand how the Indians did this," said Bud Carpenter. "I don't care how much leverage you have, these boulders are too big."

"All you need is to get one started rolling," said Sam Partridge, who owned the struggling property just east of the Newton ranch. He was a crusty old geezer, and Frank had heard that he was fighting hard to hold onto it, despite Newton's generous offer to buy it. His only ranch hand, Carl Dutton, was a little simpleminded and of little help. "Probably smashed some of the others. Must have hit rocks lower down and flown into the air."

Frank wanted to agree. It was the only possible answer. But in his heart, he knew that no man could have budged these boulders, not all of them.

"The savages set a trap," Henry Newton proclaimed loudly. "Lured them here and wiped them out."

"*Lured* them here?" Frank echoed. "Do you even hear what you're saying? The Miwok don't want these miners here, dead or alive. They certainly wouldn't have *lured* them."

"Well, they're dead now," Newton retorted, his face reddening. "And it weren't no accident."

Frank didn't have a response to that. Again, what other explanation could there be? His heart sank, for the men around him were getting angrier by the second. None of them were going to listen to reason. They were heavily armed and out for blood, and the Miwok camp was only hours away.

"Where's the evidence?" Frank asked. "I don't see any footprints, or any arrows, or sign of scalping. Nothing that says Indians were here…"

"Scalping?" Martin sputtered. "There are no heads to take the scalps from!"

"We'll find out soon enough," said Newton. "If the savages are responsible for this, we'll make them pay."

Thomas Whitford stayed silent. Frank moved to his father's side and said in an urgent whisper, "Father, you can't lead these men to the Miwok camp. They won't just punish the guilty."

Thomas shook him off. "This must be answered for." He crouched down and lifted a blanket off the ground, wincing as he saw a torso. But after looking away for a moment, the old rancher focused his eyes on the body, and Frank realized that he was looking for any sign of James. Frank joined in the search, until all were satisfied that neither Oliver nor James had died there.

Hugh was standing alone at the edge of the camp. The other men were avoiding him, but Frank walked over to him. Hugh turned to him with despairing eyes.

"It was not my people who did this," he said. "It was the Ts'emekwes."

"The...Ts'em..." Frank couldn't finish the name.

"It is a powerful creature who has lived above my village for generations. We keep away from him, and give him sacrifice. He leaves us alone...most of the time. But these white men invaded his territory. They disturbed him. He won't stop until he's killed them all."

Frank shook his head. *The Indians' superstitions keep them primitive,* he thought. "You had best worry about your own people," he said. "And yourself."

Hugh eyes widened, as if he hadn't thought of the danger he might be in.

"Leave now," Frank urged him. "Warn your village."

Hugh stood stock still for a moment. Then he gave a short nod and walked away. He slipped onto his horse and rode off without any of the other men noticing.

The ranchers were slowly getting over the shock and examining the few possessions left intact, trying to determine the identities of the miners. It was nearly impossible. They couldn't even tell how many of them there had been. Someone finally had the idea of counting only right hands, and they came up with a dozen dead men.

Henry Newton took charge, directing men where to move the bodies for burial. The next several hours were grim work, and there was nothing for it but to put all the body parts together in a mass grave.

Off his horse, Newton was surprising short, but his bulk commanded respect. His energy was almost palpable, his angry gestures and deep frown intimidating. His men, especially Dave Martin and his two flunkies, Bud Carpenter and George Banks, reflected their boss's belligerent demeanor, carrying their rifles everywhere, even in camp.

"They'll pay for this," Martin raged. "I'll kill every one of those savages."

Finally, Thomas spoke up. "We'll have justice," he said. "But we will only punish the guilty, you understand?"

Martin glared at him, but Thomas did not look away. Finally, Martin gave him a curt nod. Moments later, Newton and Martin had drawn away from the others and were conferring in quiet voices Frank could not hear. Martin kept nodding.

It was getting dark, but no one wanted to stay at the miners' camp. As they readied their horses, Carpenter noticed that Hugh was gone. "Half-breed ran off," he said. "I thought you said he was one of the good ones, Patrick!"

Patrick just scowled. Frank kept quiet, thankful that Hugh had had sense enough to leave so quietly.

The searchers left the way they had come. They couldn't follow the creek downward, for it was bordered by cliffs until it joined the main river, by which time they would have traveled far out of their way.

They were determined to find the Miwok camp, which lay in the opposite direction. The Indians moved around some, but they usually established themselves in locations higher in the mountains, thereby avoiding too many incidents with settlers. Many of the ranchers knew where the camps were most likely to be, for they had spent much of their childhood in them, when the Miwok still welcomed white men into their territory.

As they climbed out of the little valley near the ridge, Frank looked back, and he noticed a tree on the edge of the cliff catching the last rays of the setting sun. He frowned. There'd been no tree there when they rode in. Then he shrugged. He must've misremembered; after all, he hadn't been looking upward at the time. He was about to turn around when the tree seemed to move.

He looked back.

The tree was gone.

***

Henry Newton had no doubt about who had precipitated the brutal massacre, for who else would be so savage but Indians? He'd been trying to whip up anger against the useless Miwok for months, years even, but he hadn't really believed them to be a danger, not like this. No matter. They seemed half-defeated already, retreating before the white man's advances, dying from the white man's diseases.

They were in his way. Only two obstacles stood in the path of Newton's ambitions for his family: Indians and the Whitfords. With the foothills cleared of Indians, the Newton ranch would have all the grazing territory it needed, not to mention access to the rich gold fields the Indians were trying to keep to themselves.

He wasn't really concerned about Oliver. His son had mentioned that he might make a detour to check out the hidden valley. "They're hiding something," Oliver had said. "I'll bet you anything that place is full of gold."

"Take your time, son," Newton had replied, a plan starting to form in his mind. "And keep James with you, if you can."

"He'll do what I say," Oliver had said. "Don't you worry about that."

Newton had to admit he was a little surprised the Indians had actually stolen three head of cattle, for he knew that the slow drain of cattle that he complained about from his own ranch was a lie. The rustling of cattle from the Whitford ranch was real enough. Martin and his team, Carpenter and Banks, were proficient rustlers who'd learned their craft in the Midwest before coming under Newton's employ.

He'd been quick to grasp their potential.

He'd set out to weaken the Whitfords little by little, thereby combining two goals: weakening his main rival for land in the valley and turning the other ranchers against the Indians. He'd been more successful than he'd expected. Old man Whitford had come to him, offering him some of his less productive acres, but Newton had held out for the Bottoms, knowing it would diminish the Whitford ranch still further.

Then he'd set out to influence Patrick, whose youthful rebellion against his father could be twisted into hate against the Indians. He'd almost succeeded in completely winning over the young man when the other brother, Frank, had come home. Something about Frank's presence had stopped Patrick from changing sides completely, though Newton was stumped as to why. Patrick resented his stepbrother and thought him soft. But...there seemed to be more respect there than Patrick would show.

So when Oliver kept James from returning on time, Newton saw his chance to whip up some hysteria against the Indians. He didn't even have to arrange the attack on the miners! Providence had smiled upon him.

Newton almost chuckled to himself. By this time tomorrow, one of his obstacles would be removed completely. He pulled his mount aside to let most of the party get ahead of him, motioning Martin and his men to his side.

"We can use this," he whispered to Martin. "We want to get these men so riled up at the Miwok that they'll do anything."

"Won't take much, boss," Carpenter broke in. "They're already scared."

Newton dug into his saddlebags. He'd given Oliver a pair of pistols for his birthday, and before leaving the ranch, he'd realized that his son had left one of them behind. Now he pulled it out, turning his body so that only his three men could see what he had in his hands. He pulled out his knife, nicked the end of his thumb, and spread the droplets of blood on the handle of the gun.

"See if you can't slip ahead of the rest of the group a ways," Newton said to Banks. "Leave this by the trail where it can be found."

Banks nodded, took the gun, and slipped it under his coat.

"Hey, boss," Carpenter said, sounding excited. "I got another idea." He reached into his saddlebag and pulled out a worn Indian blanket. "I found this last week. We can leave it beside the pistol."

Newton nodded his approval. "When they're found, try to get the men worked up about what it means. If we're lucky, we can take care of the Indian problem once and for all."

They rode on, and Newton felt the righteousness of his plan. The Indians didn't belong here. It was the destiny of Americans to own this land, from sea to sea. He was but an agent of God's will.

Chapter Eight

Virginia left Sutter's Fort before daybreak, when no one would see her.

The previous night, she had gone back to the dead werewolf's room and searched it thoroughly. Under the bed, she'd found his rifle, which she now wore strapped to her back. Game was plentiful in the mountains. She would never again starve, not if she could help it. With the gun, she could provide for herself.

The hotel was silent as she made her way down the back stairs. She stopped in the kitchen for a day-old loaf of bread and filled her canteen. She paused in the pantry doorway. She desperately wanted more supplies. It was fall; what if the snows came early? What if the miners had overhunted the game? She bit her lip, staring at a barrel of dried beans.

Finally, she shook her head to herself. She would forage if she must, but she'd not steal from the only white woman in Sutter's Fort to offer her friendship rather than scorn.

She sighed and looked around the familiar workspace with a sudden pang of loss. She had been safe here, able to lose her history, memories, and herself for a while. But her past had found her, as she suspected it would for the rest of her life. She would not hide behind a false name, for she was too proud of her family for that. Perhaps a new name would come to her through marriage. She cocked her head, trying to imagine that. It seemed impossible.

After Mrs. Harrelson had so gently fired Virginia and told her that her destiny lay elsewhere, she hadn't thought about where she might go next. But now she realized she'd known what she was going to do from the moment she'd killed the werewolf, Strauss.

She would destroy the werewolves, wherever they might hide.

Feather called her a Canowiki, a Hunter. Maybe she was, maybe she wasn't, but that fight to the death had changed something in her. Until then, she could barely look at the mountains, but now she knew that was exactly where she needed to go. She wasn't afraid anymore. Maybe Feather was right. Maybe she was a Canowiki. It was the werewolves who should be afraid of her.

Virginia went to the back door, took a deep breath, and stepped outside.

Feather was waiting by the loading dock with a pack, hair braided, wearing a leather Indian dress and moccasins. She turned and regarded Virginia with dark, somber eyes.

Virginia hesitated, wanting to order her friend to stay behind, but she suspected the girl wouldn't take no for an answer, so she simply nodded to her and went down the steps. She couldn't keep the smile from her face as Feather followed her into the alley. They left the last houses of town behind them before any of the residents were stirring. A false dawn shone near the mountains, showing crisp morning outlines. The moon was full enough that they could see the road ahead of them. They walked briskly in the cold air until they warmed up, and then the walk became almost pleasant.

It was unusual for two women to venture alone into the wilderness, especially into the mining fields with hundreds of single men, far from home. But Virginia had heard tell there was safety in those very numbers; that the men watched out for and protected the few women in their company—at least, those who weren't prostitutes. And even the prostitutes, she had heard, were treated well, for no man wanted to be the one to deprive the others of release. There might not be law in those hills, but there was justice, she knew. Retribution was swift and final for those who broke the common accord. The mob yesterday was proof of that.

A few hardy women ventured into the mining camps and set up laundries and inns, providing the miners with home cooking and sewing, but most of all, with their own gentle presence. These women were getting rich, Virginia had heard, for miners would gladly pay a large portion of the precious metal they dug up just to have a woman's company, just to talk and innocently flirt. It seemed strange to Virginia that these men would leave their homes, their women, and their comforts, only to miss them so much that they would pay much of what they had worked so hard to earn just to have a taste of home.

There were werewolves in the mining fields, she was certain of it. If Feather was right, Virginia was able to sense such creatures, those who were part of both the civilized world and the wild, on the borders of both.

It was going to be a three-day walk to the foothills of Thompson Peak, and then another two days of hard climbing to reach the Miwok village. The girls walked mostly at night, and only had to leave the road twice to avoid oncoming travelers. The first night was still, and they talked quietly as they walked. Virginia told Feather of her experience at Truckee Lake with the Donner Party. She was relieved to be able to tell the full story—that of the suffering from the depredations of both men and werewolves.

Feather didn't question any of it, only listened intently in her quiet way.

During the day, they found shelter far enough from the road to hide their fire and to sleep, and when they awoke and waited for darkness, Feather told Virginia of the legends of her people. She spoke of Skinwalkers and Skoocooms, who to her people were a natural part of the world, no stranger than wolves or bears.

"The Skoocoom asks only to be left alone," Feather explained. "He does not attack my people if we stay away from his territory. We hold ceremonies in his valley and leave tribute. But I fear white men will not be so respectful. The Skoocoom will not be able to find a way to live with the white man, who wants everything for himself. The Skoocoom will have to go farther into the wilderness or perish."

"He should do so," Virginia agreed. "No matter how big and powerful this Skoocoom is, men will see him as a threat and a challenge. They will hunt him down and destroy him, no matter how many men are lost doing it."

"A shame," Feather said. "I saw a Skoocoom once from a distance. He was standing there among the trees, and had I not been looking directly at him, I would never have seen him. Even so, I could scarcely believe my eyes. He was as big as some of the trees, I swear, and as unmoving. I but blinked and he was gone."

"What does he look like?" Virginia asked.

"I was too far away to make out the details," Feather said. "He had the appearance of a giant man, covered in fur. He had a massive round head, but hardly any neck, and huge eyes and a large mouth. He smelled of decaying flesh, which is only to be expected. For you see, even when the Skoocoom vanishes, he leaves a pungent odor behind, like that of skunk mixed with death. It is believed that they leave this odor when they choose, as a warning.

"When I went to look at the place where I had seen him, all I found were some tufts of hair caught on the bark of a ponderosa pine near where he had been standing and two large footprints. They looked like human footprints, only broader and much bigger."

"Are there many such creatures?" Virginia asked. "I have never heard of them."

"Thou hast heard of them," Feather contradicted her. "The white man has many myths of giants and other fantastic beasts, some of which seem familiar to me."

Virginia didn't argue. After all, a year before, she wouldn't have believed in werewolves. "I wonder how many are left in the world," she mused.

Feather shook her head. "We do not know. For all we know, there may only be one. But other tribes also have tales of these beasts; when the tribes gather from far away to trade, we also trade legends and stories, so that they all become one legend. And the Ts'emekwes is always there, always at the edges of our tales."

"Why do you not hunt them?" Virginia asked. The Indians she knew were not shy about killing creatures that threatened them.

"They leave us alone," Feather said, "if we stay out of their territory. It is easy enough to ascertain the borders, for they leave their scent. The world is big enough for all of us: at least, it used to be. And also…"

"Also?" Virginia prompted.

"Even the bravest warriors have not been able to defeat the Skoocoom. They move faster than an arrow."

"*Can* they be killed?"

Feather stared at her. "Thou art a Canowiki. Hunters such as thee have fought battles with the Ts'emekwes in the past, but no ordinary warrior would dare try. The Skoocoom cannot be found if he doesn't wish to be. And if he decides to hunt you, he will be upon you before you are aware of him. No…we have learned that it is best to leave them alone. These white men who dig into the earth like prairie dogs…I fear they do not understand that."

"They don't believe in creatures they can't see," Virginia said, "or in which they don't wish to believe." Even when the werewolves had come out of hiding to hunt the Donner Party, most had refused to accept what they were seeing. Only a few hardy souls, such as Stanton and her father, had been willing to stand up to the monsters.

And yourself, came a small thought. The thought grew bigger, and the memories of how she'd felt while trying to defend her friends and family washed over her, filling her with strength.

This is what it means to be the Canowiki. It's having the willingness to fight the unknowable.

"Take me to your village," Virginia found herself saying before she knew she had made the decision. "If I can help you, I will."

Feather's eyes glowed in the setting sun as she clasped Virginia's hands in hers, her voice taut with gratitude. "Thank you, Virginia."

She was still smiling as she hefted her pack and led Virginia back onto the road in the gathering dark.

***

They heard the town long before they saw it. Even from the top of the pass, where the road led past a small waterfall into a steep gorge, they heard the sounds of men celebrating the end of a long, hard day of digging. Flickering beacons of light at the bottom of the valley reflected off the pool of water where the locals had dammed the creek. There was a single two-story building in the little hamlet, and it was lit up brightly.

"That building is new since I left," Feather observed.

"How much farther to the Miwok camp?" Virginia asked, eyeing the town with a sense of foreboding. She had the feeling that something was not right.

"Two days, at least," Feather answered. Both of them knew what that meant. Their supplies were gone, and they were already hungry. Going another two days without food and taking the risk that they could find game along the way was going to be chancy. Virginia felt the beginnings of panic rise at the thought of running out of food.

"We'll explore the fringes of the town, maybe knock on some doors," she decided. "You stay hidden."

Feather nodded. An Indian at the door would probably not be welcome in these parts.

They descended into the valley. Even here, they moved to the side of the road when they saw two men walking toward them, but the men were so engrossed in their conversation that they didn't notice the two girls.

"I spent all I had to get here," one of the men was saying as they passed. "I promised my wife I'd find enough gold to keep the farm, but I'm returning broker than when I left."

"Me too," said the other man, who was even younger-looking than his young-looking friend, "but at least I'm returning with my health. Some of those men looked completely broken down, and I don't think they were much older than I am."

They walked in silence for a few moments.

"Maybe we should wait till morning," one of them said.

"I'm not staying in that town another moment longer. There's something wrong there...I can feel it."

"You see anyone strike it rich?" the first man asked quietly.

"Yeah," said the other in a subdued voice. "I did. Son of a bitch worked no harder than I did. Just got lucky." They said no more, just kept trekking resolutely up the road, away from the mountains, toward the coast, where they would have to work for a time to earn passage East.

Most of these miners don't have that much sense, Virginia thought.

She'd seen dozens come through the hotel, and only a few found enough gold for more than a few nights of rest and relaxation and home-cooked meals before heading back to the grind again. It was possible the ones who were making real finds weren't staying on at Mrs. Harrelson's modest hotel, but Virginia doubted it.

Why do men continued to believe that riches are just over the next hill? she wondered. *Why do men believe in shortcuts?* Many of the nearby ranches and businesses needed good, honest labor…but that wasn't the way to get rich.

When they got to the hamlet, the girls walked toward the center of the street. They heard a rustling near one of the rough buildings at the edge of town and saw a man urinating in an alley. He glared at them with blurry eyes. They kept going and reached the main street almost at once. The buildings toward the middle of town were more substantial: a hotel that looked closed. A hardware store. Across the street from the largest building in town, where all the noise was coming from, they found the general store.

It was closed.

"Do you think we could rouse someone if we knocked?" Virginia asked in a whisper. She pulled out the clump of money Mrs. Harrelson had given her. She hadn't even bothered to count it, but she knew it was more money than she'd ever seen before. "If I show them how much I have?"

"Won't do you no good," a rough voice answered. Virginia jumped and stifled a scream. She shoved the money back in her pocket.

A man was leaning against the side of the store, smoking a cigarette. He pushed off the wall and lumbered toward them. He was huge, looming over them. Virginia sensed that he was fighting the impulse to grab her and take her money.

"Pickett's brother struck it rich up on Sisters Mountain," he said, his words slurring. "The whole family packed up and left a few days ago. Sold everything to Bidwell's Bar."

Virginia resisted the urge to step back. Feather edged her way up to stand beside her, as if in support, as if either or both of them could resist this man if he decided to rob them.

"Where is this Bidwell's Bar?" Virginia asked, keeping the fear out of her voice.

The man raised his eyebrows. Obviously, he'd expected a different reaction. "Why, that's the name of the whole town. It also refers to that noisy place across the street there. But I think even a brave girl like you might hesitate to go in there. And I ain't got nothing against Indians, but don't let them see your servant there."

Virginia almost objected. She felt Feather stiffen beside her, but the Indian girl managed not to say anything. "Is there no one else who can sell us a couple of days' worth of food?" Virginia asked.

"Nah," the man said. "Bidwell's bought up the town. He can charge what he wants. I would tell you to move on, except…if you'll pardon me saying…I saw how much money you have. That *might* be enough to buy you few days' worth of supplies."

Virginia felt her heart sink. The man wasn't lying, she could tell.

"Men are paying for a steak with a gold nugget, Miss. Even all your money will only go so far here. But I tell you what. You give me that money, and I'll go across and fetch those supplies for you."

Virginia hesitated. The man looked and sounded rough, but if he was dishonest, he could have simply taken the money from her. Besides, the bills Mrs. Harrelson had given her weren't going to help her much in the mountains. Just then, her stomach growled in hunger, making the decision for her. Reluctantly, she brought the money out. She pulled a few bills off the top and put them back in her pocket. Then she handed the rest of her cash to the hulking stranger.

Without another word, he turned and walked across the street, and entered the saloon.

Chapter Nine

I could fight the hunger no longer; I finally gnawed on one of the putrid pieces of gristly raw meat that Grendel leaves me each morning. It made me violently ill. Hrothgar hovered over me all day, worriedly patting me with his big hands. He responds to his name now, and has learned the words for "eat" and "play."

"Play!" he says, pushing me roughly. "Play!"

I try to indulge him, but I can barely move. The adult came at daybreak, and I am sure it is intelligent, that it knows I am dying. It either doesn't care or doesn't know what to do about it. Probably both.

I still think of Grendel as *it,* but young Hrothgar is a *he*—a child, another thinking being.

This morning, he pulled at my arm, still impatient for me to play with him, and my shoulder nearly separated. He let go when I cried out, but he was disappointed.

In the twenty-five days I've been here, Hrothgar has grown, and I have withered. He does not know his own strength, but I am so weak that it probably doesn't matter. It is difficult even to hold this stub of a pencil. But I'm determined to leave a record, as well as a confession. Let this be my last testament. I will not go to my death without telling you the shameful memories that haunt me. I've been unable to forget, but neither have I been willing to admit to them. It is the atrocity that follows that pushed Kovac and me away from the other miners and into the mountains:

We hadn't travelled far from San Francisco before we fell in with a group of fifteen men who promised us they knew the gold fields. On that first morning, we came across a family of Indians on the road. A young boy, not even five years old, rode a pony; his mother and father and older sister walked, carrying baskets on their heads. Before I knew what was happening, I heard a gunshot, and the young boy slumped over and slid off the pony. The other Indians were too shocked and surprised to run, and more shots rang out.

Our party rode on, not even bothering to move the bloody bodies off the road.

"Let that be a warning to the savages," said Harris, the unofficial leader of the men. He was a slender, consumptive-looking fellow, but we learned that with a gun in his hand, he was more dangerous than anyone we had ever met. We further learned this group of men considered themselves to be a martial troop, and killed any small groups of Indians they came across, anywhere they could surprise and massacre them. Harris had come from farther south in the state and told us that such vigilante posses (he called them "civil guards") were taking action everywhere and that the natives were on the run.

"This land will be ours, if we hold to our purpose," the man said.

Perhaps if Kovac and I had left then, we could have considered ourselves innocent of wrongdoing. But Harris then said, "No one cares. We don't talk about it, and we don't leave any witnesses."

There was a threat in that statement, and we nodded and tried to smile as we went along with the troop. The next morning, we came across a small encampment of Indians, perhaps two families, mostly women and children. This time, the men dismounted, and, carrying knives and tree limbs for truncheons, they stealthily surrounded the camp and began their deadly work, silently, ruthlessly. There was barely an outcry before it was suppressed by throats cut and heads bashed in.

Neither Kovac nor I contributed to the slaughter, but we were there, and we did nothing to stop it.

We slipped away in the night, leaving many of our supplies behind. But the guilt and horror followed us, and we found we could not look other men in the eyes, so we struck out on our own. Perhaps what has happened to us is God's retribution. With that, I cannot argue.

You who find this journal, I beg you: it may sound strange, but please show mercy to Grendel and the child, for they are not evil. They are but a part of nature that we see only in the vagueness of myth. Consider, if you will, who are the real beasts: men, or these creatures who only want to be left alone.

There are few of their kind left. They have been driven deep into the mountains, where even they have difficulty finding food and shelter.

But they have souls, this I can see. They are not monsters.

***

As soon as the stranger left with her money, Virginia felt the bottom drop out of her belly. As the minutes passed and he failed to return with their supplies, she could think of nothing hopeful.

I've just been swindled, she thought, *like an innocent girl at her first country fair.* Worse, the carny had taken her money without a fight.

"Let us leave," Feather said, after an hour passed. "He will not return."

"No," Virginia said.

"Forget the money," Feather urged. "We can reach the village in only a day or two. As long as we have water, we will be fine; we might even find game along the way. Let us move on. We do not need the money."

Virginia didn't care about the money, but she would not be taken advantage of. One thing she had learned during that terrible winter in the mountains was that "You stand up for yourself," she said aloud, "or you will forever be the quarry. The evil creatures of this world can smell weakness. They are attracted to it. You can't let them win."

She scrunched her hat down on her head and buttoned her coat. "How do I look?"

Feather's eyes widened in alarm. "Like a young girl in men's clothing!"

"Can't be helped," Virginia replied. "Wait here. I'm getting those supplies, one way or another."

Feather grabbed at her, but Virginia was already crossing the street. She marched up the steps to the saloon, staring straight ahead, ignoring the men lounging outside, whose eyes followed her progress. None of them spoke to her.

The smoke in the bar stung her eyes, and the smell reminded her of misery, of a tiny cabin at Truckee Lake where her family had nearly died of starvation, shivering and filthy.

A bar ran along one side of the long, narrow room, and it appeared to be constructed of a giant ponderosa planed to a flat surface, worn smooth by the arms of many men leaning on it. On the opposite wall was a huge fireplace, taking up half the expanse of the room. Most of the space between the bar and the fireplace was empty.

A giant wagon wheel hung from the ceiling, and candles burned along its rim. Men and women cavorted in the middle of the room, dancing to the sound of a piano near the back of the saloon. The back third of the place was filled with tables and chairs where poker players lounged, eyeing each other and measuring the depth of their pockets against the cards held tight to their chests.

Virginia suddenly felt very small and vulnerable. She felt like a rabbit who had wandered into a coyote den. But everyone was so engrossed with their own revelries that no one noticed her. Steeling herself, she moved to one side of the doorway and scanned the crowd.

The burly man who had taken her money was in the middle of the loudest group, surrounding a roulette wheel. A collective groan went up, and Virginia saw the man's shoulders slump. There were hoots and jeers, and someone shouted, "Try again, Pete! You're bound to get lucky one of these times!"

Virginia marched up behind the man called Pete. By then, some of the saloon patrons had noticed her, and the room was starting to go quiet. She tapped the man on the back and he turned around, looking guilty, as if he was expecting her.

"If you aren't going to buy me supplies," she said, "I want my money back."

"What money?" Pete asked.

"You promised to buy me two days' supply of food," Virginia said. "I want the food or the money, I don't care which."

"I don't know what you're talking about," the man answered. He said it with such sincerity, she almost could have believed him. "If I stole your money, why didn't you raise the alarm? Why didn't you call out?"

"You didn't *steal* the money," Virginia began. She stopped, realizing she had made a mistake as the men watching started to murmur. She tried to recover. "You were supposed to buy food for me with it."

Pete smirked. "Why would I do that?"

Another man pushed his way through the crowd to stand next to them. He was shorter than most men, but solidly built and very broad in the shoulders and chest. It wasn't that he was fat, Virginia sensed, but that he was solid. He gave of a sense of menace, of... Virginia shook her head. She couldn't be sure, but she thought there was something wrong with him. The whole town felt wrong, especially the men in this bar.

"He's got you there, Miss," the burly man said. "Old Pete here isn't known for doing favors." The man had a big, friendly smile on his face. Virginia immediately distrusted him.

"He is gambling with my money," she said.

The short man laughed. "Well, I think she's got you there, Pete. If I remember rightly, earlier tonight, you were so broke you were begging. Seems to me I kicked you out a couple of hours ago for stealing drinks."

"She's lying, Mr. Bidwell," Pete said. "Hanson brought my share of the claim by. It's my money, I swear."

Bidwell sighed. "Hanson ain't anywhere around. Just give her the money back, Pete. We'll let it slide."

"I can't," Pete said. "I just lost it at your damned crook..." He caught himself before he made the accusation. "...at your roulette wheel," he finished meekly.

Bidwell looked down at the saloon floor and shook his head sadly. He turned to Virginia with a regretful expression. "It would seem the money is no longer yours, Miss."

Virginia was uncertain what to do. Challenging a thief was one thing, but challenging the man who apparently owned this town was another. She sensed that she wasn't going to get very far pressing her case. What was left? Retribution? Punishment?

The sense of danger was growing with every second, a sense that came from the Canowiki part of her that she was just beginning to understand and listen to. It wasn't worth it. She turned to go.

"He ought to work off his debt," called a voice from the crowd. A young man stepped forward. He wasn't looking at Pete or Bidwell, but at Virginia.

Her heart both lifted and fell simultaneously. This was someone she had never expected to see again: Jean Baptiste Trudeau, who had been the first boy to ever kiss her, only a little more than year before.

No longer was he the handsome, dark-haired boy with olive skin she remembered. He was scarred, his hair was ragged and dull, and his eyes had a wounded look. But he still managed to give her a sad smile. He marched up to Pete, who towered over him. "You need to pay her back, Mister," he said firmly.

Pete seemed almost relieved by this turn of events. He'd been looking trapped; first by a girl he couldn't seem to bully successfully, and then by the boss of the town, whom he didn't dare stand up to. Now he eyed this younger, smaller man and puffed himself up. "You questioning my honesty, boy?"

"I wouldn't bother," Jean replied acidly. "Everyone already knows what your honesty is worth."

The room went quiet at that. A space opened up around the two men, who squared off.

Virginia stepped between them, facing the younger man. "You don't have to do this, Jean. It won't accomplish anything. He doesn't have the money."

"I won't let you down again," he said, looking away.

She fell silent for a moment, then said in a soft voice, "You never let me down, Jean. None of it was your fault."

"If you two are going to chat, then go over to bar and order a drink," Bidwell said. "Fight or don't fight; make up your mind, because until this fight is done, no one's doing any drinking, and that's costing me money."

"Please, Jean," Virginia said. "Let it go."

He turned to her with a stubborn set to his jaw.

There were footsteps behind her, and Virginia ducked out of the way. But Jean Baptiste saw the attack too late and went flying backward, landing on his back. The bigger man kept coming, kicking out and stomping down with his boots, but Jean managed to roll out of the way.

He got to his feet and started weaving and bobbing to keep the blows from landing. He finally caught an opening and hit the bigger man square in the face.

Pete only grunted and continued his advance until Jean was backed up against the bar. Bidwell pushed him away, into the middle of the floor, where Pete neatly caught the smaller man in a bear hug and started squeezing, lifting him into the air. Pinioned, Jean could move neither fists nor feet. He reared back with his head, smacking Pete in the face. Again, the big man only grunted, though blood started to pour out of his nose.

Trapped, Jean Baptiste began to Turn. His arms started to elongate; his fingers started forming into claws. His face, which had been covered with stubble, suddenly looked as if it had a full beard. Virginia glanced around, alarmed, but no one else seemed to have noticed it…except one man. Behind the bar, Bidwell looked surprised, then frowned.

"Don't, Jean!" she yelled. "Not here!"

He heard her and stopped, and a look of shame came over his face. He stopped struggling, but Pete didn't stop squeezing. Jean's head began to droop, and then, as he fell into unconsciousness, it lolled from side to side.

"Stop, Pete!" Virginia shouted. "You've won. You're killing him!"

Pete showed no sign of having heard her. She came at him from the side, making calculations, somewhere among her frenzied thoughts, about where the man was off balance. She simultaneously pushed him while tripping him, her leg curled behind his knee. The big man fell backward. He let go of Jean with a cry, and the younger man crumpled to the floor.

Pete landed flat on his back. As he lay there, dazed and trying to catch his breath, Virginia ran to Jean's side. He was starting to come around. She lifted him to his feet. To the onlookers, it must have looked as if Jean had recovered and could stand. They didn't see that she was lifting him, nor would they have expected the slim girl to be able to do that. But she caught the surprise on Bidwell's face. She met his shrewdly calculating gaze.

"What the…?" Pete said, from the floor. "What hell happened? Who tripped me?"

The crowd was laughing, though they appeared equally confused. They'd seen the young girl dart forward and seem to touch the big man lightly just as he was falling backward.

"No one, you big lunk," someone shouted out. "You fell on your own."

"That's impossible," Pete muttered, sitting up.

Virginia didn't wait to hear more. She carried Jean out of the saloon, his feet making motions as if he was walking, though he was barely able to stand. Virginia knew that a woman her size shouldn't be able to lift such a weight, but the urgency gave her unexpected strength. But even that wasn't enough to explain it.

This is the strength of a Canowiki, she thought.

Even so, Virginia felt the dead weight wearing her down. She made it as far as the sidewalk and collapsed, Jean landing on top of her. She heard running steps and then Feather was there, helping her disentangle herself from Jean's loose limbs.

"What happened?" Feather asked.

"I lost the money," Virginia said. "I'm sorry."

Feather didn't seem concerned. She was staring at the boy. "Who is he?"

"An old friend," Virginia said. "He was in the Donner Party."

Feather stepped back involuntarily, then blushed as she realized how that must have looked. "Did he...did he...?"

"He's a Skinwalker," Virginia said.

This time Feather took two steps back and looked ready to run away. "A Skinwalker? How...*Why are you helping him?*"

"He was Turned," Virginia explained. "But he never joined them. He helped me and my family survive. Afterwards, he just disappeared."

"You have to kill him," Feather said, conviction lending steel to her voice.

"No, Feather," Virginia said. "I only survived because some of the newly Turned resisted hunting humans. Mr. Stanton, Jean Baptiste...and others. They retained their humanity...their souls." Her mind shut down at the third name on her list of saviors, as it always did. She wanted to remember Bayliss as human, not wolf.

"They may resist for a time," Feather said. "But eventually they all give in to their new nature. He has Turned and hunted, of this I have no doubt. He might think he wants to help thee, but he will lapse someday, perhaps when thou least expecteth it."

"I can't just leave him here," Virginia said, looking down at the still-unconscious boy. He was breathing steadily, but his eyes were closed.

"Either thou leavest him or I continue on my own," Feather warned.

"*You* wanted *my* help," Virginia said.

"I will not lead a Skinwalker to my tribe," Feather replied.

They stared at each other stubbornly, neither of them backing down.

"Go," a soft voice said.

Virginia looked down. Jean's eyes were open.

"She's right. I have hunted humans. I can't always control myself. Go, Virginia."

"I know you wouldn't hurt me," Virginia said.

"Perhaps not, but I can't vouch for what I might do to your companion, or anyone in your company." Virginia heard the defeated truth in his voice.

"What about that man...Pete? Won't he come after you?"

"Fights happen all the time," Jean Baptiste said. He sat up and groaned, his hands going to his chest. "Feels like he squeezed my ribs right into my heart." He put one hand on the railing and pulled himself to his feet. "Don't worry about me. No one holds a grudge around here. If I buy the man a drink, he'll be my best friend. Next night, when I don't buy him a drink, he'll want to kill me again."

"He's right," a new voice agreed. They all turned toward the saloon's double doors. Standing just outside, a bag in one hand, was the owner and namesake of the saloon. Virginia wondered how long he'd been listening.

"I value a brave soul, Miss," Bidwell said. "While I have no doubt Pete took your money, you have no proof, only your word against his."

"I heard it as well," Feather said. "He promised us he would buy us supplies."

Bidwell glanced at her without changing expression, as if dismissing both her and her testimony. "As I said, Miss Reed, it's only your word against his. While justice may not be done here tonight, I can at least help you in your journey. I've given you the night's leftovers, which we usually feed to the dogs. Should be enough food there to get you where you need to go."

How does he know where we're going? Virginia wondered. *More importantly, how does he know my name?*

She took the sack. "Thank you," she murmured. She didn't like the man, but even so, she couldn't be ungrateful. The bag smelled of roast beef, and she badly wanted to tear it open and eat it on the spot.

"These are wild places, Miss," Bidwell said, "and wild times. Dangerous for unaccompanied young women to be wandering around."

Beside her, Jean Baptiste stiffened, as if he was ready to fight again over the implied threat.

"Yet...I somehow think you can take care of yourself, Miss Reed," the bar owner continued. It seemed to her that his eyes glowed red for the space of a heartbeat.

And then she knew.

"You best move along, Miss," Bidwell said, "before my patrons start heading back to their claims at dawn. You don't want to be caught on the road."

Without another word, he went back into the saloon.

"Let us depart," Feather urged.

Virginia turned to Jean Baptiste. She was shocked anew by his haggard appearance. It looked as if he'd aged a decade in the past year. He smiled at her sadly. "Go, Virginia. Your memory keeps me alive, but I'm not worthy of your company."

"Are you sure?" she asked. He had saved her life in those mountains, fighting his own kind. And she still remembered the carefree boy who had been so full of stories. They were two of a kind in those days, both of them exaggerating every little incident to feel important.

Neither of us have need of embellishment now, Virginia thought. *Our lives are so fantastic that we dare not tell people the full truth.*

"I'm sure that you're safer without me," he said with a smile, and for a moment he looked like the old Jean Baptiste. He stifled a laugh. "And I might be safer without you."

At that moment, three men came stumbling out of the saloon, laughing and hanging onto each other. They fell silent upon seeing Feather and Virginia. Their eyes lingered on the girls, as if hungry for the sight of a female. Then one of them tipped his hat and nudged the others. They straightened up and tipped their hats as well, and descended the steps with as much drunken dignity as they could muster. They were joshing with each other before they were out of view, and Virginia heard some crude commentary that alarmed her and made her blush.

"We must go," she said. She hesitated, then stepped forward and hugged Jean Baptiste.

He froze, and then his arms went around her.

"You were my first kiss," she whispered in his ear.

He nodded, his chin on her shoulder. "I loved you," he whispered back.

Feather watched the street, pretending to hear nothing. Virginia let go of Jean Baptiste and descended the steps of the saloon. Feather was caught off guard by the abrupt leave-taking, but followed. In a short time, they'd left Bidwell's Bar behind and were climbing out of the canyon. About halfway up, Virginia took the bag of food, opened it, and stared into it. Her mouth watered, and her belly ached from hunger.

She swung the bag back and threw it down the hillside as far as she could chuck it.

"What are you doing?" Feather cried.

"I won't eat anything that man gives me," Virginia said, turning and continuing her march up the hill. "No matter how hungry I am."

***

Jean Baptiste waited until Virginia was out of sight, then followed her. She was even more beautiful than he remembered. Her blonde hair seemed lighter, her eyes an even deeper blue. The soft roundness of her face was gone, and she had a refinement that he didn't remember from before. But he'd known even when he'd courted her that she would never settle for him.

He followed them, two small women alone in the wilderness. He watched Virginia chuck the food down the hillside. He looked around before removing his clothing and Turning. He wrapped his clothing into a bundle that he could carry in his teeth. In his new form, he trotted over to the food. His heightened senses told him it was only roast beef and carrots, but he understood why Virginia had abandoned the meal. He wasn't so fastidious. He gobbled it down.

Then, still in his wolf form, he stalked the two girls as they climbed out of the canyon and followed the trail along its rim, toward the mountains.

***

Bidwell marched through the now-emptying bar. "Brennan, Folkins!" he shouted. Two men standing at the bar followed him into the back room.

"Did you see that girl who was in here earlier? The one that damn fool Pete stole money from?" he asked them. They nodded. They were in human form, but they didn't look quite human. There was something feral in their movements, the way they licked their lips. "She's got a squaw friend with her. They're headed up into the mountains. I want you to follow them."

"Who is she, Boss?" Brennan asked.

"Her name is Virginia Reed," Bidwell said. "She murdered my brother during the Foregathering of the Clans. She knows about us, and she's dangerous. She has some kind of unnatural ability to fight us. Keseberg told me to kill her if I ever saw her again."

"So why didn't you?"

"Jesus, Brennan. In front of everyone?" Bidwell said. "Besides, why should I listen to that fool Keseberg? I lost some packmates to his reckless venture in the mountains. It was a dumb plan, and he shouldn't have survived it."

"You could have killed her quick, outside," Folkins suggested.

"Perhaps, but I'd just as soon she die somewhere else. Her father is an important man down in San Francisco. He'd want to know what happened. Follow the girls for a couple days and then kill them. Make sure they are never found."

Chapter Ten

Oliver could barely lift the golden rock in one hand, it was so heavy. Nonetheless, a triumphant smile played over his face. "See! I told you we'd find gold here!"
And then his face disappeared...but not his body. Oliver still knelt beside the pool, but now blood fountained from his stump of a neck, and James screamed. He tried to run, but his legs wouldn't move. A shadow loomed over him, and again he opened his mouth to scream, but no sound came out. The overpowering smell made him gag. He closed his eyes, waiting for death.

***

The smell remained when James awoke from his fitful dreams. He was in complete darkness.

I'm dead and buried, and rotting, he thought. He tried to move and was relieved to feel his arms and legs respond. He stretched out and realized he wasn't in a coffin, but in an open space. He gagged at the stench, and the sound of the retching echoed. *I'm in some kind of chamber,* he thought. But the last he remembered, he'd been far from any settlement.

Oliver. Oliver was gone. Of that, James had no doubt. He was only surprised to find himself alive. He tried to shut out the horror of his friend's head skipping across the pond. He resigned himself to the fact that though he wasn't dead yet, he would soon join his friend. So he buried his horror, but a deep sadness took its place. He wanted to mourn Oliver, but he was too frightened for himself.

James breathed through his mouth, but it was as if he could taste the smell. He gagged again, then rolled over and vomited. His head felt as though it had swelled and broken in half. He fell backward with a cry. He put his hand to his forehead and felt dry, caked blood.

James tried to sit up, but the pain in his head burst over him again. He lay back down and tried to breathe slowly, and finally the agony subsided to a level where he could think.

I'm not dying, he thought. *Head wounds bleed a lot, but I'm still conscious. I'm still able to move.*

When the pain was manageable, he tried again to rise, only this time he did it very slowly. His head pounded from the effort, but it was a steady escalation rather than a sudden explosion. His eyes adjusted to the darkness, and he saw that there was an opening to the chamber, though it was blocked by something outside.

He reached out, and his hand encountered rough rock.

I'm in a cave. Something grabbed me and took me to its cave. A bear? As soon as he thought it, he dismissed the possibility. No…it had been a giant man, bigger than anyone he'd ever seen.

James had heard stories of mountain men, who let their hair and beards grow, who dressed in fur and buckskin. He'd always imagined them as big brutes, dirty and smelly.

But he couldn't convince himself that was what he'd seen. What he'd seen was something he'd never heard of. Something most people didn't know about. Something unnatural. He stumbled to his feet, leaning against the cave wall. Slowly, he made his way toward the dim light at the front of the cave. The ground was uneven, loose, and he heard cracking sounds under his feet. He felt a breeze and knew that he was close to the entrance, and yet it was still dark.

He felt something webbed and loose, which moved when he pushed against it. It was a screen, he realized, woven together from branches. He pushed outward, but the screen immediately stopped. He tried sliding the screen to one side, and this time it moved easily.

A row of trees blocked the cave entrance from prying eyes, with just enough space and flexibility in their branches for him to move forward. With the screen out of the way, more light made its way into the cave, and he glanced behind him.

James froze.

Even his breath stilled within him. Time hung suspended for a moment, like the eternal stars whose light penetrated the cave. There was a solid wall of gold, glowing in the dim light. His mouth hanging open in awe, he stumbled toward it, reaching to touch it, before something rolled under his foot. Waves of pain radiated from his head, but he managed to not to fall. Glancing around, he noticed for the first time that the cave floor was covered in bones. Though numb with horror at the sheer quantity of scattered bones, James nevertheless moved deeper into the cave, his fingertips trailing across the surface of the gleaming gold. Behind the wall of shining metal, the cave went on, and James saw that the silky glow stretched into the darkness.

This is all the gold ever discovered, he thought. *This is enough gold to make every man in California rich.*

He looked for pockets of impurity, but the metal was solid, as if it had been melted and poured into a mold.

He reached out with trembling fingers and ran his hands over the gilded wall, and it was smooth and solid to his touch. He looked down.

The noxious smell was as strong as ever, for in walking through the bones, coated with bits of rotted meat, he had stirred up the stench of death.

I need to leave, he thought. *Come back with Father and my brothers. Leave now.*

But he couldn't help it; he reached down and found a jagged piece of bone, and used it to pry out a large, rough nugget. He shoved in his pocket and turned to leave.

It was then that he saw the other man.

His heart stopped for a moment, then resumed beating with a huge thump. The man sat propped against a golden boulder, staring at him.

"Hello?" James offered hesitantly.

There was no response. The man's face was in shadow, hiding any sign of life. James crouched beside him, ignoring his continued nausea to examine his fellow prisoner. The skin was dried and stretched across the bones and the eyes were sunken, but James had never seen a dead man so well preserved.

The man sat as if perfectly comfortable atop some moldy blankets, an open rucksack beside him. Inside was a layer of gold, and on top of that, a leather-bound journal. James slid the journal into his pocket. On the wall next to the body, James noticed small gouges, and he leaned over to see that they were rows of lines in bunches of five. He counted the rows, losing count once, but finally came up with a number. The man had been in this cave for sixty-five days.

Why didn't he leave? James wondered. *The barrier in front of the cave could hardly have kept him here.*

Near the entrance, he spotted an Indian blanket tossed to one side. James snatched it up and draped it over his shoulders against the cave's natural chill. He moved toward the front of the cave again, and as he got closer, he started moving faster.

He had almost reached the entrance when there a sound behind him. He wanted to run without even looking to see what it was. But instead, he looked back—and hesitated.

Something moved toward him in the darkness at the back of the cave. It looked like a child. Perhaps only the thought of an innocent child being held in that pit of hell could have kept him from running. It shambled toward him, like a child just learning to walk.

The figure moved into the moonlight, and James saw that this wasn't a human child. He was nearly as big as a man and was covered with fur, with arms longer in proportion to his body than any human's, and a large, broad head on thick shoulders. James should have run then, but the eyes in the strange child's face caught him.

The gaze was curious, even friendly, and the broad gash that was his mouth twisted into a smile. He moved toward the mummified body, and his broad, square hands, also covered in fur, petted the unmoving head. "Friend," the creature said, quite clearly. "You be friend?"

James backed away. He found himself with his back to the trees that guarded the cave. *Push through and run*, he thought. But some strange fascination kept him focused on the unnatural youngster in front of him. At first, as his mind tried to make sense of what he was seeing, he saw the dark shape the creature dragged as a doll. But then the child lifted it up and gnawed on it. It was a human arm. On the hand, flopping in the moonlight, was a tattoo in the same shape as the one Oliver had on the back of his hand.

James heard screaming, and as he turned and ran, he realized it was him. He pushed through the branches, which slashed into his face, but that didn't stop him. The pool was dead ahead, the small path winding around it, and he ran toward the front of the box canyon, heedless of the throbbing in his head.

He had nearly reached the narrow pass out of the hidden valley when the opening disappeared, as if a giant boulder had been rolled in front of it. James couldn't stop in time and ran headlong into the object. Instead of hitting solid stone, he hit something softer, something alive. He fell backward.

Then all he could see was a huge hand reaching down for him. The horror was too much, and his mind shut down. He scrambled between the towering legs, and then he was out.

He got to his feet, ready to run again. But as he was getting up, he spotted Oliver's pistol, glinting only inches away. He grabbed it, whirled around, and fired.

His pursuer was impossible to miss, but the huge creature didn't even flinch.

James turned, racing into the darkness, not caring what was ahead of him, knowing only that he had to escape, to run with all his might. He was running faster than he'd ever run, the downhill slope propelling him. He felt a moment of wild, unreasoning fear.

And then something grabbed him from behind and swung him into the air. Giant arms enfolded him and squeezed. James gasped for breath and was on the verge of passing out when the creature relented.

James felt hope die within him, and it was as if the monster understood that. With a giant arm, he swept up the human and slung him under one arm, carrying him almost loosely. James looked up and saw creature's jutting jaw, its canines stretching down over its lower lip.

It carried him past the brook and through the branches of the trees to where the monstrous child waited. It dropped him onto the bones with a clatter. The little beast rushed forward, grabbed James's arms, and wrenched him into a sitting position.

"Friend!" it cried.

The larger creature stood over the child, glaring down at James, and it was clear what the message was. *Stay or die*, the look said. *You live only as long as the child wants you to live.*

James heard himself repeating, shakily, "Friend. Friend."

"I'm a friend."

Chapter Eleven

The cold mountain air seeped into Virginia's bones and into her dreams. She awoke to frost and the morning light pouring through the crystals on the trees. This high up the mountains, the air was thin and sharp, every breath a blessing.

Memories of her ordeal with the Donner Party the previous winter came flooding back. She remembered how innocently excited she'd been at first, when the wagon train had reached this altitude on the far side of the mountains. After months of traveling, it had seemed they were only days away from their destination.

Then the snows came.

Then the wolves.

Virginia looked up at the sky anxiously, but it was clear. It was early fall, and the snows were a month or more away. But that's what they had believed the past winter, too. They'd nearly died because of those snows.

This side of the mountain had gentler slopes, and the salvation of the lower valleys was mere hours away. But Virginia knew how quickly that could change. The Donner Party had also thought they had plenty of time. They, too, had thought themselves a short journey from safety.

Feather walked beside her, unconcerned about the weather or anything else. The Indian girl was stoic, but sometimes in the middle of conversations, she would become surprisingly animated. Her stride was lengthening and her expression was relaxing the farther they climbed up the narrow canyons and trails that wound back and forth across the steep hillside.

They came to an indentation in the land, a small depression lined by lava rocks that looked like giants' stairs leading up to the plateau. It was like an amphitheater in the middle of the wilderness, left over from some long-gone civilization.

They sat on the giants' steps, and squads of chipmunks took turns watching them, twitching their tails from fear or interest or both. One came close, then froze in surprise, and the girls also froze until the creature ran off chattering, scolding them for blocking his path.

A half-burned log lay half-buried in the sand. That night, they started a fire for warmth. When it started to die down, the girls didn't build it back up again. They crawled under their blankets and went to sleep.

Virginia woke late in the night. It was still dark out, but she felt alert, rested even. More, her heart was pounding in her chest, and she felt tense, ready for…a sound. There was something, and she strained her ears to hear it, but heard only the whisper of the wind in the trees, and then… there it was—a soft rustling in the bushes on the hillside above them.

"It is your friend," Feather said, not moving from her blankets. There was just enough glow from the dying coals to see her glittering eyes. She held Virginia's rifle. "He has been following us."

"Have you slept?" Virginia asked.

Feather hesitated, and there was a calculating look in her eyes as she considered lying. Then she shook her head.

"I'll keep watch," Virginia said, reaching over and taking the rifle. "Jean Baptiste will not hurt us."

"Perhaps he would not harm thee," Feather muttered. "But I do not know him."

But despite her trepidation, she rolled over in the blankets and was soon asleep.

***

Virginia built up the fire, waiting for dawn. She wanted to invite Jean Baptiste to come join them, but Feather's feelings were clear, so she held back. What could she say to Jean, anyway? They had parted on awkward terms. She remembered seeing him once on the streets of San Francisco. She'd crossed the street to avoid him. She'd had enough of werewolves— even werewolves who were friends.

The warmth of the fire was making her sleepy.

The part of her that was Canowiki dreamed of the attack before it happened.

When it came, it came from behind. She was instantly awake and turning. There was a wolf leaping through the air toward her. She got halfway to her feet, swinging the rifle barrel around, then realized there was no time for a shot and swung the stock of the rifle into the leaping animal's head.

She had a moment of doubt. *Is Jean Baptiste attacking us?*

But the fur of the attacking wolf was black, and at any rate, there was no more time for ruminations. It snapped its jaws inches from her shoulder and landed behind her. It slid partway into the fire and howled with pain. Feather was rising, knife in hand, when the second wolf appeared. It was clear that it would have her in its jaws before she could react.

A third wolf, with gray fur, ran full speed into the light of the camp, barreling into the wolf charging Feather and locking his jaws on the attacker's neck. This new wolf was smaller, scrawnier than his opponent, but with the advantage of surprise.

By then, the first wolf had rolled away from the fire, its fur scorched, leaving an acrid odor of burnt hair. Virginia tried again to bring the rifle around and shoot it, but the blow to the wolf had broken the stock. The weapon misfired.

She threw the rifle at the creature, which flinched just long enough for Virginia to draw her bowie knife.

The werewolf circled her, relishing the fight, in no hurry for it to end.

The other two wolves were still locked in mortal combat as Feather watched them, knife raised. The rescuing wolf had a firm hold on his opponent's throat, while his eyes pleaded with Feather. As the larger wolf's head was held in a death grip, she stepped forward hesitantly. The attacker flailed in the clutches of his opponent, but he couldn't escape as the Indian girl approached.

The desperate look in her rescuer's eyes swept away her uncertainty.

She sprang forward and thrust the knife to the hilt into the pinioned wolf's neck. It howled, but the sound faded quickly to a gurgle. Finally, it stopped twitching. The smaller wolf let go, covered in blood. Feather watched him warily, still holding the knife, but the wolf was already turning in the direction of the other fight. So did Feather.

Virginia and the big wolf circled each other. She backed up to the fire, cutting off an angle the big wolf could use to get at her. The creature had been toying with her, but the death of its packmate put an end to the play.

The wolf tensed. Virginia knew its final lunge was coming.

It jumped for her throat, no doubt expecting her to scream and run. Three things happened at once. The wolf Jean Baptiste leapt as well and caught the creature's rear leg. Feather threw her knife with all her might and the blade punctured the werewolf's side. And Virginia, instead of retreating, shoved her bowie knife deep into the creature's chest.

The beast froze in midair, its forward momentum stopped by Jean's hold on its hindquarters as its life left its body.

It dropped among them, dead.

They stood staring at each other, breathing hard. Jean Baptiste was trembling, and he moved out of the firelight. At the edge of darkness, they saw him transform back into human form. He was naked, his body covered in blood. Feather blushed and turned away. Even in the shadows, Virginia saw that Jean Baptiste was also embarrassed. Being trapped with others in a cabin for an entire winter had stolen Virginia's modesty, but apparently Jean had retained his. Or…something had changed.

"Jean?" Virginia said, taking a step toward him.

Jean gathered up one of the blankets and covered himself. He moved into the darkness, then returned fully dressed. He was carrying one of his boots and limping because of a large gash on his ankle.

"Thou art hurt," Feather said. Instinctively, she moved toward him, but stopped in mid-stride.

Jean didn't seem to notice. He sat down near the fire and examined his wound. "I've had worse," he said.

Virginia took some linen bandages from her rucksack. She knelt by Jean's leg and started to bandage his ankle, but she was clumsy about it. Finally, Feather snorted and said, "Let me do it."

Virginia moved aside and Feather took her place beside Jean.

"Why are you here, Jean Baptiste?" Virginia asked. She'd meant to lecture him, but she was unable to keep her voice from shaking.

"A good thing I was, wouldn't you say?" he said cheerfully. When Virginia didn't smile, his face fell. "I followed you because there are others of my kind in town," Jean explained. "They know who you are, Virginia. You're…famous among Our Kind."

"Our Kind?" Virginia asked.

"That is what they…we…call ourselves," Jean said, looking uncomfortable.

Virginia softened. "It wasn't your fault, Jean," she said. "You didn't ask to be bitten."

He swallowed and stared into the fire, and when he spoke again, his voice was low. "I try not to be like them. But sometimes…the hunger comes over me, and…I no longer think like…like a human."

Feather stared at him intently, her bandaging forgotten for the moment, but said nothing. Jean Baptiste seemed uncomfortable under the scrutiny.

"Let me help you," he said. "My sense of smell and hearing will give you warning long before you realize anything is amiss yourselves."

No," Feather said, turning to Virginia. "He is a white man, *and* a Skinwalker. Neither are welcome in my village. You are the Canowiki, so you are welcome."

"I am half Indian," Jean burst out. "I pretend to be Mexican so that I won't be treated as a half-breed, trusted by neither side of my heritage."

Virginia nodded, unsurprised. Feather, on the other hand, was rattled. It occurred to Virginia that though she had always thought of the girl as Indian, a white family had raised her. She too had said that she was distrusted by both sides of her heritage.

"Thou art a Skinwalker," Feather said, her dilemma resolved by this undeniable fact. "It matters not if thou wast once one of The People."

"But I won't Turn unless there is danger," Jean pleaded. "I will stay human, I promise."

Virginia raised her eyebrows at Feather, as if to say, *It is your decision.*

Feather stared at Jean Baptiste for a long moment. "If you trust him, Virginia," she said finally.

Relief lit up Jean Baptiste's face.

Daylight was still hours away.

"Make yourself useful, Jean," Virginia said, picking up the blanket he had cast off and taking it back to her sleeping spot. "You get next watch."

***

She awoke to the sound of whispers. Feather and Jean were awake and talking softly. Virginia was surprised. Feather had never been much of a talker. They sounded almost...friendly.

"Both Bayliss and I were trying hard to win her favor, but she intimidated us both," Jean was saying.

"She had never been kissed?" Feather asked. "Never?"

"Not so much as a peck on the cheek."

"Who kissed her first?"

"Me, of course. Bayliss was just as shy as she was. Bayliss was…" Jean's voice faltered, as if he was only just remembering what had happened to his friend. "He was a good man."

"How didst thou fight them off?" Feather asked. "I heard thou wert plagued by more Skinwalkers than anyone had ever seen before."

"Not all of them traveled with our wagon train, but yes, there were more than enough," Jean said. "I think if it wasn't for Virginia, none of us would have survived. She kept us together and organized, she and Mr. Stanton. Her father too, when he was there."

"But I still do not understand how a few humans could fight off a pack of Skinwalkers."

"Because the werewolves miscalculated in leading us to that spot," Jean answered. "They were starving, just as the humans were. They were weak, disorganized, fighting among themselves. If Keseberg hadn't created so many factions, and if he'd commanded a concerted effort, he might have killed us…them…all. But he acted as though there was no hurry. He seemed to think the werewolves could have what they wanted when they wanted, without hindrance. Thus, the resistance Virginia and Bayliss and the others put up took them by surprise. It was easier to attack those who denied the werewolves' existence, or who didn't know about them."

"She is a Canowiki," Feather said. "I am not surprised at her strength."

"A what?"

"She is a Hunter," Feather said.

There was a long silence. "Of course," Jean said. "I should have realized. My people call such as her Kanati."

"I saw it in her immediately," Feather said.

"I did not," Jean sighed. "She was a pampered little girl in her hometown, a little princess. Yet when the moments of greatest danger came, she always knew what to do. You must be right."

Virginia grew more uncomfortable with every word. They were acting as though she was some kind of hero, instead of the frightened girl she really was. She groaned and turned over, as if just waking up. Then she sat up, careful not to look either of them in the face so as not to betray that she had overheard them. She imagined them exchanging a glance.

"You let me sleep?" she asked. The sun was several degrees above the horizon.

"We will reach my village before dark," Feather reassured her, smiling. "We will be safe among my people tonight."

Virginia nodded, acting as if she hadn't heard a thing. She looked down at her clothing and realized it was torn and bloody. She pulled out the gingham dress she wore in town and reluctantly changed into it, turning away but not seeking to hide herself.

"Let's go," she said.

***

The wolf pack began trailing them late in the morning. Virginia could see their sleek shapes winding among the trees, at the very edge of the horizon. They were ordinary wolves, she sensed, not werewolves. But why were they following them?

"I will see what they want," Jean said. He slipped into the trees to remove his clothes. Feather seemed determined not to look in his direction. And yet...yes, she snuck a glance.

A short time later, the lean gray shape of Jean's wolf form returned. He got dressed and joined them. "I don't speak wolf, exactly," he said. "But my sense is that they lost their pack leader. All the other males are either too old or too young to take his place. I think they were inviting me to lead them."

"What a chance!" Feather laughed. "How canst thou refuse?"

Jean Baptiste didn't join her in laughter. "I've wondered what would happen if I joined a pack," he said. "I believe I would forget what it is to be human." For a time, they walked in silence. Then Jean added, "Such a life seems very alluring."

"No one would think less of you," Virginia said.

"You don't think so?" Jean said. He didn't look at Feather, but he was obviously waiting for her reaction.

"It would be too easy," Feather said firmly. "Thou must stay human, even if it is uncomfortable. It is thy true nature."

Jean Baptiste seemed grateful for these words. "That's what I told them. Or signaled to them. Whatever it was I did, they seemed to understand."

They continued on, Feather leading, with Jean close behind and Virginia following him, watching her friends. Feather, it appeared, had decided that Jean was more human than wolf. It was a start.

Lower down in the foothills, on the wide plateau above the valley, they passed wide and shallow lakes surrounded by wetlands. Higher up, they started to see small blue lakes everywhere there was a hollow among the rocky cliffs, with broken boulders extending down into the water and beyond.

The trail wound around and between these endless and nameless lakes. It was slow going. The path would descend into a gully, run along a dry creek bed and up another hill, then down another steep gully, all the while progressing only a few hundred yards forward. But every time they were tempted to strike out overland, they saw it was impossible; the terrain was covered in deadfall trees, thick underbrush, and broken, jagged basalt rocks.

They slowly drew closer to the base of Thompson Peak.

The hills became rocky, and the trail was lined with ledges of broken stone. The air took on a crispness and freshness, as if there was less of it and it was more precious. The trees were getting smaller, and some were precariously perched on broken slopes.

They reached a small plateau at the top of a particularly steep section of the trail. There was a small meadow there, with a serpentine stream running down the middle of it. For much of the year, this was a mountain flood plain, and it was still green from the summer growth, still wet only a few inches below the surface. Wildflowers filled the meadow, small but colorful, and in their profusion, as dazzling as any garden: purple and red and white blooms, each claiming a strip of the field.

It was dry enough near the edge of the meadow to camp, but they found the banks of the stream muddy and the grass churned up.

"This is my people's fall camp," Feather said. "I hoped they would be here, but the snows have not yet fallen, so perhaps they linger on the slopes above."

She motioned for the other two to wait, strode to the middle of the encampment, and knelt. Then she returned, shaking her head. "Someone else camped here," she said. "White men. They have broken up the soil and muddied the waters. This will not be useable as a camp until the lands and waters have recovered."

"White men?" Virginia asked.

Feather nodded.

"Probably miners," Jean said. "They would use this spot, if they found it."

"This far up?" Feather sounded alarmed.

"There are more miners arriving every day," Jean Baptiste said. "Eventually, they will fill these hills."

"But where will my people go?" Feather exclaimed. "Our life is hard, living so high up the mountain. The game doesn't stay here when the weather turns cold, and neither can my people."

Virginia and Jean didn't answer.

"They stay in the summer camp, higher up the mountain," Feather said, finally. "It is another half day's journey. We cannot get there before dark."

"Shall we camp here?" Virginia asked.

"The water is fouled," Feather said. "But there is a smaller meadow a little higher."

They crossed the broken ground and climbed the steep hill on the other side. After struggling through the thick undergrowth, they found the smaller level spot undisturbed. A full hour before sunset, they set up camp, too tired to go on. Jean hovered near Feather, helping her whenever possible, but the Indian girl was too worried to notice.

Just before the sun dropped below the horizon, a series of gunshots rang out. The trio scrambled to their feet, grabbing their weapons, even though it was clear that the shots had come from a distance. It was difficult to tell with all the echoes in the ridges of the mountain, but it seemed to Virginia that the shots were coming from farther up.

Feather's face was white, as if all her fears were coming true. Jean reached out a hand to comfort her, but she shook it off. "We have to go," she said, leaning down and gathering her things.

"It's too dangerous," Virginia said. "The slopes are too steep, too rocky. We can't see where we're going."

"I know the way," Feather insisted.

"But *we* don't," Jean said. "Feather, my foot is swelling. It's difficult enough to walk in daylight, much less at night."

Virginia was thankful he had backed up her instead of Feather.

Feather said, "Then we shall leave you here. We do not need you."

He reached over and took her hand. "Please, Feather. I promise we will leave first thing in the morning."

Her shoulders slumped, and she sat back down.

The firing died away until there was only an occasional single gunshot. Whatever had happened, Virginia sensed it had been short, intense, and one-sided.

They let the fire go out.

None of them slept that night. They lay shivering and wide awake in the darkness.

Chapter Twelve

Frank mounted up and followed Patrick and their father away from the mining camp with growing apprehension. He recognized the stiff posture of Thomas Whitford's back as meaning he was angry but holding it in. It would burst out at some unpredictable future moment, raw and unrestrained.

Patrick was leaning forward in his saddle as if he couldn't wait to fight.

The Newton faction was making no effort to hide their feelings. Frank doubted more and more that there would be any discussion with the Miwok. The men had their rifles ready. There was fire in their eyes.

It was clear to Frank that whoever had attacked the miners' camp, they hadn't been Indians. But who else could it be? Other miners, trying to steal the claim? There was no evidence of that, either. If so, where were they? Why kill to claim-jump and then abandon what you had killed for?

He remembered the look of certainty in Hugh's eyes when he blamed his fairytale creature.

Frank had always believed the wilderness held more wonders and dangers than most men could see or would acknowledge. He'd spent a happy childhood in the company of the natives and saw things through their eyes, realizing not everything could be proven or shown to exist by evidence. Some things simply *were*. The world was a mysterious and magical place.

Unlike his brothers, he never lost this sense of wonder, despite being the only one of them to be educated. His brothers turned their backs on these childhood ideas and called them superstitions, treating the Indians as primitive, barely human.

The search party hadn't gone far before Frank realized that their number had shrunk. He counted twice to be sure, then spurred his horse to catch up with Patrick. "We've got a problem," he said. "I count twenty-two in our party. We're missing four men, besides Hugh."

They stopped the cavalcade. "Who's missing?" Henry Newton shouted, as if he was ready to shoot them for deserters.

"I think it's the Jordan brothers," McCarthy said. His ranch was the closest to the Jordan ranch.

"It's gotta be them," called young Peter Samuels, the schoolteacher at Old Springs crossroads, the one member of the party who was not a rancher. He was dressed in his schoolteacher's clothes and seemed out of place, but was as handy in the saddle as any of them. "The boys always talked about trying gold mining. I'll bet they stayed behind. They probably think they can just grab the claims."

Frank shook his head in amazement, the carnage at the mining camp still fresh in his mind. "I'll fetch them," he said.

Patrick nodded. "We need all the men we can get, but if they won't come with you, to hell with them. They're on their own."

Frank wheeled his mount, passing by the other riders, who looked at him curiously but didn't question him. He arrived back at the miners' enclave just in time to glimpse Billy and Jonathan Jordan pull a body out of the river. Unlike the scattered remains of the other miners, this body was whole, as though the man had drowned. The brothers were rifling through the dead man's pockets, looking excited. The other two brothers joined them, and whoops of excitement drifted up the narrow canyon.

When they saw Frank approaching, they turned their backs to hide the body from his view, then plastered fake smiles on their faces as they greeted him.

Frank sighed to himself. This wouldn't be easy. For all their simple, fun-loving ways, the Jordans were clannish and insular, and barely acknowledged the outside world except for their cousins, the McCarthys.

"What are you fellows up to?" Frank asked in a friendly tone.

Jake, the youngest brother, scowled.

"We were heading out when we saw a body in the river," Jonathan said. "Thought we ought to give him a proper burial. Go on without us, Frank. We'll catch up later."

Jake had something in his hands, and the sunlight caught it at just the right angle and it flashed, almost blinding Frank. By the time his eyes recovered, Jake had hidden whatever it was, and his three older brothers were glaring at him.

"Look, fellows, I don't care if you found gold," Frank said. "I won't tell anyone. You can come back later, but it isn't safe here."

Jonathan seemed to believe him, because he changed tactics. "Come here, Frank. You need to see this."

Frank stared down from his horse, trying to gauge whether he was being lured into a trap. But the Jordan brothers, for all their clannishness, had always been forthright in their dealings with others. He sensed no deceit.

He dismounted and approached Jonathan, who picked something up off the ground beside the body of the drowned miner. He turned around and held out a fist-sized rock that looked to be almost all gold. "This is the purest concentration I've ever seen," he said. "Whoever these miners were, they hit the big one. Someone killed them for it."

"Congratulations on the find," Frank said. "But you have to realize there were at least a dozen miners here, and they were wiped out to a man. What chance would you four boys have? Come back with us, stake the claim, borrow the money to do it right. I'll vouch for you. Hell, I'll talk my father and brothers into backing you."

"And take how much for yourself?" Jake demanded.

"Fine," Frank said. "I'll vouch for what you found and you can make a deal with someone else."

"We don't need no one else," Jake blustered. "We can do it ourselves."

"Someone killed these miners," Frank reminded them.

Billy spoke up. "They weren't on guard. Hell, they only had three rifles in the whole camp."

"That we know of," Frank pointed out. "How many do you carry?"

Billy waved off the objection. "We're armed and alert. We'll be ready for them."

Frank looked at the huge boulders half-buried in the flat ground.

Who can be ready for something like this? he wondered. But he saw the gold fever in the four brothers' eyes and doubted they could be dissuaded. "Fair enough," he said. "But what's the hurry? Why not come back to town with the rest of us and make a claim? If you don't want me to, I won't tell anyone what you found. On my word of honor."

The fourth Jordan brother spoke up. Frank couldn't remember his name because the man rarely spoke. He was smaller than the others, but despite his silence, there was a sharpness to his gaze that made Frank think he was the real leader of the clan.

"We figure that whoever jumped this claim is already in town doing the paperwork. So we're going to stick around and get as much gold as we can get until they show up." He smiled grimly. "And when they show up, we'll show them that a piece a paper ain't worth nothin' when the stake is already being worked."

"That won't matter. You've got to own it legally," Frank said.

The scrawny Jordan brother shrugged. "Then we'll take the gold before they get here."

Frank looked down at the treasure. His pulse hadn't even quickened when he saw it. The Jordan brothers must have sensed his lack of interest; otherwise, who knew what might have happened? He shook his head at the mystery of his own disinterest and mounted his horse.

"Don't be telling no one," Billy Jordan warned. "If you do, we'll be defending this claim with every weapon we have."

"Be careful," Frank said. He motioned toward the devastated camp. "This may not be the work of men."

He got puzzled looks in response, but left them without speaking further. He turned onto the trail and was about to spur his horse to catch up to the others when he spotted a small tent, out of sight of the rest of the camp, nestled among some young trees. Unlike all the other tents, it was undisturbed. He rode over to it, leaned down, and lifted the flap.

There were four barrels of gunpowder stashed inside. Next to them was a box of the new friction-type matches. Frank had used them in the East, and it made sense that the miners would have a supply of them.

Frank knew that some of the miners were starting to use explosives to unearth gold. It was extraordinarily dangerous, and thus they had prudently stored the gunpowder away from the camp. Frank frowned. He looked back to make sure the Jordan brothers couldn't see him, then got down and started breaking the smaller branches off the surrounding trees and leaning them against the canvas of the small tent.

Satisfied that the Jordan brothers wouldn't find the gunpowder and blow themselves up, he hurried to catch up with the rest of the party. He wasn't sure why he'd done that, but he had a feeling that the gunpowder might come in handy later.

Why am I immune to gold fever? he wondered. Frank knew his own brothers would act no different than the Jordan boys if they had a chance at a rich claim. Something about living among the wealthy students back East had changed his attitude toward wealth.

Frank didn't care about money. He wanted only enough to get by. When the time came, he'd tell Father to give his shares of the ranch to Patrick and James, so he would be free. Going back East had given him a taste for travel. Frank didn't want to be a rancher, stuck in one place. He wanted to roam.

***

The Jordan boys got nervous when darkness fell. They decided to camp further downstream from the destroyed encampment and not to light a fire.

"You take the first watch, Jake," Jonathan commanded. "Wake me at midnight; I'll take the next." They crawled into their blankets fully clothed and close together. The gold was in the middle of the group, as if it was most important thing of all.

It was nearly morning when Jonathan awoke. Billy and David still slept beside him; Jake was nowhere to be seen. Scratching his head, he built a cook fire, waiting for his youngest brother to return.

The sun was well overhead before the three brothers finally admitted that Jake had disappeared.

***

The search party had left churned-up tracks where they'd ascended the mountains, making it easy for Frank to track them. Instead of returning the same way, the group kept going on a northern route, and Frank knew, with dread, that they were approaching the Miwok summer camp.

They were taking the longer, easier route, though, giving Frank a surge of relief. He could still get to the Indian camp first, if he hurried. He split off from their trail a few hundred yards downslope and headed off cross-country. There was a steep but negotiable path through the forest and cliffs, and he reached the Indian camp quickly.

He stopped a few hundred feet away and gazed at the village. The Miwok cabins were mixed with lean-tos and tents, giving them a semi-permanent encampment where some of the women and children lived all season long.

At any one time, most of the adult men were off in hunting parties. At the moment, the village looked peaceful, with women and children going about their activities. No guards were posted. If the Miwok were on the warpath, they showed no signs of it.

Frank rode into the camp, expecting to be challenged, but he was among the Indians before they noticed him. They continued to go about their daily tasks in blissful unconcern. They didn't seem alarmed by his sudden appearance, but instead seemed pleased to see him, waving and smiling. He slid off his horse. A small boy ran up, took the reins, and led the horse toward the creek. By then, Frank was certain that the Indians were innocent of the havoc at the mining camp.

Chief Honon emerged from a nearby tent, followed by Hugh. The chief was a tall man, gaunt and weathered, but when he smiled, he looked like a man half his age. He held out his arms. "Franklin!" he cried. "It has been too long since you have come to visit."

Despite the urgency, Frank couldn't help but smile and return the embrace. Over the chief's shoulder, he frowned at Hugh, raising his eyebrows as if to ask, *Why haven't you warned him?*

Hugh wasn't smiling, nor did he look relaxed. "I told the chief about the mining camp, but he said he already knew."

Honon overheard this. "Yes. They disturbed the Ts'emekwes," he said. "Now the white man will learn to stay away from this land."

"The Ts'emekwes?" Frank asked. "Who are they?"

"Creatures of the mountains," Hugh said. "Our tribe has lived near a family of them for many generations. The children call them the Skoocooms. Your people must stay away."

"Does he understand that my people think the Miwok killed the miners?" Frank asked, exasperated. "That they won't believe supernatural creatures did it?"

"The Ts'emekwes are real, I assure you," Hugh said. "But, yes, I've told him. He says that your father is his friend. That Thomas Whitford would never believe that of the Miwok."

Frank turned to the old chief, who was still smiling at him. "My father is not himself," he said urgently. "Oliver and James are missing. I implore you, send your women and children into hiding, just to be safe. If you must stay, let it only be the men."

Chief Honon shook his head. "Thomas will not hurt us," he said.

"You don't understand!" Frank practically shouted. "You are in danger. Your people are in danger!"

The chief reached out with a steady hand and put it on Frank's shoulder. He looked into Frank's eyes. "What would you have me do, Franklin? We are old men and women. We cannot run."

"You can hide!" Frank said.

"We will not hide. It is too late."

Frank saw that it was useless. The Indians had seen the madness that gold instilled in the white man, but they still found it hard to believe that men would kill for shiny rocks.

The chief looked concerned at Frank's distress. He reached out with his spotted and wrinkled hand. "We will turn to stone," he said.

"I don't understand," Frank said.

Honon just smiled sadly and nodded.

"I'm going to try to intercept them," Frank said to Hugh, "to try to talk some sense into my father. But in the meantime, you must do your best to get these people to safety."

Hugh nodded curtly. "I'll try."

Frank strode off toward the creek to get his horse, but it was nowhere to be seen. He looked down to the far end of the meadow and saw that his horse was in the stockade, its saddle and bridle removed.

Frank calculated the time it would take to get his horse ready, turned on his heel, and jogged up the main path to meet his father and the others. If he could get to them in time, tell them that the Indians were peaceful, unarmed, and most likely innocent, maybe he could defuse the situation.

He glanced back to see Hugh leading a small group of women and children away from the camp. Whatever ruse the man was using was working, though the group seemed in no hurry to leave.

Turning back to the trail, Frank shook his head. Too few were leaving too slowly. He suspected the search party had turned into a vigilante mob. He feared their arrival.

***

Patrick urged his father to hurry, before the men's anger dissipated.

Henry Newton was right. Why couldn't his brothers and father see that? Clearly, the Indians must vacate these mountains and valleys once and for all. The Whitford ranch was bordered on all but one side by other ranches; they couldn't expand anymore in that direction without buying more land. No, the only way they could grow was to go upward, into the mountain pastures. The Miwok were in their way. They did not even utilize the land properly, neither growing crops nor raising livestock.

Now, with gold found on their land, the Miwok would have to change or leave...or die.

Can't they see it's inevitable? he wondered. The Indians were in the way, not just in the Sacramento Valley, but throughout California and the greater West. The native population would have to join the white man's culture: go to school, dress properly, and learn Christian values. Or they would need to be removed, taken someplace out of the way.

Even his father couldn't seem to see the necessity of this. He still saw things as they were when he'd first arrived, one of the early settlers, when there had been plenty of space for both Indians and ranchers. Old man Newton saw things the way they were now, unfettered by sentiment or old loyalties.

Patrick looked over his shoulder. Frank hadn't returned, which was probably a good thing. His stepbrother had come back from the East Coast changed. He was soft, unwilling to do the hard things that needed to be done—which surprised Patrick. Of all people, his brother should understand the necessity of moving the Indians out.

Instead, Frank seemed to be clinging to his childhood fascination with Miwok culture, naively believing that the two peoples could live side by side without clashing. Patrick had been just as glad when his brother had decided to return to the mining camp to look for the Jordan boys. Frank would have tried to calm the situation with the Miwok, whereas Patrick was hoping to get the men riled up enough to do something.

Though he wouldn't have admitted it to himself, Patrick also wanted to hurry because his own rage was eroding into a growing sense of doubt. His mind's eye went back the miners' camp, with the boulders embedded into the earth as if they had been dropped from above.

Which was impossible. No doubt they'd been rolled downward, hit some impediment, and been thrown upward. But even that would have been difficult to accomplish, given the size of the rocks. Could the Indians have done that?

He remembered the story of the Skoocoom from the time the Miwok village had been a second home to him and Chief Honon a second father. Once, when he'd spent several days with the Indian children, they'd glimpsed a huge form moving through the trees. He hadn't gotten a good look at it and had always assumed that it was a grizzly bear. But now a vivid memory came to him of huge eyes staring at him curiously, with intelligence.

It was a strange irony that Patrick seemed to be the only one to remember the story of the towering, apelike beast, and even more ironic that there was a piece of him that wanted to believe it. In his daydreaming, he drifted further back into the pack, so when shouting broke out up ahead, he was forced to push his way past the others to see what the commotion was about.

Henry Newton stood on the trail, holding a bloody pistol in his hand. Patrick dismounted, practically throwing the reins into the hands of the nearest man. "That's Oliver's," he said as he approached.

Newton nodded and looked up with an anguished expression. "I gave it to him on his sixteenth birthday."

Patrick looked around for his father and saw him slumped in his saddle, head down. Oliver and James had been together, and they had probably met the same fate. He felt his rage returning, and all doubts about the Skoocoom disappeared. He saw something out of the corner of his eye, reached down, and lifted up a torn and bloody Indian blanket. He held it over his head, making sure the men could all see it. He didn't need to say anything. Everyone could see it belonged to an Indian, and that it had been lying within a few feet of Oliver's bloody gun.

"The savages have him!" Dave Martin shouted, and the others immediately added to the mounting outrage.

Newton stood as if frozen in the middle of the trail. His shoulders were rounded, his head down. He looked a broken man…then he raised his head and howled a wordless scream of anger. The men stood still, watching him. Newton raised his arms, encompassing them.

"I was a fool," he rumbled. "I let others advise patience. I waited too long." His voice rose into a scream. "But no longer! The savages must be removed. Who's with me?"

The men responded, shouting for blood, even those who had expressed doubt before.

One of them galloped down the trail, and the others followed, shouting war whoops.

To his amazement, Patrick saw that it was his own father leading the charge. Preacher MacLeod was right behind him, brandishing his rifle with a whoop, and Patrick spurred his horse to stay with them. They were still riding at a gallop when they rounded a bend in the trail and thundered into the Indian village. Frank was there, standing on the trail in front of him, waving his arms, but Patrick didn't slow, and his brother leaped out of the way lest he be trampled.

Chief Honon stood at the edge of the village, raising his palms in peace, as if he could somehow stop the onslaught.

Someone raised a pistol and shot the old Indian in the head.

After that, Patrick couldn't have controlled the situation if he had wanted to. It was all gunshots, screams, blood, and dust. After a couple of minutes, someone within the village finally returned fire. Everywhere Patrick looked, he saw only women and children and old men. They ran away, cowered, or begged for mercy. None fought back.

A young girl was trampled by a horse, her little body kicked into the air, her limbs flopping, crushed and lifeless. The rage started to drain from his body.

It must be done! Patrick screamed inside. *They need to leave this land!*

A mother came shrieking out of a burning cabin, carrying an infant swaddled in a blanket. She was shot and fell forward into the dust, and the child went tumbling and rolling. The infant sat up, howling, and the chaos continued around it.

Patrick reloaded twice, firing into the swirling madness that surrounded him, uncertain if he was hitting anything or not. By then, all the structures were on fire, and there was thick smoke obscuring everything. With an empty feeling, Patrick lowered his gun and stared around him. The shooting was trailing off, but only because there were no more moving targets. Bodies littered the ground, all of them Miwok, as far as Patrick could see; and most of them, to his horror, were women and children.

Then Frank was standing in front of him, looking outraged. Frank pushed him violently. Patrick fell and did not rise. He closed his eyes, not wanting to see that horrified look on Frank's face again.

From the ground, he could see Chief Honon's body, crumpled under the bodies of his wives and children.

Patrick groaned. *What have I done?*

Chapter Thirteen

I'm going to die here, never to be found. The thought paralyzes me and deadens my limbs. I am not allowed to move around, and I am careful not to make too much noise. Tucker's journal has kept me sane, my only companion, even if it is only the writings of a dead man.

The journal describes what I fear will be my end as well. Nevertheless, I have read all Tucker's entries and am resolved to add my own thoughts to it. There is little doubt I face the same fate, and I too will leave a record of my last days. If anyone ever finds this, add your lament to this tale of woe or pass it along to the next unfortunate victim.

The small albino "child" that Tucker described is now almost as big as Grendel, but he doesn't venture out of the cave. He seems to want to leave, but if he tries, Grendel snarls at him, making guttural noises that almost sound like language. Language or not, his intentions are clear. Hrothgar is as much a captive as I am. Perhaps that gives me empathy for him, as strange as he appears to me—and perhaps, in turn, it gives him empathy for me.

I am certain Hrothgar's white fur has made Grendel protective of him, for he cannot blend into the wilderness the way Grendel can.

I will not have a chance to escape again. Hrothgar wouldn't let me, I'm sure. Hrothgar wants to play, but I cannot indulge him much. I do not have the energy. He kicked what I thought was ball in my direction, and when it wobbled to stop at my feet, I saw it was a human skull. Needless to say, I did not return the "ball."

He also tries to speak, and here I do try to indulge him. He can say a few words. They come out garbled, but some I can understand. He is very expressive, in his own way. Most often he is frustrated by my lack of mobility, but when I motion to go outside, he becomes still, staring at me with his wide, red-tinged albino eyes.

There is no doubt of his intelligence. These creatures are certainly more intelligent than other animals, perhaps even as smart as a young child. Great apes in the zoos of the East cannot form words, though they also have a native canniness that is beyond what any human can learn. If these creatures were in greater numbers, they might be dangerous. But if, as I suspect, they have but one offspring at a time, they are vulnerable to the ever-expanding domain of men.

They are worth saving, though they may cause my own death. I should hate them, but I do not. They are natural creatures of this world, and we are the invaders.

It has happened before, or so *Beowulf* tells us. Long ago, when mankind settled Europe, similar creatures fought them for the territory. Now they are gone from those lands, extinguished. But in the wild and dangerous places of the world, they still exist.

Tucker's naming of these beasts was apt.

They are creatures of myth and legend.

***

Frank knew from the moment he saw the riders galloping toward him that he wasn't going to be able to stop them, knew it from the look of vengeance on his brother's face and the cold, blank expression on his father's. He jumped away at the last second, barely avoiding being trampled.

The first gunshot rang out as he rolled into the brush beside the trail. He got to his feet and ran back to the village. He roared in disbelief, waving his arms futilely, but there was no stopping the carnage once it started.

Chief Honon fell, surprise etched into the lines on his face, and the women running to his side were cut down. It was hard enough to believe that his friends and neighbors were murdering unarmed men and women, but when they started killing the children, Frank almost dropped to the ground and put his arms over his head in denial. Instead, he grabbed a nearby rider by the leg as the man prepared to shoot a fleeing girl. The man kicked out at him and rode off.

Frank's mind rejected what he was seeing. He was among them, yet it was as if it was happening far away, to someone else. It was as if he was watching everything from a safe distance, observing it. He couldn't stop the horror.

And then one of the riders almost ran him down, and suddenly Frank was in the middle of it again, hearing the screams, the gunshots, the cries and pleas for help.

He saw old man Partridge, their oldest neighbor, get pulled from his horse by three young Indian boys and get pummeled by rocks and sticks. Frank ran toward them, realizing halfway there that he didn't know what to do. Partridge, bleeding from the scalp, pulled a knife. Who was Frank supposed to help? If he attacked the boys, he would be joining in the mayhem, but he couldn't let Partridge be killed.

I just want it to stop, he thought. *I want this all never to have happened. This is a mistake.*

He had known many of these men his whole life; he knew them to be peaceful neighbors. He raised barns with them, attended their weddings, and stood beside them at funerals. These weren't violent men; yet here they were killing women and children.

Partridge was still standing, slashing out with his knife, while the three boys fled. A rider coming to Partridge's aid knocked one of the children off his feet. As soon as the Miwok boy hit the ground, another rancher emerged from the smoke and dust and fired into his chest. The other two youths disappeared into the surrounding wilderness.

Frank sensed something looming behind him, and he turned to see his father pulling his horse up nearby. There was madness in his eyes, and he was trying to reload his pistol. Frank grabbed the reins with one hand and snagged his father's foot with the other, desperate to get his attention.

"You've got to stop this!" he shouted. "This is a massacre!"

It was as if Thomas was hearing a distant voice. He looked down at Frank, confused. Then he looked around. An expression of dawning horror came over his face, and he spurred his horse toward Patrick, who was leading a group of men setting fire to the cabins and tents. Frank ran after him, and saw his father being pulled off his horse by an Indian brave who jumped out of one of the burning cabins.

Frank ran full tilt into the warrior, and the knife that had been plunging toward his father's throat went flying into the air. Then Frank and the Indian faced off. Frank waved his arms frantically, showing his palms, begging his opponent to see that he meant no harm, but the warrior gave no quarter. He ran toward Frank, fingers outstretched for his throat. A rifle butt came down on top of the Indian's head from behind, and he fell. Thomas Whitford was standing there, his rifle in his hands. He walked over to the moaning Indian, pointing the rifle at the fallen man as if to fire.

"Don't, Father!' Frank cried. "He's down."

The old man stepped back as the Indian got to his feet. The warrior looked ready to charge again, but Thomas shook his head warningly and tipped his gun toward the nearby edge of the forest.

"Get out of here, Roman," he said.

The Miwok looked around. None of his people were still standing. He shouted defiance at the top of his voice, and Frank knew he'd never forget the look of pain and hate in the Indian's face. Then he sprinted for the trees.

Quiet fell in the village, sudden and complete but for an occasional shout or cry of pain. Patrick stood nearby, a stunned look on his face. Frank strode toward him and confronted his brother face to face.

"You damn fool!" he shouted. "You've killed innocents!" He pushed Patrick as hard as he could, and his brother fell without even trying to regain his balance. Patrick lay there with his arms over his head.

The massacre was over.

Into this silence came excited shouts. Dave Martin and his two followers, Bud Carpenter and George Banks, were chasing a young Miwok boy who had miraculously risen from a pile of bodies. Carpenter shot the boy in the back. Banks hurriedly dismounted and ran toward the still-moving body. Grabbing the boy by the hair, he pulled out his bowie knife.

Frank ran toward the confrontation. He drew his pistol and pointed it at Banks's head. "Don't," he growled.

The knife had already begun to cut into the boy's scalp, and there was blood flowing, showing that the boy was still alive. Banks grew still, but didn't let the boy go. Frank heard the sound of a gun being cocked behind him. He looked over his shoulder. Martin had both of his guns pointed at Frank's back.

"What business is it of yours if we take a prize?" Martin growled. Carpenter was busily reloading his own pistol.

"It's over," Frank said. "He's just a child."

"I don't know," Martin said. "Looks like he might get bigger."

"I swear I'll blow your head off," Frank warned when Banks looked as if he was ready to start cutting again.

"And I'll blow off yours," Martin said behind him.

"Stand down, boys," came Henry Newton's firm voice. "We don't need to take no prizes. We won."

Martin looked ready to argue, but Henry's glare changed his mind. Banks got up, sheathing his knife, and brushed past Frank with a baleful look.

Martin and his friends rode back to the center of the village, shouting boisterously. Frank noticed that about half the search party was joining in the celebration, but the other half had turned away.

***

They found Hugh underneath several Indian women. He'd suffered a blow to the head early in the fight, and though it was only a minor wound, he had been unconscious through most of it.

Hugh rose from the dead like an avenging wraith. The men gathering bodies backed away from his rage. Hugh marched to where Chief Honon lay, stripping off his white man's clothes until he was clad only in his trousers. He took the chief's bloody shirt and donned it. Then he turned his back on those with whom he had once longed to belong and stalked into the woods.

The search party piled the dead in the center of the clearing. There had been few men in the village, and they had been elderly, barely able to stand, much less defend themselves. The ranchers found most of them in the burned cabins: six dead old men altogether. They also found three rifles, only one of which had been fired.

There were twelve dead women and sixteen children, none old enough to be considered of age. The little bodies, laid in a row, were a bloody reproach of the massacre.

They found only one dead Indian brave, his knife in Peter Samuels's chest. The schoolteacher was the only fatality among the white men. This single warrior had also managed to wound Harold Simmons and Alan Percy. They would survive, but Simmons would be crippled for life.

The dead warrior had been shot multiple times.

Three Indian women and four children remained alive and inside the boundaries of the village, too wounded to make their escape. The ranchers did their best to save them, but in the night, the two Indians who were the least injured crawled away and left those who were beyond saving.

The Indian boy Frank had saved from scalping didn't last the night.

By the end of the next day, all five remaining Indian captives were also dead.

The white men had multiple cuts and bruises, most self-inflicted during their killing frenzy. It had been a slaughter, not a battle, and now that it was over, most of the men of the search party were beginning to realize it. Most of them were quiet and subdued, even those who had been celebrating earlier. Patrick sat staring off into space. Thomas Whitford sat at the edge of the clearing with a blank look on his face.

Only the Newton contingent seemed unrepentant. They weren't shouting and hollering anymore, but they were strutting around the village like men who had won a great victory.

**

"The Miwok braves will be returning," Frank said. "They will want revenge."

The men were gathered in a circle, but there was a gap between the two groups, as a gulf was opening between those who were ashamed of what had just happened and those who were feeling righteous glory. Frank was encouraged that the more subdued group was the largest.

His reminder that most of the warriors still lived and were out there in the woods sent the men into an even grimmer silence.

"Let them come!" Martin shouted after a time. A few of the Newton ranch hands shouted approval, but it quickly died down. The others stayed silent.

"What do we do with the dead ones?" Preacher MacLeod asked. "Maybe we should bury them, say some prayers or something."

"Savages don't deserve no Christian burial," Newton barked. "Let them rot."

Martin laughed, and the sound of it echoed through the camp. No one joined him.

"Let the Miwok men deal with it," Gerald Persimmons suggested. "They'll know what to do with their own dead, will give them proper ceremonies."

"Who cares?" Jim Perkins broke in. "I'm hurt. I need help."

"We need to get out of here," Carl Dutton agreed. "We should be getting back home. Warn others who might be headed this way."

Yes, Frank seethed inwardly. *Warn the others that the Indians will want vengeance. Warn them that the red man is dangerous and can't be trusted. Lie, until your lies become truth.*

He knew this incident would be recounted as a "battle," not a massacre. In the telling, the fight would have been desperate, the ranchers prevailing only because of their valiancy and bravery. In other parts of California, it would be repeated that the red man was dangerous and must be eliminated to make civilization safe. Wherever the tribes were in the way—for water, land, or gold—similar massacres would take place and similar lies be told.

And the white race would be triumphant and self-righteous, but the men who knew the truth would wake in the middle of the night, haunted by nightmares of the innocents they had slaughtered.

"I say we keep looking for them," Carpenter said. "Give them the same handling we gave the others."

"Let them come," Banks agreed.

Everyone turned to Newton, sensing that he had the final say.

"Let's go home, boys," he said, sounding reluctant.

It was midafternoon by the time the ranchers were packed up and organized. It was too late to move camp, but no one wanted to stay at the scene of the slaughter any longer than they had to.

They were mounting their horses when three travelers walked into the village.

***

Frank was mounting his horse, facing away from the newcomers, when they arrived. He saw men grabbing their rifles out of their saddle holsters, unmistakably alarmed. He whirled, expecting to see the braves coming at them, seeking vengeance. Instead, three forlorn figures emerged from the trees and then stopped as if stunned. One of the women was dressed as an Indian, and the man had a dark complexion and looked as if he might be Miwok.

Frank reined his horse around and spurred it, reaching the trio before anyone else. He dismounted before the horse had stopped and staggered the last few steps toward them, barely maintaining his balance. The white woman had a rifle with a broken stock leveled at him before he'd even reached the ground. He doubted it would even fire, but there was a determined look in her eye.

He ignored her and turned to face the onrush of men. "Hold up!" he shouted. "They aren't Miwok!" He didn't know if that was true, but it was the only thing he could think to say.

The men of the search party stopped cold, and for a moment, no one moved a muscle. Martin, Carter, and a few others had rifles aimed at the newcomers, but Henry Newton motioned them down.

The two women and the man were surrounded, but they didn't look cowed. Frank gave a start as he recognized the white girl. It was the girl from the Donner Party, Virginia Reed.

He stepped forward. "You might want to stay back," he warned them. "I...You might not want to see this. There has been a... a battle here." Frank was suddenly conscious that there was a long row of bodies in the clearing, but only one body draped over the side of a horse.

Some battle.

He swallowed, hating to be linked with the carnage. The Indian girl ignored him. She strode to the row of bodies, searching their faces until she found Chief Honon. She dropped to her knees, hanging her head, her hands open at her sides as if she had gone boneless. The young man, who had Indian features but was dressed as a white man, stood behind her, looking as though he wanted to help her but didn't know how.

"What have you done?" Virginia hissed. "What happened here?"

To his surprise, Frank felt defensive. He'd no more wanted what had happened here to happen than they did, but he felt he had to try to explain. "Two of our men were missing," he said. "One was my brother. We found one of their pistols by the side of the trail. There was blood on it...and an Indian blanket..."

"And you thought it was the *Miwok?*" Virginia asked. "Did you have any proof before you started killing them?"

He spread his arms helplessly, as if to say, *Who else could it be?*

"These *women,* and *children?*" the girl shouted. "*They* harmed your brother?"

Put to the question, Frank found he couldn't justify his actions or those of his companions. "It was a mistake," he muttered.

"Like hell it was," Newton broke in, his voice full of righteous certainty. "Why are you jabbering?" He stared down at the Indian girl as if he wanted to shoot her, too. He dismounted and loomed over her. "These people killed my son. If it was in my power..."

Feather had been quiet, praying beside Chief Honon. Now she rose up and whirled on the man. She was half his size, and yet Newton backed up in the face of her fury. "You cowards!" she screamed, and the ranchers flinched and turned away.

Martin drew his pistol, but even Carpenter and Banks, who were his friends, had enough sense to stop him. A lone Indian girl faced down the entire search party, and it was the men who looked cowed.

Newton snorted and mounted his horse. "Kill them or let them go, I don't care."

"What are we waiting for?" Perkins shouted. "We need to go. We need to get out of here before it gets dark."

Frank glanced up and noticed that the sun was hovering just above the treetops. He turned helplessly to the three newcomers. The returning braves would not stop to ask questions if they found them. "Come with us," he said to Virginia Reed. "We'll keep you safe."

"With *you?*" she asked, as if it was the strangest idea she had ever heard.

"It's not safe here," Frank insisted.

Thomas Whitford came up beside Frank while they were talking. "We have to go, son. She'll either come with us or she won't. But we must leave."

Frank hesitated, ready to tell his father and the others to go on without him. Virginia Reed appeared to have completely dismissed him. She went over to join the Indian girl and boy.

With a sigh, Frank mounted his horse. The others were already heading down the trail.

He'd just set spurs to his horse when he heard Virginia's voice behind him.

"Wait."

***

The young rancher turned around and looked at Virginia with such hope that she was surprised.

"Go on, Father," the young man said to the older one. "I'll catch up."

The father frowned, "You sure, Frank? I've lost one son, and I don't..."

Virginia gave the man a level stare. "We're not murderers." Neither man spoke, though the old man looked shaken. He finally nodded and left.

The young man looked anything but certain as his father rode away.

I've seen this boy before, Virginia thought, and then remembered the two ranchers she'd met in the streets of Sutter's Fort. The ones who had stared at her as if she was vermin.

The young man had a different sort of look on his face now: sadness, and compassion...and something else. She was drawn to him, though she didn't know why. She looked back at the dead bodies of the Indians and thought perhaps she should hate him.

Yet she had to admit to herself that he was right. The Miwok warriors wouldn't wait for an excuse or an explanation. They wouldn't check to be sure that she was innocent in the massacre. While Feather might be safe staying in these mountains, she and Jean most definitely were not.

"I really must insist you come along," he said. "The Indians will want revenge."

"I won't leave without my friends, Feather and Jean Baptiste," she said finally. "But if we go with you, they have to be safe."

"I give you my word," he said. "If you come with me, I will protect you."

"And them."

"And them."

"They may wish to stay, or at least not come with you," Virginia warned. "Nor would I blame them."

"Go talk to them," Frank urged. "And Miss...try your best to convince them."

"Wait here," she said. "I won't be long."

***

Feather knelt beside her people. She was leaning back on her heels, and her were eyes closed as if she was praying. A keening sound was emerging from her lips, and Virginia realized she was singing for the dead. Jean Baptiste stood beside her, looking helpless.

Virginia knelt beside her friend and put a hand on her arm. She waited until her friend met her gaze before speaking. "We have to leave here, Feather," she said gently. "It isn't safe."

The Indian girl didn't seem to hear her at first.

"If you must stay," Virginia continued, "I leave you to your grief. But I am taking Jean Baptiste with me, Feather."

This seemed to finally get through. Virginia flinched at the anger in Feather's eyes.

"I will go with thee," she said. "Not because I want to, but because my father asked me to help the Canowiki. I will do so until the task is done. After that...I vow to never speak English again and never more associate with white people."

She stood. "The Skoocoom will not stop at killing the white man now. He will kill all of us if he is not stopped. And if not for my father's request, *I would let the Skoocoom kill one and all.*"

She rose and walked away, down the mountain trail, followed by Jean Baptiste. The young rancher watched them go, not moving.

He looked down at Virginia with a concerned look she despised.

"Come on, I'll give you a ride." He reached down, offering to swing her up behind him. "My name is Frank, by the way."

Virginia stared at him in disgust. She didn't take his hand.

She started off after her friends, her rifle against her shoulder.

Chapter Fourteen

Grendel

He looked down on the Loud Ones, the ones who invaded his home, who mutilated the earth and killed the creatures that live on it.

Now they had killed the Quiet Ones, the familiar ones who brought him gifts and whom he knew and tolerated as long as they stayed away from his hunting grounds. He had not stopped the slaughter, for he was angry at all of their kind. But later, he felt some small regret.

The banging sticks hurt him, and the wounds they made took time to heal. He knew if the banging hit him in the wrong spot, he could die. But he had no choice. He had to drive them away from his home. He had to scare them, kill them, or make them go away. He had the Little One to take care of now. The banging sticks would hurt the Little One. Mother had gone away and come back, and then the Little One had come, and he'd smelled like Mother.

Grendel would no longer tolerate the Loud Ones or anyone else who threatened his kind. He would kill them all, or drive them away. His family would live in peace as they had always lived, in the glowing cave.

The Loud Ones were on guard. He understood that. He would let the Loud Ones and the Quiet Ones kill each other. Perhaps he would not have to attack them again. Perhaps they had learned.

He watched as they moved down the mountain. Good. They were leaving...all but the three who still dwelt by the mountain stream, digging into the earth like the rodent creatures he ate. It was his stream. His place.

Tonight, he decided, they would die.

But then he saw the Quiet Ones, the ones who lived beside him, approaching their camp, and he crouched to watch.

***

The more time David Jordan spent with his brothers at the mining camp, the more certain he was that it hadn't been an Indian attack that had caused the damage. The meager Jordan ranch ran along the unofficial borders of the local tribe's land, and they'd always gotten along with the Miwok. He was just as glad when the revenge-minded search party went on without them. He had no interest in killing Indians.

He hoped the search party calmed down before they arrived at the Indian village. His neighbors were good people; they wouldn't cause a ruckus if they didn't have to. Most likely, they had found James and Oliver and were heading on home.

No, whatever had caused the chaos here had been some kind of natural event. A freakish event, to be sure, but something completely natural. Had to be. So David wasn't worried about Indians. He was concerned about his youngest brother, though, who had gone missing in the night.

The three remaining Jordan brothers argued all day about what they should do about it.

"We need to find him," Jonathan said. "I saw you-all check the gold. You thought he took it."

The gold was untouched, they'd all verified that, including, despite his self-righteousness, Jonathan.

"He probably just went home," David said. He rarely spoke, so when he did, the others paid attention. "He was missing his girl."

"That's probably it," Jonathan agreed. "But shouldn't we make sure?"

"How about if one of us goes searching," Billy said, "and while he's in town, he stakes a claim to this portion of the river? None of these fellows are going to dispute it." He motioned to the hastily dug graves.

"That's what we should do," David agreed. Jonathan, who no more wanted to leave the gold camp than the others, made a show of reluctantly agreeing.

But despite the agreement, none of them made ready to leave. Eventually, in a day or two, one of them would go to town, check up on the family. They would flip a coin or something. But none of them were really concerned about their youngest brother's disappearance. Jake had skipped out on the family before, to visit Patsy Newton, though David couldn't see the attraction.

Soon Jonathan would probably wander off too, since he was the one who'd gotten all self-righteous about it. Meanwhile, they must find the source of the gold.

After the second day, however, they were ready to give up.

"I don't believe anyone in this camp ever found much gold," Billy concluded, saying what they were all thinking.

"Except this fellow," Jonathan said. They'd buried the man who'd had the gold in his pockets, and Jonathan was standing near the grave. He kicked some dust from the top of the mound. David winced at the disrespect.

Until now, the gold rush had held no appeal for David. He liked things simple. But then it occurred to him that being rich would make things very simple indeed. Since they seemed so close to the mother lode, why not search for it?

He decided it was time to let the others know what he was thinking. He had been thinking about it for a while now, and he'd come to some conclusions. David was the smartest of the brothers, but only he was smart enough to recognize it. He usually kept quiet because his thoughts were wasted on most people.

"He wasn't letting anyone else know about his find, that's my guess," he said.

"So he hid it?" Billy asked. "But where? Wouldn't the others see him digging it up?"

"I don't think these are river stones," David said. "I don't reckon these rocks have ever been anywhere near water. These here are rocks out of a mountainside, unless I miss my guess, or chunks from the boulders. But seeing as there aren't any holes around here, seems to me..." He turned and glanced significantly at the cliff behind him.

The others' jaws dropped, because once it was pointed out, it was so obvious.

So they each took a section of the cliff and started exploring.

It was Billy who found the mother lode, which was unfortunate, because that meant the other brothers would never hear the end of it.

Billy will probably want a bigger share, too, David thought, *conveniently forgetting that it was me who did all the thinking.*

There was evidence that the dead miner had tried to cover up his find, but he'd clearly been rushed and done a terrible job of it. The clay and gravel hid most of the gleaming rocks, but here and there the sun caught the metal and it flashed.

Then again, no one would have thought to look here. David had a sudden insight: the gold in the rivers had washed down from above. The real gold was in the hillside. He closed his eyes and a vision of entire mountains being knocked down came into his mind, and he felt regret. On the other hand...if it wasn't him finding the gold, it would be someone else.

The brothers excitedly cleared away the dirt and rocks, and there, gleaming like a palace in the afternoon sun, was a vein of gold so rich and so pure that it blinded them if they looked at it too long. David had been hearing stories about gold strikes for months now, but he'd never heard of anything like this. He wasn't sure anyone in the history of the world had found anything like this.

The brothers ran their hands along the streak of gold, and pulled more rocks from the cliffside, trying to figure out how far the vein went. That's when they found an opening that led to a small cave. The gold seam merged with the hole and disappeared into it. David poked his head in. He felt a small breeze that bore an odd scent, which meant there was another opening. That complicated things. If someone had found the other side of this gold vein, they might have a claim on it too. He didn't want that to happen.

"I'm going in," David announced. He took off his pack and then his coat. It was a tight fit, but when he shed everything but his clothes, he managed to get in. He stuck his hand out but wasn't able to turn his head to look at his brothers.

"Either of you happen to have a candle on you?" David shouted. His voice was swallowed up by the crevice, and he had the sense that the cavern was huge and opened up somewhere higher up.

"Stay there," Billy shouted. "I'll be right back."

David waited, pinioned in the narrow gap, letting his eyes adjust to the darkness. The cave rose steeply. Luckily, the gold was on the side, not on the bottom of the fracture, and he thought there might be enough footing for him to continue upward.

He felt a candle being put into his hand.

"Careful!" Billy called. "It's lit!"

David carefully maneuvered the candle past his chest, snagged it with his other hand, and lifted it up. The cave exploded with flickering light. The gold caught the tiny flame and accentuated it. The gold seam reached as high and far as the light penetrated. He climbed the steep corridor, using the sides to keep himself steady. The higher he went, the wider the expanse of gold became, until at the top of the narrow crack, it spread out in every direction as far as the light would shine. The crevice opened into a wider cave, and he thought he might be able to squeeze through.

Another day, David thought. *This cave is inhabited.*

He'd noticed the awful smell when he'd first entered the cave but hadn't thought much about it. The stench had gotten worse the farther he'd gone. He thought he saw excrement under his feet, streaming downward. He had a sudden feeling that he was being watched.

Bear, he thought. *And here I am without so much as a knife.*

He backed away. He wasn't up to fighting bears. He'd be a tasty morsel for the beast, something to pluck out of the darkness. The candle flickered, but he wasn't concerned. It wasn't as if he could get lost; all he had to do was follow the crevice downward. Still, he wasted no time.

David heard his brothers shouting, no doubt getting excited about their find.

I wish we had some gunpowder, he mused. They'd be able to blow a big hole in the side of the cliff. The gold might go flying everywhere, but he wasn't worried. Unless he missed his guess, there was enough of the bullion here to replace the entire national reserve. They were going to be the richest men alive—if they could keep it.

David was troubled, however. It was too much gold. He only wanted enough to be independent, to expand the ranch, maybe build a nicer house. His ambitions were modest. He wondered if he could talk his brothers into taking only a little of it at a time, or even keeping it secret altogether.

But even as he thought it, he knew there was no way they were going to be able to keep it secret. Hell, Billy would tell the first person he saw, and then the next person he saw, and then the next, and would think he was swearing them to secrecy.

Once the gold was exposed, David suspected, there was no way they were going to be able to keep it all. He had no illusions. He was smart enough to know that there were smarter people than him, more powerful and ruthless. Some big business or government or something would mostly likely swoop in and take the riches from them.

The dead miner, bless his unlucky soul, had the right idea: keep it secret—though with David's dullard brothers, that was probably going to be impossible. Well, whatever happened, there'd be enough gold in his pockets on the first trip into town to keep him solvent for a good long while. Let the others squabble over the rest.

David got the bottom of the long, narrow corridor, and turned the final corner. Light streamed in from outside. He'd expected one of his brothers to be standing at the cave's entrance, but there was no one in sight.

Then a shadow crossed the light. David frowned. He knew his brother's movements as he knew his own, and that wasn't one of his brothers. He stood in the shadows and debated going back, searching for a different exit. Something was wrong. At least one of his brothers should have been there, waiting. And he should have been able to hear them talking, loudly and boisterously, as usual.

He decided there was more than enough gold to go around. He'd argue his way out of the problem, whatever it was. He always had. Share the wealth. He didn't want it all anyway, only enough to get by.

David emerged, blinking, into the light. The afternoon sun was so bright that he couldn't see anything at first. He sensed someone moving quickly toward him, and something about the movement seemed threatening, so he put out his hands.

"Whoa, there, my friend," he said. "Whatever the problem is, we can talk about it."

He stared at the ground, away from the bright light, and that's when he saw Jonathan.

He couldn't make sense of what he was seeing. His brother was on his back, and his chest seemed to be covered with long sticks.

Arrows, came the dim, surprised thought. *Those are arrows.*

He turned and glimpsed Billy's body at the far end of the ledge, his back covered with arrows.

He raised his head and saw an Indian standing right in front of him. For a moment, David didn't recognize him. Then he saw that it was Roman; at least, that's what they called him, because of his long, chiseled nose. They'd long ago come to an agreement with Roman: he'd take the occasional stray steer, one that had wandered far from their property lines and probably would have been wolf meat anyway, and in return, the Indian would occasionally brought them a deer carcass. It was a fair trade, as far as David was concerned. Venison jerky tasted much better than beef jerky.

But Roman's face was so contorted with rage.

"Roman," David said. "Whatever happened, let's talk about it."

He felt the edge of a knife pass across his throat and the spray of blood that followed. Only then did he see the blade in Roman's hands.

He tried to talk. He tried to reason his way out. *Let me explain,* he wanted to say.

But all that emerged from his mouth was a gurgle. Blood flowed out over his collar and down his chest. His legs gave out, and the ground rushed to meet him. A rock gouged into his cheek.

It was a distant pain, unimportant and far away.

Why can't people just talk about things? he wondered.

***

Roman and the other Miwok braves piled the three white men's bodies into the cave. They climbed to the top of the cliff and rolled down boulders until one of them triggered an avalanche that covered the cave opening and glittering gold under broken rocks and loose soil.

If they hurried, there might still be time to catch the invaders who had killed their people.

If the Ts'emekwes left any of them alive.

Chapter Fifteen

Grendel brought me a knapsack containing hardtack and jerky. The canvas pack is covered in dried blood, but I can't afford to be squeamish.

It watched me eat, then lumbered away, back into the darkness at the rear of the cavern. It has apparently learned that its captives cannot live on raw meat alone. I have tried to learn from Tucker's mistakes, and have kept my little corner of the cave clean of the carnage that these creatures create. The insects are unavoidable, but at least they do not scuttle across my face as I sleep.

I'm not certain that surviving hunger and illness is going to be enough to keep me alive. Hrothgar emerges from the deeper recesses of the cave less and less. I try to engage him, but he has stopped talking to me, as if embarrassed to utter such sounds. He follows Grendel around now, and practically ignores me. Only when Grendel is not there does Hrothgar approach me.

Each time, it is the same: Grendel will leave the cave and Hrothgar will be underfoot. Grendel will notice at the last moment and howl a reprimand. Hrothgar will back away, sulking. He might kick the bones around for a few moments. Once I saw him scale the walls of the cave in a fit of temper, on hand- and footholds inaccessible to me. Once he turned to me amid one of his outbursts and glared at me as if it were my fault. If Hrothgar continues to ignore me when Grendel is around, I fear that the beast will think I am no longer useful as a companion to the smaller one.

I must either keep Hrothgar interested in me or plan my escape.

***

Images of the slaughter filled Frank's thoughts as he rode in silence: The smile fading from the chief's face as he realized what was coming. The running women and children, cut down as if they were cattle. One brave, facing them all, killing Samuels and wounding Simmons and Percy.

The Miwok's face had been so twisted with rage that Frank almost hadn't recognized him: Hesutu, a childhood playmate with whom Frank and his brothers had shared many adventures in these very mountains.

A memory came to Frank's mind: Hesutu and Patrick swimming in the river, holding each other under water, each trying to be the dominant one in their group of friends. Their dominance was never decided, for after each defeat, the loser would as often as not taste victory in the next battle.

Along with the horror of the massacre, a sense of shame hung over not just Frank, but most of the ranchers. No one looked the others in the eye. Conversations were low and were chiefly about practical things that needed to be done. There was no chitchat or joshing as there normally would be among the group.

Dave Martin, George Banks, Bud Carpenter, and a few of the others had been loudly excited at first, sounding triumphant, giddy after the battle. They'd even let out whoops of victory that echoed through the mountain canyons. But when none of the others had responded, they, too, had fallen silent.

Frank had heard stories of massacres, tales told by wandering cowboys, but he'd never really believed them. He'd reckoned they were just tall tales. He couldn't imagine his fellow settlers would be so harsh and cruel. The natives had been here long before the white man, and there was plenty of space to go around.

Oh, he realized that the ranchers, especially the new ones who scrambled for land abandoned by the Californios and other tribes, could be forceful, even brutal, but wholesale massacres? That hadn't seemed possible. Certainly not in *his* part of the state, and not involving *his* neighbors. Especially not involving his own family.

Still, the rumors of massacres, expulsions, and starvation of the native tribes had become more and more frequent.

Watching it happen was worse, far worse, than his most dire imaginings.

Frank counted the straggling line of men as they crisscrossed a steep slope. Out of the original twenty-seven men in the search party, they were missing Hugh, the four Jordan brothers, and of course, poor Samuels, whose body was strapped over the back of his horse. The addition of Virginia Reed and her two companions brought the number back up to twenty-four.

He hoped they would have enough firepower to fight off any war party the Indians might send at them.

Patrick rode with his head down somewhere in the middle of the group. Frank wondered if he also remembered Hesutu, who had once been his closest friend, closer to Patrick than any of his own brothers. He wondered how Patrick would rationalize the slaughter. Patrick thought he hated Indians, but Frank remembered a time when, of all the brothers, Patrick had spent the most time in the Miwok village.

Their father had once again taken the leadership position, riding at the head of the line. His head was up and his posture ramrod straight, as usual, but there was a subtle deflation in his demeanor.

He is going to have to find a way to justify this to himself, Frank thought. Father thought himself a moral man, and what moral man could live with what they'd done?

Henry Newton rode beside Thomas, unwilling to relinquish his hard-won leadership. Thomas Whitford ignored his presence, and the portly man grew redder and redder in the face as the day rode on.

Virginia Reed and her two friends trailed the group. Frank tried to join them, but their cold, grim silence made it clear that he was unwelcome. They'd been offered one of the packhorses, but insisted on traveling on foot, and they were slowly but steadily falling behind. Clearly, the trio wanted nothing to do with the ranchers. Frank couldn't blame them. He didn't want to be part of the party either, but there it was.

Was he any better than the rest of them? After all, he hadn't stopped the massacre.

No, he decided. *I'm as guilty as any of them.*

Lost in thought, Frank drifted back in the group until he found himself the last rider in line. He nodded to the man leading the extra horses. An overwhelming odor of horse, sweat, and leather hung in the air. The horses were nervous, some straining against the reins. Frank spoke to them in soothing tones, but still they stamped their hooves and nickered to their companions. Sighing, he took the reins of one of them and dismounted. He held on firmly until the horse settled down.

Frank breathed deeply of the fresh air, relieved to let the rest of the searchers go on ahead.

What am I doing? he wondered as he waited for the three laggards to catch up.

Virginia Reed was certainly comely, with her bright blue eyes, blonde hair, and even features, but there was a strange seriousness to her that made her beauty secondary. It was the spirit inside her that mattered, and only a coincidence that her outer features were so pleasing. She looked tired, and yet alert to everything around her. She was curious about him, and not shy about meeting his gaze. He flinched at the contempt he saw there.

The Indian girl was more guarded in her glances, and Jean Baptiste seemed to be paying attention only to her. *They seem like a couple*, Frank thought.

"Are you sure you don't want to ride?" he asked as the trio drew near. "No one is using the extra horses."

"No, thank you," Virginia answered curtly. Those three words seemed to contain a whole mountain of recrimination. He felt his cheeks grow hot. He wanted to defend himself and his companions, but he could think of nothing to say that didn't sound self-serving, as if he was trying to escape blame.

"Why did you do it?" she asked in a low, angry voice. "Why would you kill unarmed women and children?"

For a moment, Frank didn't know what to say. He sifted through all the images of the last several days; so much death. Finally, he understood her contempt. She wouldn't know about the carnage at the mining camp. She wouldn't understand why the ranchers had attacked defenseless men, women and children, why madness and the lust for revenge had overcome them.

So he explained what they'd found, the brutality they'd seen on the banks of the North Fork, and how they'd concluded that it must have been Indians who killed the miners, despite the lack of proof.

"I tried to stop them," he said quietly. "But they were enraged. They started shooting before I could do anything."

Just then, Jean Baptiste stumbled, and Frank noticed his wound. He wore a moccasin instead of a boot on the injured foot, and fresh blood seeped through the bandages even as Frank watched.

"Let your friend ride, at least," Frank said, nodding to the young man.

Virginia looked back at Jean, who was sitting beside the trail with Feather standing next to him. She nodded and went back to speak to the two of them.

"Ride my horse," Frank urged Feather once Jean was astride the spare horse. "Please."

"No, thank you," she said, echoing Virginia.

Frank hesitated, then set off on foot beside them, leading his horse. They continued on, falling farther behind the others. His thoughts again turned to Virginia. This was a girl with strength and integrity. She would die before harming anyone, no matter how long she'd been in the mountains, no matter that she'd been starving. She was also too proud to defend herself from the suspicions about her.

She was quite unlike any other girl he'd met, on either side of the continent. The girls back East were sometimes shockingly bold, though he'd still rarely found himself alone with one of them. And beneath their façade of daring, most of them were conventional in their desires and ambitions.

Strangely, the girls back home in the West were even more straight-laced, with chaperones around every moment. It seemed to Frank that he'd never had a normal conversation with a girl, at least not since he was a boy. He'd gotten along just fine with the tomboys before the girls had transformed into a different species. He didn't know how to behave around girls who played coy, and he had no sisters to give him pointers.

But with Virginia Reed, he didn't have to pretend, for she wouldn't ridicule him for speaking bluntly; in fact, she plainly preferred it. At the same time, her strangeness, her hidden depths, only made her more alluring, though her feelings for him were clearly the opposite of respect. How could he explain the massacre at the Indian village without damning his own brother and father? How could he show her that he was as horrified as she without betraying his own family?

He gave up on that and tuned to more practical concerns. "It's going to get dark soon," he said.

Virginia looked up at the horizon and nodded. "Best start looking for a place to stop, someplace defensible." She said it in the most commonsense tone possible.

Frank almost laughed. Any other girl of his acquaintance would have made a flirting joke about the coming darkness. "You think they will attack so quickly?" he asked. *I'm asking a young girl her opinion on the tactics of warfare,* he marveled.

Virginia looked surprised, as if the answer was obvious. "The Indians? I don't think so. But then, they weren't what caused the carnage in the mining camp."

Frank almost stopped walking, he was so surprised. How could she have known what he was thinking? It had been clear from the moment he'd seen Chief's Honon's face. There had been no guilt there, no fear. The old chief had had no idea what was coming.

"You think it was other miners?" he asked. "Claim-jumpers?"

"Maybe," she said. "But if so, where are they? Where did they go?"

"But there is no other explanation…" Frank trailed off. He was mystified, and he sensed that this girl somehow knew the answer.

"Do you know of the Ts'emekwes?" she asked.

Frank drew a blank for a moment, then remembered Chief Honon saying something similar. He'd dismissed it as superstition. He tried to remember where he had heard the term before. Sometime in his childhood, he had heard that name, and he recalled that it was part of the Indian myths. But he couldn't remember much beyond that.

"It is also called the Skoocoom," Virginia continued.

Then it came back to him. The Indian children they'd played with had often talked about the Skoocoom, some kind of forest creature who watched over them, playing tricks on them. He was impossible to catch, and almost as impossible to ever see. Frank had never thought of the creature as a danger.

"You don't believe that, do you?" he exclaimed. "Why, that's…" *Crazy*, he thought.

The look Virginia gave him made him falter. *She believes what she's saying! She believes in these monsters.*

"I don't ask that you believe me," she said, seeing his expression. There was no hint of defensiveness in her tone. "I have seen things that most people would dismiss as creatures of fairytales. But I know they exist. I know all too well they are real."

Frank shook his head without speaking. Apparently, the girl had not escaped her ordeal in the mountains without having suffered some damage. Perhaps it was inevitable that she would look for some other explanation for the deaths of her friends, something other than hunger and desperation, something bigger and unexplainable that would give the sacrifice meaning. He turned away.

It would explain why everyone avoided her. Such a shame. And yet…the enchantment he had been feeling about her didn't go away, though he wondered if it would be more sensible, for once, to let his mind overrule his heart.

They walked in silence for a time while Frank wondered if he should rejoin the others. There was something about Virginia's certainty that made him hesitate. He was so deep in thought that he didn't notice at first when she stopped, then suddenly realized he was walking alone.

"What's wrong?" he asked, turning to find Virginia, Feather, and Jean conferring on the path behind him.

"You must know the truth, all of it," Virginia said. "We're going to need your help before this journey is done. We will need someone to talk to the other men, to make them believe us."

"What do you mean?" The tone in her voice sent a chill down his spine.

"You don't believe me, do you?" she asked, walking toward him.

He didn't speak, just turned his head away, wondering why he felt abashed and she didn't.

"Jean, are you well enough to Turn?" Jean scowled and Virginia quickly added, "Only if you want to, Jean."

The young man stood thinking for a moment, his eyes going from Frank to Virginia and back again. "Very well," he said, finally. "If you think he can help us."

She nodded. "I don't believe we have a choice. We have to convince these men of the danger."

And how can you possibly do that? Frank wondered, shifting uneasily.

"There is more to this world than you can see. Are you willing for us to try to show you?" Virginia said.

He was silent for a moment. *What harm could there be? She cannot prove to me that mythical creatures exist...can she?* "Go ahead," he said. "But I warn you, I've had two years of higher education in one of the most prestigious schools in the world."

Virginia stared at him for a moment, then chuckled. Feather and Jean Baptiste smiled, but didn't seem to find the situation quite so funny.

"Well, I suppose, then, that you've read of such beasts, even if you were taught they were legends," Virginia said.

This girl might really be crazy, Frank thought.

Still smiling, Virginia said the last thing he thought she'd say, given the circumstances: "Give me your gun."

Much to his own surprise, Frank pulled the pistol from his belt and handed it to her. *What the hell am I doing?* Moments before, she had seemed touched in the head, but something about her no-nonsense expression made him trust her.

Virginia looked past Frank's shoulder intently, and he couldn't help but cast a glance down the trail to see the last of his party disappear into the woods. She seemed to have been waiting for that moment. "Jean?" she said, turning to her friend. "Shall we show him?"

Feather came forward and gestured for Frank to hand her the reins to his horse and the packhorse. She led the animals around a bend in the trail, where trees and rocks blocked their view. She tied them there and came back. Then she nodded to Virginia. "The riders are far enough ahead of us."

Jean started to undress.

"What the...?" Frank exclaimed. He started to flush, wondering what trick these three people—who were practically strangers, after all—were up to.

"Just wait," Virginia reassured him.

Even before he'd doffed his last bit of clothing, Jean Baptiste Turned. His chest expanded as if it was going to explode, then sprouted fur. At the same time, his arms and legs thinned and lengthened.

Frank stumbled backward with a cry, ready to run for his horse and ride away. He felt a tight grip on his arm and looked down to see Virginia's hand grasping him.

"Wait," she said. He froze, watching, waiting, Virginia gripping his arm with surprising strength.

Jean continued to transform. He dropped to all fours, and at the same time, his hands and feet turned into paws. His face changed as well, his jaw protruding and his teeth becoming fangs. His eyes grew larger and turned a dark orange, almost red. They stared at Frank with distrust throughout the whole process, never really changing expression even as the man became a beast.

Then a gray wolf stood there, appraising Frank with his uncanny stare. The creature twisted around to lick the wound on his hind leg.

The animal was real, but resembled something out of Frank's nightmares. The glistening, visceral fluid that still covered the beast was that of something at birth, something terrible. The wolf-that-was-a-boy seemed wary, turning his head to one side as if shy about being seen. Yet when it swung its head back, there was a defiant tilt to its snout, and in those dark orange eyes, Frank saw something of the noble soul behind the frightening exterior.

"All right, Jean," Virginia said. "He's seen enough."

The transformation was reversed. Frank was just as mesmerized as before, unable to turn his eyes away until the young man stood before him naked. Jean immediately reached for his clothing.

"You're a...a Skoocoom?" Frank blurted.

"Of course not," Virginia said, exasperated. "He's a werewolf, what else?"

"A werewolf," Frank repeated dully.

"Yes, obviously," Virginia said, sounding irritated. "We showed you this to prove that if one mythical beast exists, so might another."

"It's not possible," Frank said, even though he'd just witnessed it.

"All your education doesn't explain that, does it?" Virginia challenged. "Your science can't describe that which it refuses to believe exists. We've shown you this so you'll believe us. The Skoocoom is dangerous and real."

"You've seen it?" Frank asked.

"No," she admitted. "But Feather has. And I have no reason to doubt. I somehow...just know."

"She is a Canowiki," Feather said, as if that explained everything.

"A Hunter," Jean added, having fully dressed. "It is part of her nature to know these things. She fought My Kind at Truckee Lake, which they call Donner Lake now. I was Turned there, but she kept me as a friend, despite the change. I swore not to become a monster like those others, preying on defenseless men and women."

Feather reached out and took his arm as if in sympathy and support. Jean Baptiste looked down in surprise.

"Ts'emekwes are not really supernatural creatures," Virginia said. "They are as real and natural as you and I—or the werewolves. But they conceal themselves and remain unknown, for mankind is afraid of them. They hide in the shadows. The Skoocoom is no danger to us when left alone. But men have invaded its territory, and it defends its home. It doesn't care if we believe in it or not, or whether we intend to do it harm or not. It will kill anyone in its territory, even the Indians to whom it's grown accustomed. We have roused it from its slumber, and there will be no stopping it until we are all gone, or until it is dead."

Listening to Virginia, Frank suddenly got the feeling that someone or something was watching them. The forest around them had become quiet. The noise of the search party had receded into the distance, and they were alone on the mountainside.

"It's here," Virginia said quietly.

"Here?" Frank asked, becoming very still. "What's here?"

She held out her hand to shush him. "Don't speak," she whispered.

Virginia extended his gun to him, and he took it. He cocked it and waited.

The disturbance, when it came, was downslope, out of sight. There was a loud thump, accompanied by a rumbling sound that continued. When the rumbling finally stopped, they heard men screaming.

Then there was a brief silence, followed by alarmed shouts and a flurry of gunshots.

Jean Baptiste was already back on his horse, and this time, Feather got up behind him. He spurred the horse down the trail. Frank mounted his horse and held out his hand. Virginia hesitated only an instant, then took his hand, swinging up behind him. He galloped down the trail.

They reached the copse of trees to find the men of the search party in turmoil. Johnny Hawkins, holding onto a frightened horse, whirled at their approach and fired a wild shot over their heads.

"Stop shooting!" Frank heard Patrick shout.

His brother was motioning for the men to create a circle facing outward, and Frank and his companions entered the circle before it closed. Patrick and Thomas were shouted orders. The trail on the far side of the trees crossed a steep cliff face just wide enough for one horse and rider at a time.

"What happened?" Frank asked.

"I don't know," Hawkins said. "Something charged the center of our line. I only caught a glimpse of it, but it was huge. It bowled over Perkins and Dutton, horses and all. Tipped them right over the side of the cliff."

Frank stared over the precipice. It went straight down for a hundred feet before it ended in talus, a rough mixture of boulders, rocks, and gravel. Then there was another steep drop-off down to the stream far below. Frank was overcome by the vertigo he always had at heights, the sense that something, some malicious spirit, would snatch him and toss him over the edge before he was aware it was happening, and his heart lurched as he stepped back.

Standing on solid ground, and yet so close to death…this is something that no one who wants to live can ever get used to, he thought.

There was no sign of the missing men.

"Whatever…whoever it was, they're gone," Frank said. "No one could survive that fall." He glanced back at Virginia, but she was stone-faced. She gave him a quick shake of her head, as if disagreeing with him.

He swallowed, remembering the young man changing into a wolf.

"It was a boulder. It had to be," Thomas Whitford said. The old man looked frightened, something that Frank had never seen. All the confidence that his stepfather had started this journey with was gone, replaced by guilt and uncertainty.

"It's the same thing the savages did to the miners," Dave Martin said.

"Just like them to make a sneak attack," Henry Newton agreed. "Not face us man to man."

You mean, like armed men against women and children? Frank wanted ask aloud.

As they spoke, clouds covered the late afternoon sun.

"We'll camp here tonight," Patrick said. "We'll explore the path tomorrow, make sure it's safe."

"But what if they come back?" Johnny Hawkins protested.

No one responded.

They backtracked a short way into a wooded section to establish their camp. No one said why, but Frank was certain that they all felt better among the shelter of the trees. Thomas assigned two men to stand guard on each of the four sides of the camp, to be relieved twice during the night. Feeling on edge, but secure that the men on watch would rouse them if trouble threatened, the search party settled down to sleep.

There were no disturbances in the night, but in the morning, two of the guards, Jesse Sherman and Joe Foster, were gone.

Chapter Sixteen

Grendel has forgotten me. He doesn't mean to neglect me, but I am starving to death. The canteen has not been filled in more than a day.

Until thirst woke me, I spent most of the last three days sleeping. As my world diminishes to a dark corner of a cave, my dream life seems to be expanding. I dream of my brothers, and the ranch, and everything I love about being outdoors.

Then I wake to the stench and the darkness, and I can barely move, as if, instead of days of inactivity, I had walked a hundred miles. It makes no sense that I am so tired, or that my muscles hurt so.

Grendel has been absent for three days, I realize as I empty the canteen of its last drops. With Grendel gone, Hrothgar is more interested in me again. He seems lonely. He walked up to me this morning and said in his deep voice—so strange coming from a being that is no more developed than a child—"Friend."

"Friend," I agreed. I lifted the canteen and tried handing it to him. "I need water."

Instead of fetching some for me, he motioned for me to get up and follow him. He held the branches away from the entrance, and I was blinded by the enhanced daylight bouncing off the golden walls. I climbed unsteadily to my feet, using the silky golden wall for support. I never yearned for gold, but the more I am in its presence, the more beautiful I find it. I don't care if it can make me rich; its lustrous shine and soft, smooth surface is something precious in its own right. Strange that it should be the cause of so much misery.

I pushed away from the wall, tottered to the entrance, and entered Fairyland.

That's how it appeared to me. I left the awful smells of the cave, the lack of movement and air and light, and entered a scene that was the most beautiful in all the world.

Of course, I'd seen it before, and sights equally as magnificent. California is a beautiful place, a wonderland, unspoiled and pure. But I never really *appreciated* it before. It was always around me, and I took it for granted. After days in darkness, I saw it with new eyes, like a once-blind man miraculously seeing for the first time.

The trees in the box canyon seemed so straight and vibrant, each placed right where it should be. The pond beyond was a brilliant blue, the water clear to the bottom, and glittering there, like coins in a fountain, were golden nuggets. The grass was green, untouched by any animal. The cliff walls were as formidable as the ramparts of any castle.

It is a paradise on Earth, and it belongs to Grendel and Hrothgar.

I don't blame them for wanting to protect this. I recalled the mining camps, with their piles of scrap and torn earth and muddy waters. Man destroys that which he loves. I had a vision of the future of California, with all the trees cut down, all the grasses trampled and eaten, all the rivers clotted with mankind's waste. There would be no room for the wild and the dangerous. I felt ashamed.

I filled the canteen slowly, then took a long drink. I refilled it, taking my time, hoping Hrothgar wouldn't force me to return to the cave right away. The sunlight on my face was caressing, soothing. I lay back in the grass and stared at the bright blue sky and white clouds floating lazily across it.

There's wind outside this canyon, I thought. *But inside it, all is peaceful and still.*

Hrothgar watched me intently, and I could tell he was pleased that I was happy.

I looked toward the narrow canyon entrance and thought about making a run for it. But Hrothgar is bigger than I am, and even if I was a match for him, even if I had a knife to oppose his fearsome claws, I have no desire to hurt him. He is only doing that which his nature requires of him. I am the intruder here; me and my kind.

We spent the afternoon peacefully together. I taught Hrothgar two more words, "water" and "sun." Maybe he'll bring me out again, if he can only understand how much I need it. Maybe he'll want to learn other words.

When the sun dropped below the walls of the canyon, Hrothgar rose and motioned me back into the cave.

I wondered if death might be preferable. *Let it be quick, instead of this slow wasting away,* I thought as I lay in the long grass, my eyes closed, but then a glimmer of hope rose in me. Having let me out of my prison once, Hrothgar might be inclined to do it again.

My reluctance showed in my movements as I rose and followed him to my prison, finally lowering myself to sit in my little corner. Hrothgar stayed in the front chamber of the cave longer than usual. We didn't interact, simply sat companionably. He spends most of the time in the cave's dark depths, doing what, I do not know. But this time, he was near me in the cavern when I heard a sound coming from the back.

I froze, knowing Grendel had not returned.

There is someone else in this cave! I thought.

I was suddenly certain that Hrothgar and Grendel were not the only two beasts in this cavern.

Somewhere in the darkness there was another; perhaps others.

***

The night the two guards went missing was the last time any of the party slept soundly.

Preacher MacLeod raised a fuss while the party broke camp.

"This is God's judgment upon us for murdering innocent men and women!" he cried. "He will smite us for our hard-heartedness!" He wasn't really a preacher, but the nickname was apt. No one paid any attention to him, regardless, for he had helped lead the charge into the Indian village, as bloodthirsty as any of them.

The worst was not knowing what had happened to the missing men, or how they were being picked off. Among the search party, Frank alone had an idea of the foe they faced. It wasn't Indians. That idea was frightening enough, but they were men; they could be fought. A creature of myth that no one could actually see? That weighed on him. He felt helpless, and that was the most unpleasant feeling he'd ever felt. If he was going to die, he wanted to face his enemy, not suddenly be snuffed out as if he was unimportant to this world, just another victim.

The group was unnaturally quiet as they packed, eyes darting around, watching the forest as they worked, shadowed by a feeling of unease that none could shake.

The ranchers reached the edge of the cliff in short order and there, at the head of the trail, they found the heads of the missing men: Carl Dutton and Jim Perkins, who had disappeared in the rock fall, and the two guards, Jesse Sherman and Joe Foster. The heads had been stuck on sharpened stakes. Their faces were frozen in what appeared to be laughing expressions. It made them appear as if they had gone gibbering mad in their last moments.

"Why would the Indians pose them like that?" Martin asked into the silence. "If I catch one of these savages, I'll...I'll..." His voice trailed off as he tried to imagine something worse than what he was seeing.

I was wrong that it is worse not to know, Frank thought. *This is much worse.*

"Can't we go another way?" Johnny Hawkins asked, staring up at the sheer cliff, trying to see if there was anyone up there. He always had his hand near his holster now, as if ready to draw his gun at any moment.

"It will take us an extra couple days to get home if we do," Henry Newton said. "I don't want to stay out in the wilderness one day longer than I have to. We need to get back to civilization, see if James and Oliver have returned."

His forlorn hope was so dismaying that no one said anything for a few moments. Then Hawkins spoke up. "We need to inform the authorities."

His statement was greeted with another uncomfortable silence as the men wondered, *Tell them what? That we massacred a village?*

"We fought a battle; we lost some men," Thomas agreed, understanding what everyone else was thinking. "Let the federal troops take care of it now." The Whitford patriarch had been a shadow of himself since leaving the Indian village, but there was some of the old command in his voice. Meanwhile, Patrick stayed silent.

"All this proves is that the Indians are as dangerous as we thought," said George Banks. "We did the right thing. Let's get going."

There were mutters of agreement among the men.

They will have rationalized all of it by the time we reach home, Frank marveled. *It will have all been the Indians' fault. If we make it home, that is.*

No one moved. Several of the ranchers were staring at the cliff face where two of their fellows had fallen.

Finally, Fred Carter snorted, "Don't no one want to go home?" He spurred his reluctant horse forward onto the narrow trail. The rest of the search party watched him instead of following right away. He crossed the open cliff, hugging the mountainside all the while. Reaching safety, he gave a whoop, waving his hat in the air as he shouted to them, "Come on, you cowards!"

Then it was as if a curtain fell over him.

Carter only had time to give a brief cry of alarm before a dust cloud obscured him. The rumble of the rockslide reached the rest of the searchers after the rocks had carried the man away.

When the dust cloud cleared, the path was gone, and a huge part of the hillside had dropped away as if sliced off by a knife. General panic followed, many of the men wheeling their horses, nearly causing others to fall while they retreated to the illusory safety of the trees. Only after they stopped did they realize that they had left the four heads still mounted on the stakes. No one volunteered to go back and give them a decent burial.

"My God, it's happening again," Virginia said in a low voice.

"What's happening again?" Frank prompted, turning his head so she could hear him, mounted behind him as she was.

"Soon it will be every man for himself," she said. "We'll be picked off one by one. We need to stick together, to protect each other. No matter what happens."

"Agreed," he said.

Patrick and Thomas were standing apart from the others. *I should be with them,* Frank thought. *That's what is expected of me.* But he knew that Virginia would not be welcome at their side. He'd never seen men die before, and now...it was as if a lifetime of experience had been condensed into a few days. Gone were his childhood visions of glory in battle against the Indians. Amazing that he'd ever had such illusions, when most of his playmates had been Miwok children. Somehow the savage Indians of his imagination weren't the same Indians he knew: those were the *good* Indians. He realized now that Indians were simply other human beings with different customs and history. It was the white men who had painted the picture of the savage.

"We can't stay here," Patrick said. He was standing in the middle of the clearing, trying to get everyone's attention. "We need to get as much distance from here as possible before dark."

The search party reassembled reluctantly and followed the path away from the cliffs. It would mean a half a day of backtracking and a day's journey out of their way, but for once, there was no argument. In another day, their road would lead them to the lowlands and other white folk, but for now, they faced the constant threat of attacks by Indians and other, unknown beings.

Frank knew when they were nearing the high lakes, for insects attacked them in dark, swirling clouds, making everyone, man and beast alike, miserable. When they saw the green valleys in the distance, they started to relax, probably thinking the Indians wouldn't dare follow them this far. As if to rebuke them for letting down their guard, it began to rain hard. The men put on their slickers and rode on. They were recognizing landmarks now. They were close to home. Frank could sense the men's spirits improving.

When the ranchers set up camp, they again assigned two guards to each side of the campsite. They were determined to remain watchful through the night. Frank served his turn on watch in the middle of the night, and never once got sleepy or sloppy. Each time he was the slightest bit inclined to nod off, he remembered the four heads on stakes, their laughing yet horror-filled expressions, and he snapped awake.

Incredibly, they found one of the guards, Bud Carpenter, asleep in the morning, sitting with his back against a tree. When they woke him and asked about Ben Torrance, his fellow guard, he couldn't tell them anything.

"I don't understand," he kept saying. "I couldn't have fallen asleep. I must have been knocked on the head." He felt his scalp and but found no bump or bruise. "I couldn't have fallen asleep!" he insisted.

They broke camp quickly. Just outside the clearing, they found Torrance, flayed and spread out on a boulder, with the same insane, grinning expression as the other dead men.

"He waits until they've frozen in death, then sets their features," Jean Baptiste said. He was talking to Virginia, Feather, and Frank, but some of the nearby ranchers heard him, and word quickly spread through camp, though "he" became "them" in the retelling. Most of the men were still convinced it was the Miwok hunting them.

They grew angrier. Rifles and pistols were kept close at hand. Frank prayed no Indian would have the misfortune to happen to appear. He or she would be shot, regardless of the circumstances.

The ranchers made camp that night with the foothills and the mountains behind them, most of them certain they had escaped the danger.

"Where's Jeffers and Banks?" someone asked as they were making dinner. Silence fell as the searchers realized that none of them had seen the two men since setting out earlier that day.

They spent the next half hour searching the surrounding area, shouting the missing men's names, before gathering around the campfire again.

"They were riding right behind me," Hawkins said. "At least, I thought they were…"

"How's this possible?" Percy said. His wounds from the Indian village were getting worse, and it seemed all he did was complain. Now his voice had a tinge of panic. "How could they disappear without any of us noticing?"

"Maybe they just lit out," Partridge said. "Skedaddled. Banks always was a big talker. The bigger the talker, the smaller the man, I always say."

"You shut up," Martin said, bristling. "George is a friend." Carpenter stood beside him, equally angry.

Partridge just shrugged, as if to imply *Birds of a feather…*

"No," McCarthy spoke up. "My man Jeffers would never leave without telling me. Something else happened."

"Maybe the Indians have a spy," Martin said. "Maybe someone's helping them." Several of the men cast glances in Feather's direction. "I'll say it if no one else will," Martin continued. "We have one of the enemy among us."

"Now wait a minute," Frank said.

"We should bind her, at least," Carpenter said. "Make sure she stays put."

Frank got to his feet, his hand drifting down toward his gun. The other men stared at him. "No one is touching her," Frank said. "She's been with me the whole time. She's in as much danger as the rest of you."

Martin turned and faced him, and with a sinking feeling, Frank saw the man's hand fall to his own gun with a practiced motion.

Frank would never know whether Martin would have actually drawn on him, because to his surprise, Patrick came to Feather's defense. "How would she be telling them anything? And why?" he said. "They know where we are; they don't need a spy."

"But how can we trust her not to slit our throats in the middle of the night?" Carpenter asked.

Frank scoffed. "Look at her," he said. "If you're afraid of such a little thing, then you should have stayed home. You don't belong among us men."

The ranchers backed down, more afraid of scorn than of Feather. Besides, they didn't really believe the small Indian girl had anything to do with what was going on. It was anger talking, and bluster, and she was a convenient target.

Nevertheless, when Frank sat down again, Virginia put her hand on his arm and said, "Thank you, Frank."

He wasn't sure if it was his imagination or not, but it seemed as if her hand lingered on his arm longer than was necessary to express her thanks. He decided then and there that if he escaped this terrible trap, he would court her. To hell with the Donner Party. And to hell with what his brothers and Father wanted.

Most of the men didn't bother setting up tents that night. They sat wide awake, in a circle, their backs to each other and their rifles under their rain slickers, trying to keep their powder dry. Despite the danger, or perhaps because he was exhausted from the constant vigilance, Frank found himself nodding off. When he did, he drowsily imagined that the unknown creature was crouched right behind him. He woke with a start, his heart pounding, and looked behind him; then he became equally certain that it was in front of him, always there, always waiting, waiting to kill.

Virginia squeezed his arm again, as if reassuring him, but when he looked down at her, she too was staring off into the darkness. The rain continued to pour down on them.

Morning dawned, and never had the search party witnessed a more welcome sight. Frank rubbed his hands over his face, grimacing at the length of his stubble, and did a quick head count. Fifteen.

Fifteen of them were left, counting the three newcomers. Fifteen out of the twenty-three who'd left the Miwok village. When they included the Jordan brothers among the missing, more than half of their original search party was gone. From their faces, Frank guessed that the others were having similar thoughts. The men looked around at each other as if counting who wasn't there, as if suddenly realizing how many of their friends were simply gone. They had yet to see who was attacking them, much less being able to fight.

The rain let up and the ranchers could hear the river in the distance, giving them renewed hope. There was little to pack; no cook fires, no tents; no one had even bothered pulling out blankets to warm themselves. They were saddling the horses when Johnny Hawkins suddenly cried out. There in the mud, just outside the camp, were two giant footprints filled with water, with the same five toes as a man's but twice as broad and twice as long.

"That's impossible," Persimmons said.

"The water must have made the footprints bigger," Hawkins muttered, "...somehow." But the outlines of the prints were as sharp and fresh as if the creature had made them but a moment before.

When they reached the river, they found that instead of the usual quiet flow, it was a raging torrent.

It must have rained even harder in the mountains, Frank thought. *There is no chance that we can cross that.*

"What now?" Martin shouted. He raised his head and let out a shout of frustration.

From far in the distance came an answering bellow, a booming cry, impossibly low and deep.

Hawkins paled. "What was that?"

No one answered. Those who knew weren't saying. Frank glanced at Virginia, trying to catch her attention.

Maybe it's time to tell them, he wanted to say. *They'll believe us now.*

But Virginia didn't return his glance. She was staring at the river.

"Are you all right?" he asked.

She turned to him with a forlorn but determined look. "I must prepare myself for darkness," she said. "He is coming.'

"No sense standing here all day," Patrick shouted. "Stark's Crossing is a day to the north. There's a ferry there."

It was the only solution, but they were uneasy.

"It's like every mile we travel, we get farther away from home," Carpenter complained.

"The rate we're being picked off, won't be anybody left to make it home," McCarthy added.

The party started north along the muddy banks of the swollen river.

"He shall not let anyone escape alive," Feather said quietly, so that only Frank, Jean, and Virginia could hear her. "The god, Ts'emekwes, is angry."

"He is not a god," Virginia said. "He can be defeated."

Feather blushed, but didn't retract her statement.

Virginia was grim. "I must confront him."

"You?" Frank asked, looking down at the young girl who was a full head shorter than him. A party of adult men was running for their lives, and here she was talking about taking on the creature all by herself. "What can you do?"

"She is the Canowiki," Feather said. "It is her destiny."

Frank shook his head in amazement. "I'll help."

"No," Virginia said. "You're not a Hunter."

"I'll be there," he repeated stubbornly. "Whether you want me to be or not."

"We will all help," Feather said. "But in the end, she will defeat the Skoocoom. She is the Canowiki."

It was as if this statement decided the issue, for the threesome, at least.

But Frank would not allow Virginia to face the danger alone.

If that meant he had to confront the monster, so be it. He would do what was necessary.

Chapter Seventeen

For a second night, no one went missing. The ranchers continued on in higher spirits. The river's opposite shore seemed so close. If they reached the far side, most would consider themselves almost home. Surely there they'd be safe. Surely the beast wouldn't follow them that far.

The sun broke through the clouds for several hours, and soon there was joshing and banter among the men, which hadn't been heard for days. It was strange; more than half of the friends and neighbors who'd set out with them were gone, and yet somehow they managed to carry on casual conversations, even to laugh. Perhaps laughing in the face of death gave them courage.

Frank felt none of the relief the others felt. Virginia turned her head this way and that, as if she sensed something no one else could. And then, as the sun sank toward the horizon, the clouds and the rain returned. It turned dark in moments, and it seemed as if it was nighttime already. It was as if nature itself was reminding them that they weren't yet out of trouble. The men fell silent and rode on, miserable and wet.

From the foothills in the east came a long, eerie cry, as if someone with a deep voice was giving a deafening bellow. It wasn't an animal; it sounded almost human, but unlike any voice they'd ever heard. No human voice could go so deep or carry so far.

"Skoooooooo! Cooooooooom!" the voice proclaimed, again and again. It sounded closer with every howl, and then, right when it seemed to reach the very edge of the trail, it stopped. The horses were skittish; the men took up their rifles and looked about with watchful expressions.

"Skooo! Cooom!"

The party turned toward the sound, rifles gripped in trembling hands. Despite the constant howling, nothing emerged from the thick brush.

"Move on!" Patrick shouted. "The ferry is only an hour's ride away. *Move!*"

They hurried the pace then, breaking into a trot, and as they saw the ferry in the distance, they broke into a gallop.

They were at the crossing within an hour. Against expectation, the ferry was at a wider spot in the river, but the water ran smooth and easy here, as if it were a lake. Frank had taken this ferry once before, but after paying the outrageous toll, he had found other, cheaper crossings thereafter. He remembered a dock with a square building built on top of it. There had been an equally expensive dining room there, and—this Frank had gladly paid for—clean, hot water for baths. In the meantime, the ferryman, Joshua Stark, had made enough money for a larger ferryboat, which was attached to a narrow chain that ran all the way across the river between two large derricks, one on either side.

As the party approached the crossing, it became clear to all of them that their unseen enemy had beaten them there. The structure on the dock was lopsided, as if it had been knocked off its base. The ferryboat rode deeper in the water than it should have. The derrick on the other side of the river was knocked over. The derrick on their side of the river still stood, but the guiding chain strung between the two was broken, one end lost somewhere in the depths of the smooth water.

A man hung from the other end.

He was a fat man. His neck had stretched under his weight, and his body was barely hanging by a shred of skin. His face was unrecognizable, but had the same gargoyle rictus of a smile as the other dead men. Frank had no doubt it was Joshua Stark, who had been obese and who had only gotten fatter as he got richer.

Frank passed the body with his gaze averted. He could see the man was dead; he didn't need to see more. He continued on to the ferryboat. There was a huge hole in the bottom, exactly in the middle. It was as if someone had punched through the thick wood with one blow. Over the side of the sunken boat, Frank saw other, obscenely bloated bodies floating in the river. He quickly counted eight people. It wasn't only men. There were women and children among them.

No one said a word. Frank glanced at his companions, who were either slumped in their saddles or staring at the swinging body. They looked defeated. Not even Preacher MacLeod mentioned giving the dead a proper burial.

"We can still cross," Patrick said at last. "I've crossed here before. It's shallow most of the way across. There is a deep current only in the very middle. It will push us downstream a ways, but there are plenty of places to land on the other side."

The others worried over the decision. It was getting dark. The current would be stronger than normal because of the runoff from the recent rain. Some of the ranchers couldn't swim, and the horses were tired from being pushed so hard. If the ferry had been operational, there was no doubt that they would have braved the crossing in the darkness. But now? Exhaustion robbed them of their adventurousness.

On the other hand, their enemy was on this side of the river. Their foe hadn't remained in the mountains, but had followed them to the river's edge. Some of the men were muttering about a beast, perhaps having overhead some of Feather and Virginia's conversations. Most seemed to understand now that it wasn't Indians who were killing them.

"I'm going, whether the rest of you come or not," Patrick said. "I'm not staying here another minute."

Thomas Whitford rode to the edge of the river and stared across. Dark was falling, but the other side was still visible. He sighed. "Go ahead, son. You scout it for us. Take Carpenter and McCarthy with you. Their horses seem to have some stamina left."

Now that he'd been given permission, Patrick seemed uncertain. He turned to Carpenter and McCarthy. "Uh...you ready, boys?"

"Hell yes," Carpenter said. "Let's get it over with."

The rest of the party watched from the dock as the three riders waded into the river. As Patrick had claimed, the water only reached the horses' knees until they were about halfway across. Finally, almost two-thirds of the way across, they reached the swift, deep channel and hesitated. One by one, each bent his head to whisper to his mount, stroking it, encouraging it. Then they spurred the horses into the current.

They were carried downstream but still made swift progress crossing what was left of the river. They were heading toward a wide, shallow bank. Patrick's horse gained footing and lurched up the sand, and Patrick's heart rose and he stifled a whoop of joy. There was still enough daylight for all of them to get across, even the most tired. The men on the other side of the river started cheering.

And then Patrick's horse was jerked backward. Suddenly, it was struggling in the current again, bobbing up and down. Patrick's shouts could be heard clear across the river. The other two riders never even made it to the bank. First McCarthy, then Carpenter abruptly vanished, as if their horses had been yanked straight down underwater. Patrick and his horse struggled to stay afloat, and he abandoned his mount and swam for it just as the horse disappeared into the current.

He almost made it. He was upright and wading desperately toward the bank when something rose out of the water behind him. It seemed as if the river itself had risen up, but as the water splattered down, the monster that was hunting them was revealed.

It resembled a man, but was half again as tall as Patrick, and twice as wide. Its huge head seemed to be attached directly to its shoulders. Its arms and legs were extra-long and wiry, and strong…so strong. It grabbed Patrick by the neck with one hand and lifted him out of the water.

Patrick's deep voice had gone shrill and high; when he cried out, it didn't sound like him at all. The beast held Patrick at arm's length, as if examining him curiously, then twisted Patrick's head from side to side, as if he was a doll. What happened next, Frank didn't understand for several moments. He couldn't make sense of it. Had Patrick's hat come off?

But it was Patrick's head that had been pulled away from his body, and even in the distance and the gathering dark, Frank could see blood spurting high into the air. Patrick's arms moved upward, as if searching for his missing head, then flopped to his sides, like a scarecrow full of straw. Not a man. Not a brother.

Silence fell on both sides of the river.

Then the creature disdainfully, almost casually, tossed the body into the water. Still holding Patrick's head in one hand, it faced the onlookers.

"Skoooooo! Coooooom!" came the call. It was a challenge. *Come across,* the creature was saying. *Or I will come and get you.*

None of the men took up the challenge. Their cries were not of defiance, but fear. And rising above them all was the forlorn wail of Thomas Whitford as he lost the second of his three sons. He teetered in his saddle and fell, landing with a splash in the soft mud of the riverbank.

The monster twirled Patrick's head by his hair, around and around, faster and faster, and then released it to fly far out over the river. For a second, Frank thought it would land at their feet, but it splashed into the deepest part of the river and was carried away.

***

The remnants of the search party made camp. They had no choice. The rain was coming down even harder than before, if such a thing was possible. There was dry firewood inside the broken ferry building, and the fire they made comforted them for a time, but the wood diminished, the rain increased, and the fire slowly went out.

The men sat back to back, rifles in their laps, none of them certain whether the gunpowder in the weapons would even fire. They sat in misery, waiting for their doom to come. There was no light, for thick clouds obscured the moon and stars. Frank found that his hearing was enhanced, so the slightest shift in position by one of his companions, the merest brushing of a branch against a tree, was easily discerned. Someone had taken the ferryman's body down, he noticed.

Frank spent the evening at his father's side, watching over him as he slept and listening to the growl of thunder. The image of Patrick being killed ran over and over again in his mind. In a strange way, he was glad that his father wasn't awake, for he would have wanted to talk about Patrick. Frank wasn't ready for that yet. He'd been so angry at his brother, and now Patrick was gone. The anger was gone, too, replaced by guilt and grief.

When Thomas Whitford woke, it was with a howl more bloodcurdling than that of the beast, a scream of pure, unreasoning grief.

Nor did it stop. Frank tried to console him, but the old man seemed not to know him. Preacher MacLeod stepped in. McLeod was calm in the face of death, consoling the elder Whitford.

Suddenly, the clearing was filled with light as a giant bolt of lightning flashed across the sky, bringing an acrid odor. Its flash illuminated the ferry derrick, the long chain empty and swinging.

The Indian girl, Feather, had called the creature a "god." Could it control the weather? Had the ranchers offended nature itself? It certainly seemed as though everything that could go wrong had gone wrong, that everything in nature was conspiring against them, including the skies, water, and earth.

Or perhaps it wasn't the beast doing it, but the Christian God, who had looked down on their sins and was meting out justice.

In the darkness, Frank had a hard time believing in gods, big or small. *We just aren't important enough*, he thought. *We don't deserve either God's grace or his wrath.* Nature and bad luck were against them. There was no larger meaning.

What about the creature? Frank wondered. It seemed a natural creature, motivated by revenge and territorial instincts. *No more mysterious than a grizzly bear or a pack of wolves.*

Then how to explain the girl beside him? Virginia wasn't a normal girl. There was something extraordinary about her. She seemed neither frightened nor at a loss. She was always focused and resolute, no matter what happened around her. She was eternally vigilant, aware of her surroundings. When Feather called her a Hunter, the description was exactly right. She was a Hunter; a defender. The Canowiki.

But how could this slim young girl hope to fight that beast? All the grown men in the party were defeated. Frank could see that. She should have been in the center of the circle, surrounded and protected by the men, but instead, she seemed the only one who still had the will to fight. She was the only one standing, waiting for the beast to appear.

And, because of her spirit, he felt hope, as did Feather and Jean Baptiste, who stood and joined her, waiting for battle. They were slightly apart from the others, in their own little group, as if they intended to take on the beast all by themselves.

In the midst of the gloom, the rain abruptly stopped. The ranchers lifted their heads, and could make out the trees for the first time. The clouds parted, revealing a full moon, and soon the clearing was filled with soft moonlight. For a moment, all of them felt a glimmer of hope.

And then, in the middle of the clearing, there stood the beast, as still as a statue.

The men started firing wildly, those who still had a good load of gunpowder. The moon passed behind the clouds again, and the creature blinked out of sight. There were cries of alarm and at least one shout of pain. Frank thought it likely that one of the shots had gone awry, catching one of the other men in the crossfire.

When the moon appeared again, the creature didn't look as though it had moved, and there wasn't a wound on it. But there were two men sprawled motionless at its feet.

Dave Martin marched toward the monster, a gun in each hand. He raised his weapons to fire. Darkness descended again and two muzzle flashes lit up the night. When the moonlight returned, half of Martin's body lay at the beast's feet, while the creature held Martin's head and torso in his hands, seeming to stare into the dead man's eyes.

Frank aimed at the creature. As if the beast could sense him aiming, it turned its head toward him. Frank saw the intelligence in its gaze. He hesitated. *I was wrong*, he thought. *This is not an animal…this is a thinking being.* From that moment on, he saw the beast as a *he* instead of an *it*.

One of the men at the creature's feet stirred, and with a single stomp, the monster crushed the man's head, splattering blood and brains across the clearing.

Frank gulped and his finger twitched. By the time he pulled the trigger, the monster was already moving. Again the moonlight dimmed, and again there were cries of pain.

Then the creature became visible again. Everyone else had fled. For a moment, it seemed to Frank that he faced the monster alone. And then, as the moon came from behind a cloud, he saw Virginia standing directly in front of the beast. She reached as high as his waist and was about as wide as one of his legs. She was armed only with a bowie knife.

How can she possibly fight this monster? Frank thought despairingly. He stepped forward, but felt a restraining hand on his arm. He looked down to see Feather shaking her head at him.

"But we have to help her!" he said. It came out as a whisper.

"She is the Canowiki," Feather whispered back. "Thou wilt only be a hindrance to her."

Frank looked up at the sky. There wasn't a cloud in sight. Whatever happened, he would see it all.

If the monster could have laughed, he surely would have laughed at the sight of the girl brandishing her knife. Yet he did not. He examined her, tilting his head slightly, as if bemused and curious. It was her demeanor that he assessed; she stood as if unmovable, as if she fully intended to defeat him. Therefore, he considered the possibility.

He swung a massive fist at her head in a motion so fast that Frank caught only the end of the swing and cried out after it was over. Virginia ducked, moving to one side, and yet, she seemed to have barely moved.

"Skooooo! Cooooom!" the creature rumbled, and stepped toward her. She ran at him and darted between his legs. Then she climbed onto his back, scrambling upward by using his fur for handholds. He twisted and spun, but her swift blade kept him from dislodging her. Reaching his shoulder, she dug the point of her knife into his right arm socket. He gave a bellow and swung at her with his other arm, and almost connected. Virginia leapt away, landing on her feet.

She ran.

He lumbered after her, if such a fast movement could be called lumbering. Virginia was ten steps ahead of him, but with every stride, he drew closer. She clambered onto the derrick, swinging on the chain till she could grab one of the struts. There, she adjusted the chain in her hands as she watched the creature approach.

She waited till he reached the bottom of the chain's arc before leaping, the chain clutched tight in her small hands as she swooped toward him. The monster grabbed for her and missed, and then she swung past him.

Swinging round and round, fast and faster, she wrapped the chain around his upper arm, swinging under, then up and over it, until the chain was wrapped securely around the wounded limb. Twice more she swung while the monster howled and tried to catch her. Each time, she avoided his grasp.

Dropping to the ground, she ran behind the derrick. The Skoocoom turned to chase after her. The other end of the chain was hanging near the top of the structure, and she jumped up and grabbed it. The chain's slack was quickly taken up as it rushed across the wood with a *rurrring* sound, and then Virginia was hanging in midair. The creature moved toward her, then suddenly stopped.

His arm was extended behind him, and slightly upward. As Virginia put her full weight on the chain, it became even tighter. Blood streamed down the creature's dark fur. The beast's other hand was only inches from Virginia, but the pain of his bound arm kept him from getting nearer. Virginia turned her head toward her friends, and a signal was passed.

"*Now* we help," Feather said, and she sprinted toward Virginia, followed closely by Jean Baptiste. With one flying leap, Feather caught hold of the chain, adding her slim weight to it...just in time, for the monster had decided that he could stand the pain and was pulling against the chain, his bound arm raised awkwardly behind him. He managed to get within inches of Virginia.

Then Jean was there, jumping higher than both of the girls and grabbing the chain right above Virginia's whitened knuckles.

Now the creature was frantically struggling, howling and spinning around, but instead of freeing himself, he was only getting more tangled. Frank hesitated below the friends, looking for a way to add his weight to theirs, for there was no way he could jump high enough to grab the chain without knocking one of them off.

He scrambled up the timbers of the derrick, finding handholds where he never would have thought possible, at times bracing himself between the struts, stretched out in midair, amazed he was still aloft.

He looked up at where the chain passed over the top of the derrick, and as he felt himself slipping, he leapt and grabbed it. His weight pulled the chain down only another couple of inches, but it was enough. If Frank thought the creature was making a racket before, he hadn't heard anything yet. The deep, booming voice became an ear-splitting scream.

Suddenly, all the tension on the chain was released. Frank fell, still holding onto the now rapidly sliding chain, and saw, below him, that Virginia and the others had crumpled to the ground. He hurtled toward them and managed to twist himself to one side before he landed on them.

He hit the ground hard, and couldn't breathe. He was certain that a splinter had stabbed into his chest, for he felt a heavy weight there.

The monster is loose! he thought, panicked. He couldn't move. Then he saw Virginia standing over him, looking concerned. She checked him over for injuries. Finally, she smiled and took his face in her hands. She impulsively kissed him on his forehead.

"You'll be fine," she said, seeming embarrassed.

As if she had released the bonds around his chest, Frank gulped in a mouthful of air. He gasped for a few moments, then rose to one elbow.

The beast was nowhere to be seen.

But hanging above Frank's head was the monster's long arm, torn from his shoulder, swinging gently in the wind.

Chapter Eighteen

The beast's arm swung from the chain, the breeze scattering drops of blood. Someone took it down, and once it was on the ground, the limb seemed even bigger than it had before, longer than a tall man and nearly as thick around. It was covered in black hair, and the long fingers were clawed. There was dried blood on the hand and up the forearm. The limb had come off at the socket, and bone protruded from amongst the gristle.

It was flesh and bone, though; that was incontrovertible. That was a relief, for most of the men in the party had begun to believe that it was a demon attacking them, that a creature from Hell itself had risen from the ground to take them away. Dave Martin was barely recognizable. Harold Simmons and Alan Percy were also dead, their bodies torn apart, their heads crushed. The two men wounded in the attack on the Miwok village had been left in the middle of camp while the others scrambled to get away.

The ranchers were not as joyous at the beast's defeat as might have been expected, for they were remembering the lost, and fearing repercussions.

Most of the men were sure that all that had happened was retribution, believing the worst because of their guilt. They all knew, by then, that Indians hadn't slaughtered the miners. They all realized that they had attacked the wrong people; innocent people, even if they were godless savages. The ranchers were decent folk in their day-to-day lives, but mob fever and gold fever had transformed them into vigilantes.

Most of the ringleaders were gone. Henry Newton stood alone and uncharacteristically quiet. His men had been wiped out. Thomas was still a pale shadow of himself. Preacher MacLeod, the eldest member of what was left of the search party, seemed to be directing things now.

If Virginia, Feather, and Jean had been apart from the ranchers before, now the distance was a gulf. Anger burned in Frank until he realized the men weren't shunning them out of contempt, but out of awe. The distance was attributable to their respect for the trio as much as to their fear of them. To his surprise, Frank was included with the three of them, for the men had seen how he had joined in the attack on the monster.

They crossed the river at dawn. Partridge and Persimmons lashed the severed arm of the Skoocoom onto one of the spare horses. Three more of the horses were given to Virginia and her companions. Once they were loaded up, though, no one wanted to be the first to brave the river.

"Well, hell," Sam Partridge said. "If no one else is gonna do it…"

He spurred his reluctant horse into the river and crossed the swift current, landing safely near where Patrick's body lay. The rest followed without incident.

Thomas Whitford was among the last of the party to cross, and then only because Preacher MacLeod guided him. He didn't speak; he hadn't spoken since Patrick's death the night before. His gaze was directed in front of him, unseeing.

Frank watched him make it to the far shore, feeling as though he should have been the one leading his father instead of MacLeod. But his father had not responded to him, while, childlike, he would follow simple instructions from MacLeod. From a distance, Frank watched as the old man was helped down from his saddle. Thomas stood over the body of his son. MacLeod pulled a shovel off a packhorse and started digging a grave farther up the bank.

"I need to help him," Frank said to the others. "Ready?"

Virginia nodded. She turned to mount her horse, but hesitated when no one else moved.

Feather and Jean Baptiste were standing nearby, Jean with his hand on her shoulder.

"We are not going back," Feather said. "I have done what I set out to do. I found the Canowiki—and helped her defeat the Skoocoom." Her eyes found Virginia's. "I will never live among the white man again."

"I'm staying with her," Jean added.

Virginia started to object, but hesitated. Finally, she nodded. "I understand. Will you be safe, Jean?"

"I have been counted as a white man, because that is what I pretended to be, because I mimicked their clothing and speech," he said. "But I spent the first half of my life as an Indian."

"Then go with my blessing," Virginia said. "I wish I were free to seek my own way, but my job is not done. The werewolves of the town must still be dealt with. That isn't your task; I understand that."

She stepped forward and took Feather into her arms. "I will miss you, Feather."

"Litonya," the Indian girl corrected her. "I will no longer answer to the name the white man gave me."

Virginia just hugged her tighter. Frank had thought Virginia was small, but when she enveloped the smaller, slimmer Indian girl, it emphasized her strong and healthy body. Jean Baptiste waited his turn for a hug and was rewarded by a big one.

"Take care of each other," Virginia said. She turned away and mounted her horse. Frank nodded at the pair, and they waved back. Then they turned and started across the river.

Preacher MacLeod had dug most of the grave by the time Frank was safe on shore. He took the shovel from Preacher MacLeod's hands and finished the job. It felt good to put his muscles to work, to sink a pickaxe into the tougher areas of the ground. They put Patrick's headless torso into the grave and covered him with earth and rocks to keep the wildlife from digging him up. Then the surviving members of the search party stood at the graveside while MacLeod recited the Twenty-third Psalm.

Frank held his trembling father upright. When the brief ceremony was done, he turned the old man gently, as you would a sleepy child, and helped him mount his horse. MacLeod took the reins and led Thomas away.

***

Several hours later, Virginia turned aside, pausing on a gentle slope near the Plumas River. There was a green lea there with red wildflowers rimming the edge. The morning dew was turning into a fine mist, and the river flowed by peacefully.

"Can we stop here for awhile," Virginia asked, "while the others go on?"

"Of course," Frank said, his heart beating faster.

Enough trees surrounded the clearing to create a windbreak. The sun was shining and the ground was sufficiently dry for them to make camp. It was midday, but for once there was no reason to push onward. Starting the fire took some doing, but they soon had enough of a blaze to keep it going, even with the damp firewood. Frank got up and pulled the last of his food from the saddlebag. He handed Virginia part of a loaf of bread and his waterskin, and dared to plop down next to her.

Virginia sat tantalizingly close to Frank as they enjoyed the fire's warmth in silence.

He wanted so many things: to take her in his arms, to hold her, to lie back and listen to the murmuring river with her. But something made him hold back. *How does she feel about me?* he wondered.

He looked inside himself and realized he held her in the same awe as the rest of the men did because of what she had done. But he'd come to know her, so what he felt toward that warrior aspect of her seemed to be distinct from what he felt toward the girl herself. The hero was the Canowiki, as Feather would say; the girl was Virginia, a straightforward, brave young woman who loved her friends. But, he admitted to himself, really, they were both her.

One thing was for certain. She was never going to be like other girls.

It had never occurred to Frank that he could meet a woman stronger and more capable in a fight than he was. He realized, somewhat to his surprise, that it didn't bother him.

Virginia was a wonder, true, but she was also a young woman, and he could help protect her, could help fulfill her needs. And that's what he would do—he would help her on her journey, wherever it led.

If she would have him.

How can I be feeling this way with my brother barely in the ground? Frank wondered. *With James still missing?* His grief and desire became one large tangle of emotion, his heart aching with it.

"I'm sorry about your brother," Virginia said, as if reading his mind. "He was a brave man."

Frank didn't answer. He sensed she had not liked Patrick. She had heard the men talking about the massacre at the village and blaming much of it on him. But she must know that Frank had loved Patrick, despite their differences.

"I...I feel...That is, I shouldn't..." she stuttered, so unlike the confident woman he had come to know. She paused, took a deep breath, and tried again. "I shouldn't be feeling what I'm feeling for you right now. Not now, when you have suffered such a loss."

Frank turned toward her in amazement. Could it be true? Was she feeling the same way he was?

He brushed her cheek with his fingertips, and she turned, finally meeting his gaze. She buried her face in the hollow of his neck with a sigh. He tightened his hold and drew her closer.

Somehow, love gave meaning to the loss. That was good; otherwise, he'd be like his father, who felt only desolation and emptiness. The love of this girl could save him from that devastation, Frank knew.

"Virginia," he breathed, and kissed the top of her head. "When you walked up to the Skoocoom, I thought you would die and I would never get to hold you like this."

She looked up then and they stared into each other's eyes for a long time. Then, slowly, her eyes closed and their lips met in a long, deep kiss.

Then she pulled away. "We can't," she said sadly. "I want to, but we can't. Your father will need you."

"Virginia..."

"No, Frank," she said. "It can never be. I am a Canowiki. I can never be like other girls. I can't go home with you and be a rancher's wife."

I don't care! he wanted to shout, but he kept silent. She was right. Without Patrick...without James...his father would need him.

But though she had pulled away from him, he couldn't help but notice that her gaze lingered on him whenever he wasn't looking.

There had to be a way.

***

In the foothills of the Sierra Nevada, Litonya and Jean Baptiste also stopped early for the night. They made a fire and sat on opposite sides of the flames.

"I hate being a Skinwalker," he said after a long silence. "It was not my choice. I've never wanted to kill anyone."

Litonya looked at him gravely. "I have," she said.

She got up and went to his side. When she sat down, she fit comfortably into the curve of his arm. They kissed, for how long, Litonya couldn't tell. It seemed forever, and yet only an instant.

Litonya rested her forehead in the crook of his shoulder, sighing deeply.

"What's wrong?" Jean asked.

"I am not worried about thee being a Skinwalker, as long as thou hidest it," she said. "But I fear my people will not accept thee because thou art a white man."

He laughed. "So I can be a wolf, but not a white man?"

"I am serious," she said.

"But I am as Indian as you are," he protested. "Well, I'm half Indian."

She gave him a small smile. "Perhaps by blood. But thou art not like me. Thou thinkest like a white man."

He began to protest, but she set her fingers on his lips. Then the fingers curled in a come-hither sign, and he moved toward her, and they kissed again. "I will make them see..." she murmured.

In the morning, Litonya found herself comfortably settled in Jean's arms, and it felt as if she'd always been there, as if she'd spent a hundred mornings being held by him.

"Feather..." she heard him say as he awoke.

"Hush," she answered. "I am Litonya now."

"Sorry," he muttered. "I'll try harder to remember."

They set out before the sun was an hour above the horizon. They followed the same trails they had used in the days before; they were drying out now. The gray rock cliffs were dry already, and the ponderosas' bark was turning from dark red to soft orange. They were glad of the horses, and they rode companionably, and without their guard up.

So they were caught by surprise when several Miwok braves appeared before them on the path. Litonya recognized Lokni, the one the white men called Roman. He was probably the chief now, she realized. He was the nephew of Chief Honon and a renowned warrior.

The Indians walked quickly toward them. They didn't even look at Litonya. They bypassed her and went directly to Jean Baptiste. They pulled him roughly from the saddle, knives in their hands.

"Stop!' she cried in her own language. "He is one of The People!"

Lokni grabbed Jean by the hair and prepared to cut his throat. He stopped at the last moment, then twisted Jean's head to one side, letting him go with a disgusted sound.

Jean managed not to cry out in pain. He rose, holding his throat. "I am Apache," he said in English, not knowing the language Litonya and the others spoke.

Lokni stared at him for a long moment before speaking to Litonya in Miwok. "I don't care. He has lived too long among them."

Litonya slid off her horse and ran to Jean's side. "Are you going to kill *all* the white men?" she asked.

"Was he there?" Lokni demanded. "Was he one of those who attacked the village?

"No," she said. "He was with me. I swear it."

Lokni turned to the other braves, who gave their adamant opinions. Though she couldn't make out the conversation, Litonya could tell they were opposed to letting Jean live. When Lokni turned toward them again, the knife was clenched tightly in his fist. Litonya used the last and only argument she had left.

"I am bound to him," she said. "He is mine. We have become one."

Lokni stopped at this, and stared at Jean Baptiste as if seeing him for the first time. He didn't look impressed. "*Him?*" was all he said, but a world of disgust was contained in that one word.

"He will be allowed to live…for now," Lokni said reluctantly. "But when we arrive back at camp, it must be approved by the elders. I am not yet chief."

Litonya breathed easily again. He was confident enough to say "not yet," as though his being accepted as chief was a foregone conclusion. It was a troubling thought, for Lokni had always been more aggressive than Chief Honon. But perhaps when he held that authority, he would see, as the former chief had seen, that there were too many of the white men and they were too well armed to fight.

"Thank you, Lokni," she said. They were safe for now. He would not go back on his word.

"Why are you not with the Canowiki?" he asked abruptly, still displeased.

"She fought the Skoocoom and defeated him," Litonya said. "My duty was done."

"The girl killed it?" he asked. "By herself?"

"We helped," Litonya said. "Jean Baptiste and I."

Lokni seemed to realize that she hadn't answered his question. He repeated, "The girl *killed* it? The Ts'emekwes is dead?"

"He is gravely wounded," Litonya answered. "He will not attack us again."

"Why are you so certain?" Lokni demanded.

Litonya suddenly felt uneasy.

"Chief Honon was wrong to seek the Canowiki," Lokni said. "The Ts'emekwes were never our enemy, as long as we left them alone."

Litonya didn't argue with him. She didn't mention the attack on the village that had precipitated her quest. If the white man hadn't come to mutilate the earth in his search for the yellow metal, the Skoocooms would have left them alone. "It is done," she said. "The Ts'emekwes is defeated. He is gravely wounded. He will not confront us again."

"You are wrong," Lokni answered. "If it was only the one, or even him and the white child, then perhaps we would be safe. But there is another."

"Another Skoocoom?"

"The mother of the others," Lokni said. "She is bigger and stronger than the one who attacked us. Our people have moved our village to the far borders of our territory. We hope that she will inflict her vengeance on those who harmed her children, not on us."

Litonya was stunned. They'd known about the white-haired Skoocoom, but they had always thought there were only the two of them. Now it made sense. Somewhere, there had to be a mother of the child. "I have to go back," she said. "I have to help the Canowiki."

"Go!" Lokni said. "But don't come back with the half-breed. He is not welcome here."

"You forget," she said softly. "I, too, was raised by white men."

Lokni didn't respond at first. Then he looked her in the eyes, and she felt her heart sink at the coldness in his voice. "I did not forget," he said.

Chapter Nineteen

Frank was in no hurry to return to town, and it seemed to him that Virginia wasn't eager to return either. He recalled how she had been treated by the townsfolk and became indignant in retrospect, even though he'd been one of the people who had shunned her.

From now on, he vowed, *I won't allow anyone to treat her with disrespect in my presence.*

Virginia surprised him again by appearing in a heavily worn and stained set of men's clothing the next morning. Not one of the boldest Eastern girls of his acquaintance would dream of appearing so, but oddly, it suited her, especially given her preference for riding astride the horse.

She was a strong and capable young woman, and it would have been a shame to ask her to conform to convention, especially when that convention made no sense. This girl was unlike any Frank had ever known, completely feminine, yet as tough and capable as a man. Actually, he'd always suspected the women around him hid their unconventional thoughts and feelings, as well as their own capabilities. Virginia made no effort to act "ladylike," and yet she was completely captivating.

They stopped twice along the way, dangling their feet in the cold waters of the river, taking turns sharing their life stories. Up until that horrible winter in the mountains of the Sierra Nevada, Virginia's life hadn't been that different from any other emigrant girl's, but now it was forever changed.

Frank didn't scoff as she described how the werewolves caused the Donner Party's troubles. He listened to her tell of the growing hunger and cold, and though it wasn't that chilly for a fall night, he shivered in sympathy. "I'm going to hunt them down," she said, setting her jaw in a way that he was beginning to recognize. When she did that, she meant what she said. "I will find all the werewolves who preyed on us in our helplessness, and they will pay."

"Not today, I hope," Frank joked.

Virginia laughed, and some of the tension went out of her. "No, I've done enough for today."

When they arrived at the outskirts of Bidwell's Bar, it was almost dark, and the streets were deserted. The only lights and sounds came from the saloon.

"Strange," Frank mused. "When I was here last, this was a thriving town. Murphy was just putting up his saloon, and new families were arriving. But Father did mention that things were changing."

"There's a reason for that," Virginia said darkly.

There must have been a fire roaring in the saloon's huge fireplace, because the front doors were wide open, despite the autumn chill. Frenzied shadows from inside were being cast into the street. Virginia fell silent as they approached.

"What's wrong?" Frank asked.

"I'm pretty sure the owner of this saloon sent two of his employees after me," she said.

He reined in his horse. "After you? Why would he do that?"

"Because he meant to kill me," Virginia said.

"But why?"

"Because they were werewolves, Frank."

As that sank in, Frank realized what it meant. "That must mean...then Bidwell is a werewolf, too?"

"That's what I believe," Virginia said, stopping in the darkness of the street.

Frank stared at the light spilling out of the saloon's open doors, and saw movement inside and heard laughter. "He can't do much to us right now," he said. "Not with so many people around."

"Unfortunately, neither can I." Virginia gave him a sideways smile.

Frank nodded. They put up their horses in the stable in the back of the saloon before approaching the door and stepping into the middle of the revelry.

Virginia tensed, her slim body seeming to gain an inch in height. "What is it?"

"I'm not sure," she said in a low voice.

Most of the people dancing and drinking were strangers. It took awhile to make sense of the chaos, but eventually Frank spotted the remnants of the search party huddled in one corner. Each man had a full glass before him, but none wore an accompanying smile.

"There she is!' came a loud voice. "The hero of the expedition! Here's the little lady who they claim fought a grizzly bear all by herself! Wrapped the beast in chains and tore its leg off, the way I hear it! It's a feat that shall never be forgotten in these parts. Seems almost...unnatural, don't it?"

The loud voice belonged to Bidwell, who stepped from behind the bar with a big smile that did not reach his eyes.

Virginia looked at Frank with raised eyebrows. He glanced over at the men in the corner and caught Preacher MacLeod's eye. The man just shrugged, as if to say, *What else could we tell them?*

"In celebration, the next round of drinks is on the house!" Bidwell called as he stood in front of them, beaming.

The room erupted in celebration. Bidwell returned to the bar, poured a couple of drinks, and brought them over to Virginia and Frank. Frank took his and downed it. He didn't drink often, but this seemed to be exactly what he needed. Virginia waved the barkeep off.

"Come now," Bidwell said. "I ain't never heard you were so picky about what you drink, Miss Reed. A big, strong girl such as yourself can drink with us boys, can't you?"

Virginia flushed.

Frank stepped forward, took the other drink from Bidwell, and downed it, too. Then, fortified, he leaned down toward the shorter but much broader man. "She doesn't want to drink …with you."

Bidwell pushed him away, so fast Frank didn't see it coming. By the time he recovered his balance, Virginia and the stout man were toe to toe, and appeared to be ready to come to blows. A hush fell over the room.

"I'm sorry," Frank said, intervening. "The offer of free drinks was generous of you, but we're exhausted from our trip."

"Yeah, sure," Bidwell said. He glared at Virginia, but his words were soft. "I can understand that."

Frank took Virginia by the arm and led her to the corner where the other survivors watched in miserable silence.

"Where's my father?" Frank asked Preacher MacLeod. "Is he all right?"

"He's feeling better," MacLeod said. "He's taking it hard, but he seemed to come back to himself about halfway to town. Finally remembered that he has a surviving son. He wanted to wait up for you, Frank, but I made him go to bed. Bidwell gave us the whole top floor, free of charge. But he insisted we stay and join the celebration. Most of us didn't feel like we could refuse."

The preacher downed the drink before him, and Frank noted that his speech was slurred. "Besides, he's been pouring us whiskey, and I was never one to turn down free drinks, God help me." The final words of his little speech were muttered under his breath, almost a prayer.

One of Bidwell's men brought them all another round. Virginia gave him a hard stare, and every muscle seemed to be at alert, as if she was gathering herself for action. The man walked away, and she relaxed slightly.

Frank leaned over and whispered, "Is he one of them?"

"I think all of Bidwell's men are Skinwalkers," she said.

Frank looked around the table at the last few survivors of the search party: Partridge, who owned the smallest spread and worked for the Whitcombs most of the time. Johnny Hawkins, the young man from New York. Gerald Persimmons, the old, weathered ranch hand. Preacher MacLeod, who had obviously been knocking back drinks all night. Henry Newton sat a table by himself, his bullet-shaped head down, staring at the bottom of his glass, his son still missing and all his men gone. And there was Frank's father, who—he hoped—was safe upstairs.

These battered few were the last seven survivors of the once strong and vibrant group of men who had volunteered to help find Frank's missing brother. Seeing how few of them were sitting there made it all come home to Frank, who was overcome with a strong sense of sorrow.

"Why is Bidwell being so nice?" Virginia asked, interrupting Frank's reverie. "Why is he giving us free drinks? He doesn't strike me as a generous soul."

"Just showing off his power," Partridge said. "The son of a bitch is a bully. The man has ruined this town."

"But he doesn't need to off show his power," Virginia pointed out. "He already owns the town, top to bottom."

"Hell," Persimmons said, "who cares, as long as he keeps giving us drinks?"

"Don't seem right, though," Hawkins said. "Most of our friends are dead, and we just sit here getting drunk."

"Getting numb," Persimmons corrected him. "I don't mind admitting I want to forget some of the things I saw." He lifted another drink to his lips before adding, "And some of the things I did."

"Yeah, well I've had enough," Partridge said, getting up. "I'm going to bed." His chair made a loud scraping noise, and it seemed as though everyone in the room looked over at them.

Bidwell came over, a bottle in his hand, and put his arm on Partridge's shoulder, applying downward pressure. Partridge's legs gave out on him, and he sprawled awkwardly back into his chair.

"Sit down, my friend," Bidwell said. "Drink up. This entire celebration is in honor of you and your friends. Seems kind of ungrateful to up and leave."

Partridge flushed and looked ready to object, but there was something in Bidwell's eyes that made him look away. He took the proffered drink and drank it down, shakily.

Virginia examined the room as Bidwell walked away. Then she leaned over to Frank. "I don't like it," she said quietly. "Something's going on."

"You think they mean us harm?"

"Bidwell's been encouraging some of the crowd to leave and discouraging others. Most of those who remain, besides us, have a strange aura about them. Unless I'm mistaken, they are all Skinwalkers, the whole lot of them."

It was as if Frank suddenly saw the room with Virginia's eyes. The celebration looked false, a sham. The glittering eyes of the revelers kept sneaking glances at the subdued survivors of the rescue party as though waiting for something.

As a final group of men and women left, Frank noticed Bidwell walk from behind the bar to shoo them the final few feet. "See you tomorrow night!" he cried heartily. He closed the barroom doors and locked them. Turning, he looked Frank in the eye. The smile was gone.

That was the signal.

A dozen men were suddenly removing their clothing.

"Wha' th' hell?" Preacher MacLeod's words were slurred. He tried to stand up, but fell back into his chair.

"Where are your guns?" Virginia asked Partridge desperately.

"Bidwell took them away," Persimmons answered instead. "Said he preferred not to have firearms around when the drinking got heavy."

"Do you have knives?" Virginia demanded. She reached behind her and pulled a bowie knife from its belt sheath at the small of her back.

"What the hell do we need knives for? I don't see any reason..." Hawkins began. He'd had his back to the room, and as he turned around, his voice trailed off and he reached for the small of his back, too, and drew the biggest knife that Frank had ever seen. "Got this in St. Louis, a genuine blade made by Bowie himself!"

Aw, hell, Frank thought as he pulled out his pocketknife with a grimace. Not enough.

He picked up the nearest chair and slammed it against the table, breaking it apart. He grabbed one of the legs and swung it. It had a solid heft. As he turned to face the Skinwalkers, there were crashing and splintering noises behind him as several other men broke up chairs.

The small group of survivors turned as one to see men transforming into beasts of nightmare before their disbelieving eyes.

"What now?" Partridge asked. A few moments before, he had sounded resigned. Now his voice had an edge of panic.

"What's going on?" Hawkins shouted at the sight. The big knife he'd been so proud of moments before dropped onto the floor.

There was no escape. The only two windows were on either side of the double doors, and between the windows and the ranchers were a dozen snarling beasts.

"You might want to pick up your weapon," Virginia said to Hawkins, who gulped and snatched up the blade. "These creatures *can* be killed. Even with only a knife. I've done it."

Bidwell came out from behind the bar and removed his apron, then his clothes. He stood naked in front of them, raised his arms, and grunted. His arms and then his legs extended with a crackling sound. Bidwell fell to his hands and knees, which weren't hands and knees anymore. His muzzle protruded from his lower face with another cracking sound, accompanied by the slithering of moist skin.

Frank looked away. The light of the fire sent eerie shadows across the bar and up the walls, revealing the evil within the saloon. Jerking and snarling, the beasts pushed against each other, as if reveling in their transformation and the feast they expected.

***

Virginia wished she was alone. It complicated her task, worrying about Frank and the others. They were outnumbered. If they'd had guns, it might have made a difference, but hers were in her saddlebags, and Bidwell had taken away the men's weapons.

There was still one way that they could win. If she could kill Bidwell, the others would flee, she was sure of it.

She ignored her instinct to plant herself at Frank's side. He and the others would have to survive long enough on their own for her to get the job done.

With Bidwell in the center, the werewolf pack was Turning.

Virginia didn't wait. She rushed them while the Skinwalkers were still glistening with gristle and raw muscle. Her knife plunged straight down into the skull of a wolf in mid-Change. The malformed creature thudded to the floor. It had the body of a man and the head of wolf.

Frank realized what she was doing. "Attack before they shift all the way!" he shouted, rushing forward.

The nearest wolf lunged toward him, attacking with half-formed jaws. Virginia fought the impulse to turn aside to help Frank. He jumped on the werewolf's slick back, grabbing it by the neck and sawing at its throat with his tiny blade. Luckily the knife was sharp and struck the jugular, turning the creature's howls to a gurgling sound. It stumbled, then its front legs collapsed and it rolled onto its side, whining like an injured dog.

Another wolf lunged toward him. He batted it away with his club. It grunted and rolled, but got right back up.

None of the other men followed Frank and Virginia into the fray. They were either too frightened or still frozen in disbelief. Instead, they watched as the ten remaining wolves retreated and continued to Turn.

Virginia was able to get close to another half-Changed werewolf, striking with quick stabbing blows into its chest. The wolf-man quivered, jumping a yard into the air. Its legs collapsed under it. Still twitching, its back legs pushed it sideways across the floor.

But now the biggest wolf transposed himself between Virginia and the other wolves, his transformation much swifter than the others. She stepped back and they eyed each other. Bidwell's fur was red and thick, and he was wide across the chest. Unlike the body he wore as a man, there was no fat on this creature, only muscles swelling at the shoulders and thighs.

He snarled, and it seemed to Virginia that the building shook from the vibration

.***

Virginia looked tiny beside the giant red wolf.

Frank leapt to her side without faltering.

She glanced at him, and there was a welcoming gratitude in her face that made his heart swell and fill with courage. But as she turned away, he saw the hopelessness that passed for a moment over her features, and he quailed.

If this brave girl despairs, he thought, *we have no chance.*

Someone was behind him, and Frank whirled. It was Preacher MacLeod, brandishing a knife of his own.

"They're going to kill us anyway," MacLeod said grimly. "Heaven awaits those who fight the Beast."

The other survivors hung back. Frank couldn't blame them. *If not for Virginia,* he thought, *I would be hiding under the table.*

The wolves separated again, and Frank found himself surrounded. Something snapped at his legs, barely missing. He couldn't move forward or back.

He assumed something similar was happening to Virginia. He was wrong.

Virginia had ignored the other wolves and was charging Bidwell.

With growls that nearly froze Frank in place, the rest of the wolves abandoned their attack to rush to their leader's side. It was as if a signal had been passed among the pack, and now that Virginia had committed herself, isolated herself, they were focusing on her.

Frank rushed forward to strike at the wolves surrounding Virginia, and he saw MacLeod leap forward at his side as both groups rallied to the defense of their leaders.

MacLeod slashed one of the wolves, which turned and leaped for his throat. Frank was unable to help; he was struggling to defend Virginia from the wolf pack. He stabbed his knife into a wolf's hindquarters and swung his club at another.

He couldn't get to her.

"Hey, come get me!" Frank shouted at the wolves, brandishing his pocketknife. One of them broke away, snarling, but the other three kept heading for Virginia.

"Behind you, Virginia!" he cried in warning as the wolf leapt for him. He tumbled to the ground, the heavy weight of the creature on him, its foul breath in Frank's face as it lunged for his neck...but the wolf missed, snapping its jaws shut mere inches from his throat.

Partridge had entered the fray. The old man had the monster around the throat. The wolf reared up, dislodging him. Then the werewolf squirmed around and its jaws closed on the rancher's throat. There was the snap of bone breaking, and Partridge fell and went still.

Frank spun to cover Virginia's back, but there were too many wolves between them, and he cried out in frustration. The wolves stopped, forming a half circle with Virginia at the center and Frank on the outside.

Virginia didn't take her eyes off Bidwell, despite the threats surrounding her. Knife in hand, she stared him down.

The challenge was obvious. The giant wolf gave a low growl, and his packmates slunk away.

Frank slashed wildly. The wolves jumped away, easily evading his blade, and circled him.

Out of the corner of his eye, he saw Virginia and the big wolf moving toward each other in a blur. They seemed to merge, and then both fell back as if pushed. Both of them were injured, but soon they were moving toward each other again, faster than before.

Then Frank was surrounded and fighting for his life. He whirled around as first one wolf and then another snapped at the tendons of his ankles. He wasn't going to be able to keep it up much longer. He was a little slower with each second that passed, and the scent of blood made the wolves faster and more frenzied.

Virginia fell.

Frank heard her cry out and, ignoring the wolves at his heels, ran toward her. There was a ripping sound as the fabric of his shirt was torn. Virginia was lying on her back, and the giant wolf was crouching to spring.

Virginia started to get up, but she would be too late. Frank felt as if he was moving in slow motion.

Bidwell's massive body jerked slightly, and a second later there was a loud bang. He dropped to the ground and rolled away. Then the red wolf was running for long bar at the side of the room, the wolf pack at his heels. Another shot rang out as the monster disappeared around the massive bar, and a section of it splintered where the bullet struck it.

Frank turned to see the stocky form of Henry Newton facing the bar, a smoking pistol in each hand.

***

It was the werewolves that finally shook Newton from his lethargy.

Oliver was dead. Newton couldn't remember when he'd realized that fact; it hadn't been a single revelation, just a slowly dawning awareness that there was no other possibility. One by one, his men died under the onslaught of an impossible monster, but Newton didn't care. All his hopes, all his careful plans: it had all been for Oliver and future generations of Newtons.

All gone; and none of it mattered. Nothing mattered. Henry Newton hated everyone equally now, Indian or white man. He despised them all.

He rose from his chair as the fight became desperate. He had half a mind to shoot Frank Whitcomb, or that interfering girl, Virginia Reed.

Hell, he just wanted to kill someone...or something. He still had his own gun, and he hadn't given up his son's blood-smeared pistol, either.

He pointed Oliver's pistol at the giant wolf and fired. He could swear he hit the beast, but the creature fled. Newton took careful aim, but the next shot only succeeded in splintering the end of the bar.

"I don't give up my weapons for no one," he growled.

He paused to reload.

***

Partridge lay on the floor, unmoving. MacLeod was on his side, crawling toward the back, trailing blood. Hawkins stood beside him, his giant bowie knife dripping crimson. Persimmons was still alive, but bleeding from bites on his head and shoulders.

How long does it take to Turn? Frank wondered. *How long before Persimmons becomes one of them?*

The old ranch hand sounded completely human when he said, "Mr. Newton, I never much liked you, but if you got bullets for that thing, how about you load it up and fire at will?"

A naked Bidwell emerged from behind the counter, seeming untouched, with a revolver in either hand. The rest of his pack swirled around him.

"Here I was, fighting fair," the barkeep said. "Using a gun ain't fair. But if that's the way it has to be…"

Newton fumbled with the gun, trying desperately to reload, and all the while, Bidwell and his wolf pack came closer. He finally threw the useless weapon at Bidwell, his face contorting with hate.

"Be damned, foul creature!" he cried. "My son is gone. What do I care…" and then half of his face simply disappeared and a red cloud floated over the remains of his body. He fell forward, and his huge torso slammed into the floor.

Bidwell dropped the empty guns onto the floor and said, "Now, where were we?"

He Turned again, quickly, almost casually.

Virginia was hunched over, breathing deeply, claw marks on her arms and face. The knife hung at her side, as if she didn't have the strength to lift it.

Frank wanted to fall to his knees in exhaustion, but Virginia straightened, staring her enemy defiantly in the face, as if the odds hadn't changed, as if they weren't outnumbered and overwhelmed.

Frank swayed but managed to stay upright. The wolves lowered their heads, slinking forward as a pack this time. This time, there would be no individual skirmishes. This was to be a coordinated action by a pack that hunted together, in which each wolf could anticipate the reactions of his packmates. They would begin by separating out the weakest of their prey.

It took Frank a few moments to realize the weak link was *him*.

The wolves may have sensed Virginia would fight to protect him, making her a defender, not an attacker. Frank wanted to yell to her to forget about him, but he knew it was useless. It was all useless. There were too many of them.

The wolves circled him, crouching to spring, their eyes never leaving him as he stood stock still, uncertain which way to move. As he'd feared she would, Virginia jumped in front of him, but she could only engage the first wolf while knocking the second wolf to one side. Seven other wolves flowed around her fight, fixating on Frank. He raised his club desperately, realizing that he might at best get in a single blow before they were upon him.

This is it, Frank thought desperately.

***

Virginia heard a crashing sound from the front of the saloon, but for several moments, she was so intent on the battle that it barely registered. Then the left front window shattered.

Everyone, wolf and human alike, stared around the room in confusion, trying to make sense of what had just happened.

A slim young Indian girl was climbing through the broken window.

"Feather?" Virginia cried out.

A few moments later, a gray wolf jumped in after her.

Their sudden appearance was so startling that Bidwell hesitated in his attack, and then retreated to the bar again, as if to try to make sense of the newcomers. Again, the wolves retreated with him, surrounding the big red wolf.

In wolf form, Jean Baptiste raced to Frank and Virginia's side, where he turned and growled menacingly at the wolves by the bar. Litonya also ran toward them, and despite the desperation of that moment, Virginia couldn't help but smile at her.

Johnny Hawkins came up beside them with his big bowie knife.

"Persimmons?" Virginia asked.

The young man shook his head.

The five survivors turned to face the wolf pack, still outnumbered, but everyone sensing, both wolves and humans, that the odds had somehow changed.

Chapter Twenty

Grendel's heavy tread, so unlike his usual stealthy animal movement, woke me. The branches covering the cave exploded inward, and the huge beast nearly toppled in, but he regained his footing at the last minute. He breathed heavily and groaned; then, as if realizing he was home, he howled, a strangled, wounded cry I had never before heard from him.

"Skoooo coooom! Skoooo coooom!" The cave seemed to reverberate and echo like the inside of a bell.

Grendel stood in the cave's front chamber and howled like a child in pain. There was something strange about his profile, as if he had grown thinner. Then I realized that he was missing one of his arms. His remaining hand clutched the terrible wound in his shoulder, and even in the nighttime dimness, I could see the blood flowing. Answering howls echoed from below. With a start, I realized it was not a single howl, as from Hrothgar; another, even louder response shook the cave floor. I lay still and quiet, hoping none of the creatures would remember me.

The albino child came from the back of the cave, running to Grendel and grabbing him around the waist. Grendel's howls muted slightly, as if he was comforted by this. Then came the heavy, terrifying tread of another creature. The bones that lined the chamber cracked under the weight of this newcomer. She—for it was clear even in the dim light that it was an older female—strode over to the wounded beast. Grendel wanted comfort, but the female just stared at him, as if trying to gauge how hurt he really was, like a mother with a child who came running to her with a skinned knee.

I realized that this was Grendel and Hrothgar's Mother. Both of the smaller creatures, if they could be called small, were her progeny. Where the male parent is, I have no idea. I sense it is not part of the family group. Perhaps males wander alone and only come in contact with others of their kind to mate.

Finally, the Mother took Grendel into her arms. His head turned against her huge breasts, and I saw his eyes grow large as he saw me, remembering I was there.

"Skooo coooom!" he cried as pulled away from his Mother to get at me. I didn't even raise my hands, knowing escape was impossible and hoping for a quick end.

Then Hrothgar was there, standing between us, holding his palms up beseechingly, but he simply didn't have the mass to stop his older brother in time, nor did Grendel show any sign of relenting or slowing down.

I should have been terrified, but a strange calm overcame me. This was the end, then. I'd expected it from the moment I awoke in Grendel's cave. I'd thought all along it would be a violent death, but instead—like Tucker before me—I was dying slowly of starvation, of thirst, of disease—of simply not having enough freedom of movement to give my muscles and mind the necessary vigor of life. Perhaps it was better this way.

A quick death was almost welcome, and though I knew those first moments would be agonizingly painful, it would soon be over, or so I prayed.

The Mother barked a short, simple command, and Grendel stopped as if he had come to the end of a leash. He let out a howl of frustration. The Mother came toward me, but I wasn't reassured by this last-minute reprieve. She stared down at me curiously.

I'd noticed before that Grendel seemed to be crafty, almost adult in his gaze. Hrothgar too, though only a child, displayed intelligence. But the Mother! I stared into the depths of her eyes and had the eerie sense that she could read my thoughts, that she could outthink me or any other human. There was an ancient wisdom there; but overlaying it was anger and a ferocity that gave me no hope of comfort.

"Fire," she said simply. The English word was distinct but thick, as if she had once spoken the language but had almost forgotten how to form the words. She pulled Grendel to her and took his hand away from his wound. She pointed at the bleeding hole and repeated, "Fire."

I nodded in understanding, but then raised my palms as if to say, *I have no fire and no way to make any.*

The Mother snarled something to both Grendel and Hrothgar, and they dutifully retreated to the other side of the cave, staring at me, while she returned to the deep darkness of the back. She returned with a knapsack I'd never seen before. Inside were the contents of a miner's kit, including some rather large matches and fuses, which were probably used to set explosives.

"I need tinder," I said. "Wood."

She uttered another batch of commands and Hrothgar hurried out the entrance.

There was a small hammer inside the pack as well. I hefted it while the Mother watched me. *Don't even try to escape*, said the look she gave me. I shook my head and set the hammer on the ground. Its head was broad, but not as broad as Grendel's wound; still, it would have to do, unless I wanted to use the open flame at the end of a branch. Using the hammer would require more than one application, and I wasn't sure Grendel would sit still for it, or that he wouldn't kill me for inflicting such pain. But it would be the cleanest way to cauterize the wound.

Hrothgar returned with an armful of dry wood that was easy to ignite. Soon I had a small blaze, thanks to the small sacrifice of my shirtsleeve. I built up a fire. I looked around the cavern once, and regretted it. I had not seen, until then, the human skulls, some with hair still attached, or the many little creatures and insects that scurried away from the light. Some of the bones were old and brittle, as if they had been there a hundred years.

I placed the hammer in fire and waited until it glowed red.

The Mother grabbed Grendel almost roughly and made him kneel by the fire. Already, he was glaring at me as if he wanted to kill me. I lifted the hammer gingerly and approached the giant beast. Even standing, I was no more than shoulder high to him. The Mother gave me a short nod and I drew a deep breath.

I pressed the glowing hammer to the center of the wound, where the blood flowed fastest. Grendel raised his head and screamed, and the gold walls seemed to gather the horrible, tortured cry and send it echoing back and forth, again and again, across the cave.

The wound stopped bleeding, but the edges were still raw. Grendel was held in the strong grip of his Mother as she nodded her head toward the fire and the red-hot hammer.

I lifted it again and plunged it deep into the wound. Then Grendel's hand came flying toward the side of my head, and I tried to duck as I thought, *Not again!* But he caught me full on the temple. I fell back against one of the gold walls and into darkness.

I woke later that day and found Hrothgar curled up next to me, regarding me with concerned eyes. I moaned and touched my head, not certain it was still attached after all the knocks it had gotten.

"Friend," I said, and it was as if my head split open from the effort.

"Friend," Hrothgar echoed, and it was as if I was healed, just a little.

Grendel's moans were audible from the back of the cave, and I wondered if my ministrations had done the creature any good.

There was a heavy tread, and when the Mother appeared, the huge chamber suddenly seemed crowded. She stared down at me, and I wondered if this was end, now that I was no longer useful.

Hrothgar left my side and scrambled over to his Mother. He climbed up her legs and body and up to her shoulder, where she nuzzled him. Then she lifted him and gently placed him next to me again. There was a look on her face that was very human: sadness and resignation, and a little fear. But her demeanor was determined. After she put Hrothgar down, she turned and marched out of the cave, and I shuddered.

Without the Mother to protect me, I wasn't sure how long Grendel would let me live.

Whoever had injured Grendel was about to get a visit from his Mother.

I had a feeling she was even stronger and faster than he was.

***

Jean Baptiste sprang at Bidwell, who was surprised by the attack and drew back momentarily. Jean kept coming at him from under the massive wolf's chest, going for the throat. The bigger wolf rose upward on his hind legs, and Jean had to settle for lunging at his flank. Faster than the eye could follow, Bidwell struck out and knocked Jean to the side.

Litonya rushed toward him, but two wolves broke away and waylaid her. She kept them at bay with her knife, but barely.

More wolves were circling Frank, who was fighting back to back with Hawkins. Three others kept Virginia busy, and every time she tried to help Frank, it made her vulnerable.

There was a cry from Hawkins, followed by a thump, and Frank was left to fight alone. He looked away and waited for death. Jean Baptiste was down; the giant wolf had him by the shoulder. Virginia was furiously battling three wolves, but the rest had already passed her, their strange eyes on Frank as they crouched, waiting for an opening so they could spring for his throat.

That moment seemed to last forever.

***

The crash was so massive, so unexpected, that everyone in the room, human and wolf, was thrown off their stride. The entire building shook. A log rolled out of the giant fireplace and lay burning among the combatants, the wagon wheel chandelier swayed, and the wax from the candles splattered onto the floor. There was one more enormous crack and the saloon doors teetered wildly on broken hinges. A cool wind blew through the long room and the fire flared up, sending sparks high into the air.

An enormous shape loomed in the doorway, silhouetted in moonlight. Each footstep echoed like thunder as it entered the dim bar.

Howls broke the stillness as the werewolves backed away, eyes riveted on the creature before them. It was clear they understood three things: that the creature was a fellow predator; that it was an enemy; and that everyone in the room was in danger. Their pack instinct took hold. The wolf that was Bidwell charged the creature while his packmates surrounded it, going for the tendons of the back legs. Once the monster was down, they would make short work of it. No doubt they thought it would be no harder than bringing down a buffalo or an elk.

But this was no common prey. Buffalo and elk didn't think; they reacted by instinct. By the time the wolves launched their attack, the Ts'emekwes had figured out their stratagem. She broke through the circle of wolves, punching one of them so hard that it was flung completely across the room, where it slammed back first into the bar's edge. There was a crack and the wolf slid to the ground. Frank saw life in its eyes, a burning desire to rise and attack, but it couldn't move.

The Skoocoom's back was to the wall, the fireplace to one side of her, so the wolves could no longer get behind her. The pack had no option but to attack from the front, and when they did, two more were flung into the air. One crawled on its front legs, not away from the fight, but back toward it. The other didn't move at all, the fierce light going out of its eyes.

Then there was a moment of stillness. The fire crackled in the sudden quiet, and there were whimpering sounds from the wounded wolf that was dragging itself toward the battle.

The two types of predators examined each other, each the master of their own world, afraid of nothing.

This isn't the same Skoocoom as before, Frank realized with a start. This was obviously a female; her hair was red instead of black, and she still had both arms. Despite being female, this creature was larger than the other. Frank sensed that she was older, much older than the male that had attacked them. But the rage in her eyes was every bit as fierce as that of the Ts'emekwes that Virginia had defeated at the ferry crossing.

This is the Mother, Frank understood instinctively.

The predators measured each other, and it was the werewolves who gave ground.

Bidwell backed away. The other wolves followed him to the broken doors. Bidwell-as-wolf hesitated in the doorway, and, raising his muzzle, howled one last time in defiance. The others joined him in filling the air with howling insolence.

Then they were gone.

Only Virginia still faced the Skoocoom. Litonya lay on the ground, unconscious or dead, bleeding from a gash to the head. Jean Baptiste had turned back into a man when the wolves retreated, revealing a gaping shoulder wound. Ignoring the pain, he knelt at Litonya's side, lifted her over his good shoulder, and carried her from the battlefield.

Frank fell to his knees in despair. This beast was beyond any of them. Upstairs, the humans must be cowering in fear. No townspeople would come to their rescue; the events of this night were beyond them, too. These creatures were things that men hid from, denying their existence so they could carry on with their lives, could continue to believe they were the masters of this world.

The room filled with a terrible stench, and Frank gagged. The Ts'emekwes would attack and they would die. There was no other possibility.

The Skoocoom lumbered forward, her eyes fixed on Virginia. Reacting without thinking, Frank snatched Johnny Hawkins's huge knife off the floor, doing his best to ignore the detached hand that was still clutching it. He caught up to the Skoocoom just as she reached Virginia, who stood waiting. The girl looked defiant, but Frank could see the exhaustion in her face. He stabbed at the creature's back leg, hoping to slow her down or distract her.

Virginia, meanwhile, didn't do what the monster probably expected. She didn't turn tail and run. Instead, she attacked, leaping into the air, pushing off against beast with a double kick. It barely budged the huge creature, but the Skoocoom stepped back and bumped up against Frank, knocking him off his feet and against the burning log that had rolled out of the fireplace.

Frank kicked the log toward the Skoocoom, and it rolled under her raised foot.

The creature tried to catch her balance, but she stumbled on the log and toppled backward. Frank rolled away, just managing to get out from under her. Her head cracked against the stone mantelpiece over the fireplace, shattering it.

The whole building shook from the beast's fall, and she howled as the long red hair on her back and shoulders caught fire. She rolled on the flames till they were out, knocking the tables around like toys.

The hair on the monster's face had burned away on one side, and when she rose and turned toward Frank and Virginia, they saw that under her pelt, she was strikingly human. She had a heavy brow and a wide nose, and her skin was red and black from burns, but her visage could have passed for a human's.

The monster seemed to enlarge, her shoulders bulging and chest expanding, as if the pain and rage had redoubled her strength. She raised her arms, reaching the ceiling. Her face was blistering and oozing, and she was shaking from the pain. She opened her mouth, her huge teeth seeming longer and sharper without the fur to cover them.

"Skooo cooom! Skooo cooom!" she thundered. Virginia and Frank both took a step back, but there was no escape.

The saloon rattled and the floors shook. Frank knew that nothing could stop the creature's next charge. He turned to Virginia to say good-bye, but her eyes were darting about the room as if she was calculating something, as if she had a plan.

She grabbed his ragged sleeve and tugged him toward the long bar on the other side of the room. "Run, Frank!"

She stepped toward the creature, who roared again.

He hesitated, unwilling to leave her alone.

"I'll follow you!" she cried. *"Run, dammit!"*

The floor shook beneath Frank's feet as he sprinted toward the bar. Virginia stood her ground for a moment, and for the first time, the Skoocoom showed caution, slowing down. When Frank had gotten far enough away, Virginia followed him, the Skoocoom lumbering after them. Frank was certain one of those giant hands would close over his head, but then the bar was in front of him, and he vaulted over it. He landed in the narrow space behind the bar, and Virginia landed next to him a second later. She scrambled toward the end of the bar, and he followed her.

The Skoocoom didn't stop and didn't jump over the bar; she went through it. The giant log shattered, breaking in half. The creature slammed into the big mirror behind the bar, and all the glittering bottles of liquor on the shelves there rained down on her, shattering, spraying her with alcohol. For a few short seconds, they smelled the stink of liquor rather than creature.

Without the reflected light from the mirror, the room dimmed. Virginia gripped Frank's arm. He winced at the small woman's unexpected strength, but managed not to cry out. "I need you to lead the Ts'emekwes toward the fireplace," she said, her voice tight and urgent. "Can you do that? Can you make it that far?"

Frank looked at the end of the bar, only a few feet away. Beyond were the shattered doors and escape. He wanted to yell at Virginia to flee. They were foolish to think they could defeat this creature. But then he remembered that Feather...*Litonya* and Jean Baptiste were still among the wounded and that his father was in one of the rooms above. They couldn't leave.

"I'll try," he said grimly.

The Skoocoom shook her head, recovering from the collision.

Frank rounded the end of the bar and sprinted toward the fireplace. He gathered his last strength, more than he'd thought he possessed. The saloon had seemed so much narrower when they'd first come in. Frank ran with all the energy he had, knowing he had nothing to lose.

"Hey, you ugly beast. Come and get me!" he shouted at the top of his lungs.

The creature started after him, making him regret his words, for the Skoocoom accelerated with a fearsome burst of speed. Suddenly, Frank wasn't so sure he would reach the fireplace.

And if I do, what then? he asked himself. *Do I just stand there with a stupid grin on my face?*

He cast a quick glance over his shoulder to see that Virginia had scrambled up to the highest point on the shattered bar.

Then she leaped.

What is she doing?

Her outstretched hands caught the edge of the chandelier, an impossibly long jump. The candles rained down like falling stars, splattering about the floor, splashing hot wax everywhere. Most blinked out, but a few remained lit, starting small fires on the rough wooden planks.

Not that Frank noticed any of this, for the Ts'emekwes grabbed him around the middle, a grotesque smile splitting her half human/half beast face.

Virginia emerged from the billowing smoke feet first, flying through the second half of the expanse directly toward the Skoocoom's back. The beast was completely focused on dangling Frank by one arm, her smile widening as she reached for his leg with her other hand. She didn't see Virginia coming. Then Virginia slammed into the creature's back, right between her shoulder blades.

It wasn't much, perhaps, Virginia's small weight compared to the monster's huge size, but it pushed the creature forward just enough so that she dropped Frank as she toppled into the fireplace again. The alcohol that drenched her fur ignited, and bright fire flashed over her body. It was almost beautiful, the flames of different colors, greens and blues and reds and yellows. The stink that pervaded the room became stronger still, now accompanied by the smell of burning flesh and fur.

The Ts'emekwes screamed, no longer the majestic boom of a battle cry, but the tortured sound of a creature in pain. She rose to her feet, batting at the rainbow flames, but out of the air came more bottles of whiskey and other spirits, shattering against her, spewing out their contents, which flashed into even more flame.

Frank backed away, feeling his own hair singe in the heat. He turned and saw Litonya and Jean on the other side of the room, hurling bottles of alcohol with all their might.

The Skoocoom rose, stumbling toward the open doors, sprawling and rolling, putting out some of the flames as she escaped. But she was still burning as she leaped over the steps and ran screaming down the dark street. Pale faces peered out dark windows in neighboring buildings, frightened but curious, watching as an impossibly huge, manlike being ran by them in flames.

And then it was over, and it was as if Frank's bones melted in his body. He slumped to his knees and pitched forward in exhaustion. He closed his eyes, but didn't quite pass out.

He looked about, expecting the saloon to be in flames, but the fires were sputtering fitfully on the green timber. Citizens were showing up with buckets of water, and when he saw that the problem was being handled, he collapsed.

He felt Virginia's hands on his forehead and cheeks, and murmured "I'm all right" in response.

"Stay here," she whispered into his ear. "I'll check on the others."

Frank nodded. The sense of relief he felt was so strong that he wanted to bask in it for a while. He heard Litonya talking to Jean, urging him to stay awake, and then his father's voice, and footsteps coming toward him, the same comforting, familiar footsteps he'd remembered from childhood.

"Son! Son, are you hurt?" He heard panic in Thomas's brusque voice.

"I'm alive," Frank said, opening his eyes. "A little charred around the edges, but nothing that won't grow back."

His father's eyes held a look of concern Frank hadn't seen since he was a young boy. His son, his "soft" son—now his only son—had fought off demons with only the help of a small woman. That's how Thomas would see it, at least, even if the reality was that Frank had helped *her*. Litonya and Jean likely wouldn't even count in his father's estimation.

"What was it?" Thomas marveled. "Some kind of bear?"

"It was the beast's Mother," Frank said.

"Are there more of them?" his father exclaimed.

Frank shook his head. "No, Father, I don't think there are many of them at all."

***

Less than a day later, all the blame had fallen on Bidwell . He hadn't built the bar; he'd started out as a bartender, working for an Irishman named Murphy who wanted to create a fine establishment, with a theater and grand music. Murphy had disappeared one day, and Bidwell claimed that he'd won the saloon in a poker game. He'd produced the receipt, and everyone ignored the brown stains on the corner of the note. Bidwell and his companions began buying up the town, for far less than the properties were actually worth. He didn't overtly threaten anyone, but there were more suspicious disappearances.

So it was easy for everyone to believe that all the ruckus had been between Bidwell's men and the party of ranchers, one of whom was the girl from the Donner Party, Virginia Reed.

People fell silent when she passed.

Everyone wanted to believe the more prosaic explanation for what happened, though they sensed that there was more to it.

No one mentioned the flaming giant that had screamed its way out of town.

"Shouldn't we tell them the truth?" Frank asked Virginia.

"Would you have believed me if I had told you the Donner Party was attacked by werewolves?" Virginia responded.

He fell silent at that.

As far as the events in the mountains went, the decimation of the search party was attributed to Indian attacks. Perhaps if there had been more than a few survivors, the real story might have emerged. Only Preacher MacLeod told the truth, but people just shook their heads at his wild story, thinking the trauma had driven him crazy. He'd been badly wounded, after all.

A few days later, they found his clothes in the middle of his room— but he was gone.

Frank screwed up his courage enough to ask Virginia to accompany him back to the ranch. The least he could do was give her shelter, he pointed out. There was no obligation on her part, he hastened to add.

"Not yet," she finally answered. "There is something I must do first."

"I'm too forward," he said, his heart sinking. "If I misunderstood..."

"Shush, you," she whispered, putting her finger to his lips. "If your heart is saying what mine is, you haven't misunderstood anything."

"Then why?" he asked, crestfallen.

"It isn't *over*," she said. "The Ts'emekwes weren't killed, either of them. When they take their revenge, they will take it on both the innocent and guilty. I can't allow that. It's because I'm the Canowiki, I suppose. Something compels me to put an end to it."

"Is Feather...Litonya...going with you?"

Virginia shook her head. "It is up to me to finish this. She is staying with Jean Baptiste until he heals."

"Then *I'm* going with you," Frank stated.

"I can't ask that of you. You saw how dangerous it is."

"I would rather be in danger with you than be safe at the ranch without you," he said. "Besides, these creatures killed my brothers. I have more of a reason to seek revenge than you."

She started to object, but he interrupted her. "The only question remaining is, when do we leave?"

Virginia smiled at his tone of voice. Then her smile wavered and she looked away. "I think my life is going to be difficult, Frank. Not only in the near future, but from now on. You should find a nice girl to marry and settle down."

"I want *you*, settled or not," he said. And there was not a single doubt in his mind.

"We leave in the morning," Virginia said. "Before the others wake."

Chapter Twenty-One

It was still dark when Virginia and Frank rode out of town the next day. He suspected half the town was peering at them from behind their curtains. They were fully outfitted for once, with plenty of food, as Virginia had insisted. The merchants of Bidwell's Bar were so grateful that the tyrant was gone that they gave Frank and Virginia nearly anything they asked for.

Still, most of the townspeople wouldn't look Virginia in the eye, as if they were afraid of her. Now she was being shunned not only because she was a survivor of the Donner Party, but also because stories were circulating that she was a strange creature herself, perhaps even a witch. It was difficult for Frank to grasp that anyone could believe such things in this day and age.

Then again, he had just fought werewolves and giants.

They accept Virginia's help because they need her, Frank thought. *But when she's done, they'll go right back to spurning her.*

Virginia didn't seem to notice. She seemed to always have a far-off look in her eye. It was only when they were alone, talking, that her eyes focused on the here and now…on him. He didn't always know what to say to her, but he made sure she knew he would always be there.

He was grateful for those moments alone with her, and understood that she would always be drawn away from him by the inexplicable and the strange, but that he would be her companion and her safe harbor from the world at large. And he was glad to be that, if that was what she needed.

Late the previous evening, Litonya again volunteered to come, but her reluctance was plain. Jean Baptiste had collapsed after the battle and still hadn't regained mobility. She was never far from his side.

"No, Litonya," Virginia said, taking her friend's hands in hers. "Please, stay and take care of Jean."

"If thou refusest to let me accompany thee, I must tell thee how to find the Ts'emekwes," Litonya said. She proceeded to describe a high mountain valley with a single entrance that couldn't be seen until one was right on top of it.

"When thou comest to the pass, thou wilt see a small stream flowing from the northeast corner of the high plateau," she explained. "It will appear to be nothing more than glacial runoff, but it is the source of the

North Fork. There is a spring at the end of the canyon, enclosed on three sides by high cliffs. On the north side of the spring, thou wilt see trees lining the cliffs. Concealed behind that row of trees is the home of the Ts'emekwes."

"Draw me a map?" Virginia asked.

At that moment, Jean Baptiste cried out, and Litonya flinched. "The map will be ready by the time thou leavest," she said over her shoulder as she hurried to his side.

The weather cleared, and Thompson Peak loomed over Bidwell's Bar, a fresh coat of snow atop its rocky summit. There was a nip of chill in the air, but the skies were blue as the sun rose over the mountains. In the light of day, the events of the past weeks seemed impossible, like a dream fading in the morning sun.

***

It was an enjoyable journey that first day. When Frank and Virginia reached the river, it was placid and easy to cross.

They talked about small things, making observations about the weather and the countryside around them, as they started up the path into the mountains. It was a pleasant fall day. Frank became conscious of the squeak of the leather saddles, the breathing of the horses, the buzz of the mosquitoes surrounding them.

Despite the bright sun, it grew colder as they climbed the foothills. It was so peaceful that Frank felt his apprehension starting to fade. When they stopped for the night, Frank was glad just to be with Virginia. They started a fire and then sat close to each other, not quite touching.

"We should get married," Frank blurted. The proposal had been on the tip of his tongue for days, but he'd been afraid to say it out loud, afraid of driving her away. But he realized that if he didn't say something now, he might never have another chance. "My father will give me part of the ranch for our own," he continued, the words spilling out of his mouth. "He can't...he won't object to you."

"You know that can't happen," Virginia said. "You must take care of your ranch. I must be the Canowiki, wherever that leads."

"But..."

"You can't go," Virginia said bluntly. "And I can't stay."

"But what if..." he countered, "what if I stay, so that can you go do what you must? I will be here when you need me. I will not stand in your way."

She appeared to be trying to find an answer to that, and it seemed that she was actually considering the offer. Then a strange expression came over her face, and she turned away.

"What is it?" Frank asked.

"I just realized that I have once again turned a year older without noticing it," she said.

"How old are you?" He'd been wondering. Sometimes she seemed so young, like a little girl, and other times she seemed as mature and wise as a grandmother.

"I turned sixteen a couple of days ago," she said. "I'm old enough to make up my own mind about who I want to be with...and how I want to be with him."

Frank sat there, trying to interpret her words in a way he could trust, for he was afraid his fear for her safety and his desire for her were combining to twist her message. But then Virginia leaned toward him and took his face in her hands, bringing his lips to hers.

This was plain speech, no doubt about it. Frank let go of doubt. His kissed her, and a hunger like he'd never felt before overwhelmed him. It was if the world had narrowed into that single moment, as if all creation had been waiting for this, for him and her to come together. They merged, becoming both the whole world and the only two people in it.

He knew this time together would define their entire future...if they were to be lucky enough to have one. It was a vow, a commitment, a promise to be together forever.

Afterwards, they slept in each other's arms under the soft glow of the moon, in a darkness that, for the first time in days, brought peace, not danger.

***

The trail was clear; the dried tracks left by the original search party were still visible. There were no miners in sight, but they'd be back.

Frank tried to imagine this winding trail becoming a road, flat and wide enough for wagons, but it was impossible. It was reassuring to know that the alpine vistas would remain forever out of reach of man's destruction—reassuring until he came across the remnants of mining camps and realized that nothing was out of reach.

It was a hot day, and it stayed hot no matter how high up they went. The trail passed in and out of shade, the trees blocking the sun like the slats of a giant fence. Frank let his mind drift. When he closed his eyes, he sensed the shadows and light through his eyelids, and it all seemed peaceful and eternal. The breeze in the shade was tantalizingly cool.

On the second night, they camped at one of the same spots the party had used on the way down the mountain. Frank volunteered for first watch. Virginia fell asleep instantly, and when it was her turn to watch, he decided not to wake her. What he really wanted to do was crawl under the blankets with her, and he knew she would welcome him.

Instead, he stood guard for the rest of the night, giving her the rest she needed.

As he watched her sleep, he marveled that this miraculous and one-of-a-kind woman had come into his life. He didn't deserve her, but he did give himself credit for seeing how impressive she was. Most men would've had difficulty accepting her strength and her power, but he recognized that his destiny was to help her on the long and difficult path ahead of her. He was no coward. His life with her would not be simple or safe, but he was glad for it.

In the morning, they would rise and enter the secret canyon that Litonya had described, and there they would face not one, but two of the giant creatures. Frank had no illusions that he, by himself, could do anything effective against them. But he would do whatever Virginia needed; whatever the *Canowiki* needed.

He smiled to himself. His life with Virginia Reed might not be long, but it would be interesting.

Perhaps if he hadn't been sitting there shivering all night, he never would have remembered the cache of gunpowder at the mining camp. When Virginia finally awoke in the morning, the sun was well above the horizon. He told her about the nearby explosives.

She brightened at the suggestion. It wasn't until then that he grasped that she was equally doubtful of success; perhaps more so, for he had the simple faith that she knew what she was doing. Now he realized that she had no plan.

"We can blow up the entrance to the cave," she said. "Trap them inside. Since they are wounded, they may not know what is happening until it's too late."

There was a single rocky trail there, going up the slope at a slight angle. It was a narrow path, with tree roots showing through the soil on both sides. Thick treetops towered above them, allowing little light below. Frank's eyes were focused on the light above them, at the end of the tunnel of trees. He gradually realized how silent the forest was; even the background noise of birds and insects had died away.

Virginia was tense, staring resolutely ahead. It was this stiffness that made Frank glance to the side of the path.

At first, he sensed rather than saw their silent companions. When an Indian finally revealed himself, about midway along the corridor of trees, it was because he wanted to be seen. The Miwok was tall, with a noble countenance. His nose was long and straight, and his eyes glittered in the shadows. Standing next to this tall Indian was Hugh, dressed as a Miwok brave, war paint on his face. He glared at Frank as if he didn't know him, as if he was just another intruder he wanted to kill.

Virginia rode by the silent Indians without looking at them, as if they weren't there. Frank followed her lead, his back itching from the vulnerability of their position. Emerging into the light, he expected an arrow in the back at any moment, but they made it to the other side of the corridor.

It wasn't until they had climbed several hundred feet above the forest that Frank spoke. "Why did they let us pass?"

"Because the Ts'emekwes hunt them as well now," Virginia explained. "This is why Litonya sought me in the first place."

"But why now?"

"The Skoocooms and the Indians lived together in peace until the white man came to dig up the mountainside," Virginia explained. "The Skoocooms are only responding to the threat, defending their territory. But what the beasts don't understand is that there are more white men coming, and more after that. Soon, the Indians will be driven off the land or killed. And the wild creatures of the forest—the wolves and the grizzly bears and even the Skoocoom, *anything* that is a threat—will be hunted until they are gone."

It had never occurred to Frank that the predators of the wild could be extinguished. They were an ever-present danger, and always had been. Every year, they lost a few head of cattle to the wolves and cougars, and when you wandered into the forest, it was prudent to make lots of noise so that you didn't stumble across a mother grizzly and her cub. It was just the way of things.

Suddenly, Frank had a vision of the West settled the way the rest of America was settled. What a strange thing to contemplate! Miles and miles of roads and fields and fences. Domesticated animals where wild creatures once roamed. Cities and bridges and dams. It was a future that seemed impossibly far off, but now that the vision had come to him, he knew it was inevitable.

I should be happy the dangerous creatures will be gone, he thought. Certainly Patrick would have been.

Instead, he felt a strange sadness, despite or because of what the Ts'emekwes had done to him and his family; he wasn't sure which. The Skoocooms were creatures from the far past, from the time of myths and legends, that had somehow survived until today, but not for much longer. Not unless they learned how to hide themselves so that no one could ever find them or prove they existed.

Virginia brought out Litonya's map, and Frank looked over her shoulder as she examined it. The path split here, one fork going up the ever-smaller creek to the hidden valley, the other following the North Fork south along the hillside.

They turned away from the hidden canyon and rode downward along the edge of the creek. The mining camp was just out of sight, but far enough away that Frank had time to wonder how he was going to persuade the Jordan brothers to give him their gunpowder. From what he'd heard, gunpowder was worth nearly as much per ounce as gold these days, it was in such short supply.

But the Jordan brothers were nowhere to be seen at the mining camp. Frank wondered why he was surprised. Despite all the death over the past weeks, he'd longed to think of the jovial boys pulling gold out of the river. If they had been part of the search party, their levelheaded cheerfulness might have even kept the others from getting out of control.

The camp was undisturbed. The Jordan boys had simply disappeared.

The tarp over the gunpowder had been untouched for several days, and half the barrels were uncovered and useless. Only two containers seemed dry enough to ignite.

They loaded one barrel on each side of Frank's horse. He started leading the way back up the trail on foot. Virginia followed, still riding her mount, her head bowed in thought.

His heart in his throat, Frank trudged up the trail, following the small creek upward.

Chapter Twenty-Two

<u>James's Journal, Day 12</u>

I awoke and was surprised to find that not only was I alive, but that the front chamber of Grendel's cave was empty. Grendel was in the dark corridors below, I suspected, licking his wounds. Grendel's Mother must have ordered him to stay away from me. She must think I am useful. But for how long?

Hrothgar's interest in me and his need for a playmate has kept me alive until now, but he grows bigger every day. He is already taller than I am. His large red eyes are no longer all innocence. The craftiness of his brother appears in his face now and again. Sometimes I find him staring at me, and I'm frightened by his coldness. It's as if the young albino is asking himself why he ever liked having a pathetic human around in the first place.

I've tried to engage his curiosity, to teach him new words, but he no longer seems interested in human language. He hasn't said "friend" in days.

Soon I will simply be in the way.

I dream about escaping, but I wouldn't get far out of the hidden valley before they caught me, much less down the mountain trails. Even Hrothgar could easily catch me.

Still, if they are truly losing interest in me, perhaps they won't notice me long enough for me to make my escape, or perhaps they won't care. Perhaps they will let me live simply because they have become familiar with me. Perhaps they are grateful to me for helping them. So I have been telling myself.

Until this morning.

A ray of light penetrated the cave, shooting across the surface, flashing red behind my closed eyes. I awoke when Grendel's Mother came through the entrance. Pine needles flew through the air, the last of the pollen shimmered in the sudden light, and I saw in the brief illumination that her fur was scorched and singed, showing the raw, red skin beneath. I couldn't make sense of it at first. She was dripping water, as if she had plunged herself into the spring outside. She must have been in great pain, but she didn't make a sound, though her footsteps were awkward and labored, instead of having the grace I remembered.

She passed me without looking my way, and I was careful not to catch her attention.

Moments later, I heard the howls of a creature in pain, but it was Grendel and Hrothgar I heard, not the Mother. They were alarmed, angry, and frightened. To my astonishment, I understood what their utterances meant now. They were asking her what had happened.

I could hesitate no longer.

Grendel's Mother had left the miner's pack at my side. There, at the bottom, was a small container of gunpowder, as well as flint and steel and fuses, enough to cause a small explosion if the damp hadn't ruined them. The cave narrowed as it plunged downward, and I knew, from previous explorations, that this tapered opening must be a tight fit for the giant creatures.

I snuck to the opening and set the gunpowder down. There, I hesitated. Obviously, there had been a cave-in. The ceiling of the cave still looked unstable. It would take but a few moments to put some explosives there and seal the exit. I could simply light the fuse and run.

Grendel, his Mother, and Hrothgar would all die. I was certain of it. This was the only exit from the cavern. There had been drafts at one time, but after the cave-in, days ago, the air had become close and still, plunging me deeper into misery. Now I recognized it as an opportunity.

Grendel and his family were scared. Something or someone had maimed Grendel and burned the Mother of Hell, as I thought of her. When Kovac had wounded Hrothgar, he had set into motion events that had escalated.

I could do it. I could close these monsters in, shut them away forever.

My heart pounded in my ears as I considered how simple it would be to be free of the beasts. Why did I hesitate?

I returned to my nesting place, wondering with every step what the hell I was doing. Even that much movement exhausted me. I was taking too long. One of them could emerge from below at any moment. I needed to escape. I had no choice. There was no doubt in my mind that Grendel's Mother would no longer stop him from killing me. Hrothgar might be reluctant to see me die, but he wouldn't face the wrath of his brother to defend me.

Yet…I put the pack of explosives down and started toward the entrance.

I won't kill these creatures. They are simply responding to the threats from the world around them. In a way, Grendel was the manifestation of

Nature fighting back. I have little sympathy for the miners who tore up the mountainside in their greedy search for gold.

But Nature isn't going to win this time. Mankind destroys everything he touches, killing the wildlife and forests, digging up the earth and soiling the waters. The Indians, who live in harmony with both prey and predators, whom these beasts had left alone, are as much victims of the coming of civilization as all the other creatures.

Who are the real savages?

Patrick and Oliver wouldn't think of it this way, I know. They would demand revenge. Perhaps Frank might have second thoughts, but even he would do what was necessary. Being the youngest son, I have always watched others take action and observed the results.

I haven't always liked what I've seen.

I'm as good as dead anyway, I thought. *My family has probably all given up on me. So what difference does it make? I'm a dead man.*

I decided I would escape rather than wait here to be slaughtered.

At the last minute, I dumped the contents of the pack onto the floor and scooped up as many gold nuggets as I could carry. Strangely, I felt guilty at doing so, as if I was succumbing to the same greed that caused all this misery in the first place. But if I escaped, I would live again in the world of men. At that moment, I wanted nothing more than to be wealthy enough to escape their expectations, especially those of my father and brothers. I grabbed this journal too, shoving it into the pack with the nuggets and the empty canteen.

As I left the cave, blinking and squinting into the morning brightness, I decided to go back East. Maybe there was enough gold to buy me the education that Frank had accepted so reluctantly.

I would go my own way, never to return.

***

It occurred to Frank, as they drew closer to the cave, that they were going to have trouble making their plan work. For one thing, they hadn't any fuses. Whatever material they used—cloth, wood, or rope—would either burn too fast or too slow. Their only plan was flawed.

Virginia looked grim. Once again, she had that far-off look in her eyes, as if she was seeing the future and it didn't include Frank.

All these thoughts ran through his head as he gazed at her, studying her features, trying to absorb her face perfectly into his memory. So it was that he was gazing at her when she suddenly straightened up and pointed uphill. He saw a figure stumbling down the slope toward them. Frank immediately recognized the form, the movement, the combination of grace and awkwardness that his baby brother James had always had.

"James," he breathed, "It's my brother, James!"

James veered toward them, falling down once in what looked like a painful tumble. Frank heard Virginia dismount, and then she was standing next to him. But for once, she did not have his attention.

"James!" he shouted with joy, but her hand covered his mouth before he could further alert their enemy. James paused, then headed for them.

Frank nodded to Virginia. "I'm OK," he whispered. He wanted to whoop and holler, but restrained himself as he remembered where they were. But he couldn't resist the huge grin that came over his face and the flood of relief that washed through his body.

Smiling, Virginia took the reins of the horse carrying the gunpowder from his hands. "Go," she said. "He needs help."

Frank scrambled up the slope and met his brother halfway, just as James was teetering on the verge of another fall. Frank caught him and held him up. It was like holding up an empty suit of clothes. James was pale and painfully thin, his face filthy and splotchy. He smelled of the Skoocoom, and Frank realized that, impossible as it seemed, his brother must have been with the beasts the whole time.

"Where's Oliver?" Frank asked. "Is he with you?"

James gave him a miserable look and then shook his head slightly.

Frank put his brother's scrawny arm over his shoulder and helped him down the hill, almost carrying him. Now that he'd been saved, James appeared to lose what little strength he had.

Virginia was waiting for them with a canteen and some biscuits, and they sat James down on a flat rock beside the trail. At first, James waved away the food. "We have to get away. Grendel will come after us."

"Grendel?" Frank echoed. Then, *"Beowulf...*of course. I know the reference." While at school, he'd written a paper on *Beowulf.* Grendel was an appropriate name for the Ts'emekwes.

"That's what Tucker called him," James explained.

"Tucker?" Frank asked.

"The man who wrote the journal I found...never mind. He's dead." James gobbled down a biscuit and took a long drink of water. "We need to get out of here! Grendel and his Mother will be coming after me. And probably Hrothgar, too."

Hrothgar? But Frank didn't voice the question. Later, when they were safe, they would speak of Oliver and Patrick and tell their stories. For now, it was enough that James had survived.

"How is it you're alive?" Virginia asked. She was studying James as if he posed a dilemma. The Skoocooms showed no mercy, yet here was a man who had lived among them for days, if not weeks.

"Later," James said. He staggered to his feet. "They're angry, wounded, and in pain. They won't just capture me...us...this time." He tried to rise, but Frank pushed him back down. His younger brother looked alarmed. "We don't have much time," James insisted.

Frank turned to Virginia, eyebrows raised. He was overjoyed at finding his brother, and this spark of hope forced him to reassess their plans. Maybe James was right. Maybe they should escape while they could, let the others deal with Grendel and his family. Let those who invaded the creature's territory deal with the consequences.

"We aren't ready," Frank said to Virginia. "We need fuses, and we need to find others to help us."

"No," Virginia said. "Today. Now."

"But James needs help!" Even as he said it, Frank realized that he wasn't pleading for his sake, or even for his young brother's sake. It was Virginia who would have to face the Ts'emekwes, no matter how much he might want to help her.

Virginia hesitated. "Take him to safety. I'll go alone.

Frank shook his head. "You know I'm not going to let you do that."

"Let?" Virginia's mouth was a thin line, and her jaw was set.

"Go on alone?" James exclaimed. "Haven't you heard me?"

But Frank and Virginia ignored him. They were staring at each other, communicating on a level James couldn't recognize or understand.

"You've found me," James was almost yelling now. *"We need to get away from here."*

"He's right, Virginia." Frank tried one last time. "James is safe. That's what we came for."

"Take him with you," Virginia said bluntly.

Frank lowered his head, defeated. Virginia was going on without him, he could see that now. It had always been her plan.

"Escape was never my goal," Virginia said to James. "I have come to end these creatures."

James's mouth dropped open. "That's not possible. You can't imagine how strong and dangerous these monsters are!"

"We know all too well," Frank said. "We were part of a search party looking for you and Oliver. The…Grendel…killed most of us." Frank stopped there, wondering if he should continue, then decided his brother had the right to know. "He killed Patrick."

James hung his head and put his hands to his face. He looked ready to weep. "I knew it! I should have done it. I was going to blow up the back of the cave, but…I took pity on them. If I had known…" He stopped and looked up at them, desperation written all over his face. "You have no chance against them."

"Yes, we do," Frank said. "Virginia can do it. She *will* do it." His pride was unmistakable as he stared at her. She could not hide a smile in return.

"Who?" James asked. His eyes focused on Virginia, who was a full head shorter than either of the brothers. "*Her?*" His voice rose in disbelief.

"She's tougher than she looks," Frank said. "Come on, we can at least get you down below the tree line." He looked up at the sun, which was still several hours from dropping below the horizon. "We have time."

He started to lift James's pack and nearly fell over. He barely got it off the ground. "What the hell have you got in there?" he exclaimed. He opened it. There was a torn and tattered journal on top, and below it were gleaming nuggets of gold.

"Grendel's cave is the mother lode," James said. "I suspect that all the gold the miners are finding below washed down from that cave. The walls are near solid yellow metal."

Virginia examined the bullion. "If that is true, it will draw more miners, and still more. The Skoocoom will keep killing them, unless he is stopped," she said. "Or *they* are stopped," she corrected herself, as if suddenly remembering that there was more than one of them.

James' mouth gaped open, as if he couldn't believe what she was saying. He looked around as if wondering where they were hiding the others. His gaze landed on the barrels of gunpowder. "You're going to blow up the cave?" he asked.

"Yes," Virginia said.

"I had the same idea. There are fuses and matches on the floor near the front of the cave. At the back, there is a narrow gap right where the cavern deepens. You won't need anywhere near this much gunpowder to close it." The food and water had brought some color back to James's face. "I should have done it myself," he added. "But I…I felt sorry for them."

Virginia gave James a strange look. "A moment ago, you were scared to death of them," she said.

"I am…I was…I can't explain. They aren't what you think. Dangerous, yes. But…they have souls."

Virginia squinted up the slope. "Frank, take your brother to safety and stay there."

"No, I won't le…"

"I can't worry about you!" she interrupted, her voice rising. Her eyes bored into him as she drew in several deep breaths before continuing in a more rational tone. "Besides, your brother needs help."

Frank finally nodded his assent. "We will wait for you down the trail."

"No," she said. "If I don't succeed, you need to be farther away."

"Very well," he said, with no intention of obeying her. When the fight came, he would be nearby to help. Virginia would go in alone, but if she didn't return…

She took the reins of the packhorse and turned to go.

"Miss?" James called. "They aren't evil. They are only protecting themselves."

She looked at him puzzled, and he looked away. "I just thought you should know," he muttered.

Chapter Twenty-Three

Virginia led the packhorse up the trail, following James's tracks. She didn't look back.

She'd always intended to leave Frank below the canyon, but she hadn't been sure how she would accomplish that. The appearance of Frank's brother had been a godsend in more ways than one. It gave her a reason to leave Frank behind, one he would accept, and James's description of the cave and the leftover fuses gave her real hope that her plan might succeed.

As Virginia approached the hidden canyon, she began to feel as though she'd been there before. James's description had been simple and accurate, but not detailed. The green grass, so startling this high up the mountains, the blue spring ringed by the dark evergreen of the ponderosas; it all seemed completely familiar, as if she'd dreamed more than once of such a place, even though she had no memory of such dreams.

The walls of the canyon rose impossibly high on three sides, hiding a small opening at one end, guarding a paradise worth defending.

Virginia found the entrance to the cave easily, and once inside, the stench of the Skoocooms was overwhelming, but it did not deter her. The fuses and matches were exactly as James had described, as was the cavern narrowing toward the back. He'd been right: a small amount of gunpowder would close in the Skoocooms forever.

She stopped and listened. She could sense them below her, but perceived no movement. She went back for one of the barrels of gunpowder. She drew her bowie knife and hacked away the branches at the entrance.

The late afternoon sun hit the entrance of the cave just right, and a blinding light flashed from inside it. Virginia held her hand up to shield her eyes, avoiding the worst of the glare, and slowly, her eyes adjusted.

The sight that greeted her was so beautiful that for once she didn't question mankind's lust for gold. Until then, she'd managed to ignore or dismiss the fact that gold was the reason for everything that had happened. Oh, she'd been aware that it existed, of course, but it had seemed unimportant. Now she grasped the full extent of its power. She caressed the shining wall, and it felt so soothing, so seductive, that she understood at last. The walls were almost solid metal on both sides, reflecting the light so that the cave glowed. The expanse of yellow metal continued on deeper into the cave, and if anything, it looked to get broader, extending to the ceiling and floors.

This is going to attract hordes of miners, Virginia thought, hefting a nugget the size of her palm and rubbing it with her thumb—not a few hundred men scratching for gold in the creek bed, but hundreds, thousands of men, and their families, and all those who supplied, transported, fed, and clothed them. It would create, and bring, big money, and huge businesses from back East.

This mountain would be whittled away to nothing. It would change, she sensed, not only this small part of the state, but the entire breadth of the land, drawing men from all over the world. With more miners arriving every day, the cave would inevitably be found. There were rumors that the Oregon Trail was full of wagons heading their way. Discovery of Grendel's cave would only hasten that change.

Virginia tossed the nugget into the debris littering the cave floor. The glittering metal caused too much death and destruction. She wanted none of it.

She carried the barrel of gunpowder into the cave, setting it near the opening in back. She took one of the matches in hand…and then hesitated.

It was all too easy, somehow. With a spark of fire, she would destroy these creatures and their threat to humans once and for all. But she could not lift her hand to strike the match.

They aren't evil, James's voice echoed in her memory. She remembered the look of determination on the face of Grendel's Mother. There had been no anger, no hate in her expression. There had been something almost resigned in her face, as if she only did what she felt she must.

Clutching a handful of matches, Virginia ducked into the narrow opening at the back of the cave.

The golden path was slippery and strewn with bones. She went slowly, bracing herself against the slick cavern walls with one hand. As the floor leveled out, it widened slightly. She drew her bowie knife with her other hand.

What am I doing? Virginia wondered. She probably had no chance against the Skoocooms, even with their injuries. Why was she risking everything to see them one more time?

But she went on. Ever since her first heart-pounding experience facing monstrous, impossible creatures along the dangerous Oregon Trail, she'd learned to trust her instincts, learned that her destiny was somehow different than others'.

Unlike the front of the cave, the back was clean and clear of refuse. Even the smell seemed to fade into the background. Virginia hesitated, quieting her breath. Her heart pounded, but from excitement as much as fear. There was no other sound. She sensed the creatures were waiting for her.

She lit another match and continued on. The cavern seemed almost to have been constructed, like the hallway of a building. The floor was flat, as if worn down by generations of very large feet. The walls were smooth, and the gold shone with a soft, almost comforting light. The temperature was warmer, as comfortable as the inside of a home.

It is a home, she realized. The thought reassured her.

She glimpsed the white fur of the child first, and then his red eyes reflecting the light. Behind the child was the huge shape of Grendel's Mother on the floor. Trying to stand was Grendel himself, but he was struggling. Hrothgar charged at Virginia, and she raised the bowie knife, hoping that the match in her other hand would last long enough for her to fend him off.

Then it went out, and she was blind. She waved the knife back and forth, and could sense the albino circling her, looking for an opening.

From the back of the cave came a loud barking sound. It sounded like a word, but like none Virginia knew. The small Ts'emekwes moved away. As she squinted, trying to peer into the darkness, she realized that it wasn't completely black. Slowly, her eyes adjusted and she saw that a thin streak of light was penetrating the chamber, the gold in the walls reflecting and amplifying the light. Once again, she could make out the three shadowy shapes against the shining gold that surrounded them.

The floor was covered by a soft layer of needles and moss. There were blankets or skins against one wall, and squared-off rocks and flattened spaces, evidently where the creatures sat. She wondered what they did here. Did they tell stories to each other? Did they play games?

She was certain now that these were thinking and reasoning creatures. But more importantly, they were feeling beings. They loved each other, and wanted to protect each other from the threats from outside their home.

From her.

She approached them slowly, lowering her knife. She held out her other hand, and even though Hrothgar growled at her, he didn't attack. Then she stood above the Mother.

The female Ts'semekwes was in a bad way. Some of her burns were inflamed. Mud and mosses had been applied, as if they were medicine. Virginia looked into the Mother's eyes…

…and fell into them. The Mother's thoughts enveloped her in warmth, and Virginia almost fled from the emotional depth that filled her consciousness.

This creature was long lived, far beyond human years. Virginia saw the years pass in her mind's eye as if she was reading the Mother's thoughts and memories. There came a vision of the Mother as a young child, part of a large family, happy among her brothers and sisters. There had been many more of them then, and there had been gatherings, and the changing of mates, and things brought from far away.

Then the Quiet Ones had come, and at first there had been war, but eventually the two sides learned to live with each other. But the others of her kind, the ones that had come from far to the east, no longer came. The Loud Ones came, and there were no more gatherings, and her brothers and sisters died, one by one. Always before, there had been young ones to take their places, but that was no longer so.

Then, a miracle: a lone male appeared, primitive and almost feral. He stayed long enough to mate, and then the youngest one had come. Then new men had invaded the cave and wounded her young son, and she had sent her older son, who was as old as the oldest man, to warn them to stay away.

He had been too zealous, too aggressive, she saw that now, and she had tried to rein him in, but his anger could not be controlled. Then he too was injured.

They were at Virginia's mercy. They had met humans such as her before. Some brought them death, but others looked into their eyes and hearts to see and understand. Moomaa, for that is what her name was, hoped this was such a Hunter.

More visions came, images of a long life, dangerous and always on edge, yet also fulfilling, filled with love for her children and hope that there were still others of her kind out in the world.

And then the visions ended.

Virginia blinked. How long had she been standing there? The light from the small crack was dim, almost gone, but she could still see, as if she had been granted the same vision as the Skoocooms.

She bowed her head to Mother in respect. "You must hide from us. You mustn't attack us, for you cannot win." Her voice rose emphatically.

"Hide, and never let them see you. Disappear into the woodlands and high into the mountains, or you will never survive."

She felt the Mother's acceptance of her words.

"Disappear and become myth," Virginia said, and turned away, sheathing her bowie knife.

She climbed back up the corridor and through the front chamber of the cavern. She gathered up the matches and gunpowder, still in its barrel, and carried them outside. It was almost dark. She led the packhorse to the entrance of the canyon, where she unloaded both barrels and set them on either side of the rocky enclosure. She set the fuses again, lighting them from the torch she still carried, and leapt onto the horse and galloped away.

The explosion lit up the twilight skies, and Virginia was pelted with small rocks, though she had ridden as fast as she dared. When the dust finally settled, she wheeled the horse around and went back. The opening to the canyon was gone. From the outside, it looked as though it was a sheer cliff all the way up the mountain.

She found Frank and James not far down the trail. They hadn't made much of an effort to get away. Frank hurried toward her. "You blew up the entrance to the canyon?" he asked. "Not the cave?"

Virginia didn't answer.

"I don't understand," he said. "I think those creatures are capable of climbing out."

She nodded. "Of course they are. I expect they probably will. But I didn't close off the canyon to keep them in. I closed the entrance to keep us out."

He stared at her uncomprehendingly.

She smiled and approached him, and draped his arms around her.

"Hold me, Frank. It's over."

Chapter Twenty-Four

Litonya ministered to Jean Baptiste until he regained his mobility. He was weak, but in time, he recovered. The townspeople were generous, giving them a spacious room, food, and medicine.

At first, Jean wasn't aware that Virginia had left. When he discovered it, he was alarmed. "You should have gone with her!" he cried, nearly getting out of bed.

"Frank is her helper now," Litonya informed him.

"But how can the two of them alone hope to defeat the Skoocoom?"

"She is a Canowiki," Litonya said. "She will do what is necessary."

Jean didn't have much choice but to accept her judgment, for he couldn't get around without her help.

To distract him, Litonya shared some of the tales of her people, including the myth of Coyote and Lizard creating the world and the little story of how Coyote, in his anger, created a small world of his own, hidden from all.

"I searched for it when I left San Francisco," she said offhandedly. "I wanted nothing to do with white men, and I was too afraid to join my own people, for I did not believe they would accept me. So I wasted time seeking a place that does not exist. I wasn't in my right mind."

Jean Baptiste was riveted by the story. "Did you find any hint of the place?"

Litonya hesitated, and he caught it. "Tell me, Feath…Litonya," he insisted.

So she recounted the story of the day she'd almost been ready to give up looking. She was north of Thompson Peak, outside the territory of the Miwok. She'd discovered that the tribe that had once inhabited the area was gone. No one would say why, though from the averted eyes of the white people, she suspected the worst. For some reason, the white men left her alone. A single "squaw," as they called her, was not a threat.

On the highest pass, she found a man perched on a rock as if he was waiting for her. He wore a strange hat, round and wide, and Litonya remembered seeing drawings on rocks of such a thing. His age was impossible to determine. At first glance, he seemed but a boy; when she looked again, he appeared to be ancient. His eyes were deep and sad, and yet she felt him laughing at her.

She asked him the usual questions, and he listened for a time without speaking. "I have seen this place," he said finally.

Litonya was so stunned that it took her several seconds to respond. When she did, she couldn't hide her excitement. "Where is it? Will you tell me?" she cried.

He held up one smooth hand. "You are not ready," he said.

"What do you mean?" she demanded.

But he didn't answer. His head sank to his chest, and the wide hat completely covered his face. When he looked up again, he had the aspect of an old man. "Come back when it is time," he said.

He rose and walked away. Just as he was about to disappear around a bend in the path, he turned and pointed to the peak of a mountain whose name she didn't know.

"Did you keep looking?" Jean Baptiste asked.

"I spent a week looking in every canyon, every little cave. I found nothing."

Litonya thought that was the end of the conversation, but a few days later, when Jean Baptiste was finally back on his feet and able to get around, he looked at her and said, "We must search for Coyote's Land."

"Jean, it is just a myth."

"As is the Skoocoom," he said. "As are Skinwalkers."

Litonya shook her head. She'd had enough of adventures. She had done her duty, finding the Canowiki and helping her make her way. Now she wanted to settle down with this man and live the rest of her life in peace.

"Where else can we go?" Jean asked abruptly.

She didn't have an answer. As kind as the people of Bidwell's Bar were to them now, she didn't want to stay. Nor could she join her own tribe in the mountains, not as long as Roman was chief. *Lokni*, she corrected herself—and that was part of the problem, for she often responded as a white woman would respond. She still thought of herself as Feather, not Litonya. And yet, there were times when she looked at the way white women acted and couldn't understand them at all.

"Very well," she said. "We shall go. Perhaps we will find Coyote's Land, or perhaps we will find some other place where we can make our home."

She did not speak her secret thought, that Jean's answering smile was all the home she'd ever need.

They set out together, just the two of them. They avoided the territory of the Miwok, journeying north to the place where Litonya had met the old man. They asked questions of those they encountered, and a few of the aimless Indians who had lost their own lands joined them in the search.

Word got out among the scattered tribes, and more and more people showed up every day, speaking every language, so that English became the common tongue, to Litonya's chagrin. They became a new tribe, one that they dubbed Coyote.

They searched the hills and they searched the valleys, but always they returned to the place to which the Old Man of the Mountain, as he was now called, had pointed.

One day, the youngest of them, a five-year-old girl, came running. "I've found it!" she cried. "I've found it!"

Epilogue

"Hello, Bidwell," Virginia kept her voice soft. "We have unfinished business."

He turned around, and when he saw who it was, he gave her a slow grin. He started to take off his clothes, and she let him.

"It took me some time to track you down," she said conversationally.

He snarled, no doubt saying something nasty in werewolf.

"Here you are again, pretending to be a barkeep again, in another town." She'd waited until after closing, when he was alone in saloon's back room.

The floor was covered with the gory, rotting remains of the bar's previous owner. It was the same thing he'd done in Bidwell's Bar, and Virginia wondered how many times this scenario had played out across the country.

Frank thought she was visiting her family in San Francisco. She often made up excuses about why he couldn't accompany her. There were things she needed to do that he could not help her with.

He always volunteered to help, he wanted to come with her, but she needed him to be at the ranch, comforting and supportive, taking care of what needed to be done at home. She would handle Bidwell herself. She just needed to trust her instincts.

Visions of the Ts'emekwes came back to her. That's when she'd truly known that Litonya was right: she was a Canowiki, a Hunter. When the compulsion came to intervene, she had to embrace it.

"Ready?" She smiled grimly at the slavering, growling werewolf before her. He was even bigger than she remembered.

In reply, the beast leapt at her.

Virginia raised her bowie knife, embracing the rush of energy that came with a righteous task.

About the Author

Duncan McGeary is a native Oregonian, who has lived most of his life in Bend, Oregon, on the dry side of the Cascade Mountains. (His stories are often located in this western terrain.) After graduating for the University of Oregon (Go Ducks!) he returned to his hometown, having had his first three fantasy novels published in the early 1980's.

He bought a bookstore, Pegasus Books, in downtown Bend in 1984, got married to Linda, raised two sons, Todd and Toby, and spent the next 30 years trying to keep the store alive.

With the store thriving, he is now devoting his stored up creative energies writing again. Visit his website at www.duncanmcgeary.com.

Made in the USA
Columbia, SC
11 March 2019